T0271496

Maggie Su is a writer and editor. She received a PhD in fiction from University of Cincinnati and an MFA from Indiana University. Her work has appeared in *New England Review, Four Way Review, TriQuarterly Review, Puerto del Sol, Juked, DIAGRAM,* and elsewhere. She currently lives in South Bend, Indiana, with her partner, cat, and turtle.

BLOB

A LOVE STORY

Maggie Su

Sceptre

First published in Great Britain in 2025 by Sceptre
An imprint of Hodder & Stoughton Limited
An Hachette UK company

First published in the United States in 2025 by Harper, an imprint of HarperCollins
Publishers, New York

The authorised representative in the EEA is Hachette Ireland, 8 Castlecourt Centre,
Dublin 15, D15 XTP3, Ireland (email: info@hbgi.ie)

1

A CIP catalogue record for this title is available from the British Library

Hardback ISBN 9781399731935
Trade Paperback ISBN 9781399731942
ebook ISBN 9781399731966

Typeset in Bell MT Std

Printed and bound in Great Britain by Clays Ltd, Elcograf S.p.A.

Hodder & Stoughton policy is to use papers that are natural, renewable and
recyclable products and made from wood grown in sustainable forests. The logging
and manufacturing processes are expected to conform to the environmental
regulations of the country of origin.

Hodder & Stoughton Limited
Carmelite House
50 Victoria Embankment
London EC4Y 0DZ

www.sceptrebooks.co.uk

FOR MY FAMILY AND FELLOW BLOBS

CHAPTER ONE

It's May, freshly turned and drizzling, when I find the blob
outside a dive bar. A beige gelatin splotch the size of a dinner
plate sits next to a trash can, tucked between glass shards and
chewed gum. It reminds me of the slime I made as a kid with
my brother: a concoction of Elmer's glue, baking soda, shaving
cream, contact lens solution, food coloring, and water. Before
Alex abandoned me for the neighborhood boys with their N64s
and X-Men cards, we spent hours sticking it on each other and
peeling it off.

"You're a monster," we would say.

The blob looks like those times when we made the mixture
too liquidy and the whole thing slipped from our hands and dis-
integrated on the kitchen floor. I bend down to get a closer look
and make out a mouth and eyes. Its lips form a downturned
crescent moon, an exaggerated frownie face. Two beady black
eyes look up at me, no eyelids.

"Shit," I say. This thing isn't slime.

I take a picture of the creature on my phone, reverse-search
the photo, and an animal called a blobfish appears on my screen.
There are some similarities; it's about twelve inches long, and
seems to lack bones and teeth. The problem is, blobfish are

native to Australia and live a thousand meters underwater. It shouldn't be in a landlocked midwestern college town.

I shiver through my thin jacket. The street behind me is empty—it's too early for Friday revelers. A knotty branch sticks out from the bushes, and I grab it. Without questioning my instinct, I return to the blob and extend the stick. Gently, I poke. The wood meets flesh without any resistance. I push deeper, and the stick glides through the blob. I've gone too far, made myself a blob kebab, but when I pull back, there's no puncture wound. I poke again and see the blob flinching away from the intrusion, forming a tunnel of open space to avoid the stick. I stumble back, regretting my encroachment.

"What are you?" I ask.

I receive no response.

FIFTEEN HOURS EARLIER, I stood behind the front desk of the hotel right off the highway. My job is to answer the phone and say "Start your experience at Hillside Inn and Suites. This is Vi," using a phone voice that's half spa receptionist and half sex worker. I like this greeting. It sets low expectations, promising nothing helpful or enlightening from the phone call or subsequent hotel stay. All we can give is an "experience."

I work the 6:00 a.m. to 3:00 p.m. shift. Rachel, my front desk co-attendant, doesn't have to get in until 9:00 a.m. because she started a month before me and has seniority. Both of us are twenty-four-year-old "townies," born and bred minutes from the college we would end up attending. In the two years since we started this job, Rachel graduated with a degree in acting and I dropped out of a biochemistry program. I instantly forgot everything I ever knew about organic compounds and covalent bonds, but Rachel still takes small acting gigs and talks about moving to LA. She books the annual local theater production—this year it's *Grease*—and more than a few quinceañeras.

Rachel walked into work with two coffees from the strip-mall Starbucks across the street.

"Good morning," she said, and smiled at me with the whitest teeth I've ever seen in real life. I've debated asking if she uses whitening strips or has invested in veneers, but I don't want her to know that I look at her so closely.

Rachel and I never met before getting this job. Our high schools were on the opposite sides of town—I went to Westside and she went to Pinewood—and I can say with some degree of certainty that we ran in different crowds.

"Morning," I said.

"How's it going?" she asked.

"It's going."

I grabbed one of the coffees from her without saying thank you or offering to pay. We repeat this interaction every day with minor deviations. According to the Hillside employee handbook, daily rituals are important to maintaining professional work-place friendships.

Before Hillside Inn and Suites, I'd never held a job for more than three months. The summer before college I spent a few weeks in a ten-square-foot parking booth with no air-conditioning. My entire job was taking money and pushing a button to let cars in and out. I got fired for running to the Dunkin' Donuts to go to the bathroom and trapping an angry zigzag line of cars in the lot. While pursuing my doomed biochemistry studies, I worked in an animal science laboratory, injecting piglets with the common cold. As karma for this violence, the piglets peed and shit constantly, so I spent most of my time cleaning up feces slurries from the lab floors. I only lasted two months before I got too attached to piglet number twelve and protested by refusing to show up for three shifts in a row. By comparison, this job's not bad. In fact, it almost suits me.

As I sipped coffee, Rachel checked tasks off the manager's to-do list with a militant cheerfulness. She listened to the voice-mail and returned a call I'd missed from a mother trying to book a room for her daughter's college graduation two years in advance. She watered the dying spider plants in the lobby and checked on the indoor pool. She chatted with handyman Rich about the weather as he measured the pool chemicals. She's too perfect, one of those tall strawberry-blond white girls so overeager and performative, you can't wait to see them crack. I hadn't yet seen Rachel stumble. She fake-laughed at Rich as he pretended to fall into the pool. Through the window, she saw me watching. I looked away, turned back to my solitaire match, and found I'd run out of time to make my next move.

I'D FINISHED SOLITAIRE and moved on to online Scrabble when a twentysomething couple approached the desk, the man's arm wrapped around the woman's waist like they were competing in a three-legged race. He was built like a swimmer, with gym shorts that rode low on his hips and a Cubs hat on backward. Her high ponytail was secured with a pink scrunchie. They looked wholesome enough to be in a life insurance commercial. I wasn't surprised when the conjoined creature made its way to Rachel's register, even though mine was closer.

"We have a block of rooms reserved. Jenkins wedding?" the man said.

Pink Scrunchie squeezed his bicep, and I caught the glitter of a giant diamond on her finger.

"Congratulations," Rachel said, flashing her perfect teeth as she searched the computer for their rooms. "We're glad to have you here. . . . Okay, we've got you on the third floor, and I'll put you a few rooms away from the elevator because they can get pretty noisy."

The man smiled back at Rachel, and something tightened in my throat. It wasn't just the smile that reminded me of Luke. It was the tilt of his head, the squareness of his jaw, the easy way he stood with his shoulders back. Rachel was still talking about room selection, so I interrupted—there aren't any rooms next to the elevator, anyway, just supply closets.

"Do you know someone named Luke Meyer?"

Everyone went silent. The man, presumably Mr. Jenkins, turned to me with surprise.

"No," he said, slowly.

"I think you two could be related."

Pink Scrunchie exchanged confused glances with Rachel.

"Because your tooth, the right incisor"—I tried to point it out with my pen, but Mr. Jenkins flinched away—"it's pointed and has a notch. Identical to someone I know."

When Luke and I were still together, I used to run my pinkie across the sharp edge, tug at his receding hairline till it stood up on its own. I liked his irregularities; they seemed to contradict Alex's decree that Luke was "the most generic white man in the world." Sometimes I messed with the tooth when he slept, half hoping he'd bite down and break skin. He never did.

"It's like you keep mistaking me for someone else," Luke said once toward the end, a week before he broke up with me, when every conversation was charged with significance and every question was a metaphor: Were we out of Oreos? Had the milk soured? Who killed the supposedly unkillable African violet? His accusation struck me as ironic. It was clear to me by then that Luke was the one who woke up every morning hoping I'd transformed.

Under the bright lights of the Hillside Inn and Suites front desk, I realized I'd been silent too long. I had just asked an absurd question, and my pen was still hanging, accusatory and flaccid, in the air.

Mr. Jenkins looked me up and down. "What the hell are you talking about?"

Something about the question and the look of annoyance on his face broke the illusion. He wasn't Luke, not a cousin or a stepbrother of Luke's, he was just a guy with a pointed tooth. A guest who wanted to put his bags down.

"Nothing. My mistake," I said.

"Can we just have the keys to our room?" Pink Scrunchie said to Rachel.

"Of course."

Rachel's cheeks were red, but her hands were steady as she swiped their room cards and checked them into the online system.

"You're all set. We have complimentary breakfast from seven to ten a.m.," she says.

Usually we tell guests about the pool and the business center, the toiletries available upon request, and the twenty-four-hour security, but they were already halfway across the room, no longer physically intertwined, walking with four distinct feet.

"Best wishes for your wedding," Rachel called out as they slipped through the sliding doors toward the elevator. Pink Scrunchie lifted a hand in acknowledgment.

"What was that?" Rachel asked me.

Even embarrassed, there was a part of her that loved this. Every crisis needs a savior, and no one plays the part better than Rachel.

"Nothing," I said.

I felt her gaze on my profile, full of pity and moral superiority. I ignored her and played the word JOUST against the Intermediate Computer for 28 points. The phone rang three times, and Rachel answered it. Someone on the fifth floor had requested extra towels.

"Okay, well, I'm here if you need to talk," Rachel said, clutching the freshly laundered linen to her chest.

As soon as she left, I opened Facebook for the first time in a year. I ignored the fifty-five red notifications that I was sure were inspirational messages from my mother and typed his name in the search bar in all caps: LUKE MEYER. I wanted to see his photos—I'd taken most of the ones on his page. It embarrassed him to be photographed, but I loved looking at him through a camera lens, his face placid and calm like a mountain reflected in a lake. I wanted to remind myself that I would still recognize him if he walked through the door, that he's specific—not just a conglomeration of every other man. But when I clicked on his name, his page wasn't visible. Only his profile picture, a shot I took from the grass as he stood over me, just his silhouette against a blue sky. He had unfriended me.

I MET LUKE when he was a freshman and I was a sophomore, still pretending to be a scientist. I poured liquids back and forth between beakers in the lab, and during bathroom breaks I googled things I should've learned in high school biology. *What's the role of RNA in DNA transcription? What does the mitochondria do again?* I was a fraud, and I couldn't even blame my misery on parental pressure. My dad is the opposite of any Asian parent stereotype. He's forgetful and preoccupied, has never once looked at my grades. Before his retirement, he spent his days and nights behind a computer screen developing programs for the university's admissions office, and now, without work, he spends most days outside with his hands in the dirt, growing award-winning tomatoes. My mom is midwestern white and supportive to a fault. I once called her after failing an exam that I admitted I hadn't studied for, and she sent an email to the professor railing against the unfairness of exams as measurements of academic success. *What innovation has ever come from the blind memorization of the Krebs cycle?* she wrote. He caved and bumped me to a C-minus.

I didn't meet Luke in lab, though. We met in the laundry room of the dorm we both lived in, known for housing the quiet nerdy kids. Not the cool misfits who connected over their shared weirdness, but the truly socially dysfunctional ones. It was a place where we could be partitioned off, left alone to marinate in the darkness of our own difference, instead of being forced into mandatory dorm "team-building" activities like Red Rover or Capture the Flag.

It was Friday night, and I was waiting for my clothes to dry while running my eyes over my chemistry textbook and underlining words at random. Normally I would've returned to my newly single room. My sophomore roommate Faith had gotten busted for selling Adderall to the entire fourth floor. The only words she'd ever spoken to me were, "Can you please type softer?" But there'd been rumors of someone stealing clothes from the dryers, specifically undergarments. It'd gotten so bad that one of the RAs posted signs in every bathroom stall warning residents against leaving their underwear unattended: "The Underwear Bandit has taken lacy red thongs and tighty whiteys featuring a cartoon bunny. UB doesn't discriminate. Do not underestimate UB or YOU! WILL! BE! NEXT!" This was posted next to a sex-positive informational poster that claimed cum could whiten your teeth.

I had given up on the properties of lipids and was watching my laundry spin when Luke walked in. He glanced at my book and smiled, showing me his pointed, notched tooth. "I got a D in organic chemistry."

"You're seeing into my future."

"I'm in mechanical engineering."

"Biochemical," I mumbled.

He kept talking even when I reopened my book and flipped through the pages, pretending to read. He was from Gardiner, Montana, a small town outside Bozeman, and his dad was a nuclear engineer for a company that built missiles for government contracts.

"He wants me to go into business with him one day," he said.

I was confused by him, even then. What was he doing sitting here, this Montana boy with his sandy hair and college sweatshirt? He looked too normal to be in this dorm, and in fact he was. He'd missed the deadline for dorm preferences, so they assigned him one at random, and he never complained. I wondered if part of him liked it, being surrounded by people who were so much weirder than him.

"Is that what you want? To work with your dad?" I asked after a long pause.

"I'm not sure," he said.

He didn't ask me anything in return, and we sat in silence as my clothes spun and the fluorescent lights hummed. I became aware of what I was wearing—a used-to-be white sweatshirt, no bra, Alex's old oversized basketball shorts, and fuzzy blue socks covered in peace signs. I felt hot and embarrassed and tugged at my sleeves as if covering my hands might make me invisible. Usually eleven p.m. on a Friday was the perfect time to do laundry; the partiers were out, and the shut-ins were already tucked in bed. I hadn't expected to see anyone.

"What are you doing here?" I asked finally.

"I'm Luke. I live on the fourth floor."

He took the highlighter from my hand and twirled it from his thumb to his pinkie. Across the hall in the computer lab, the first-floor gamer boys yelled obscenities at each other.

"You're the underwear bandit, aren't you?" I asked.

"That's exactly the type of accusation the real underwear bandit would make."

I laughed in spite of myself.

"And your name is?"

"Vi."

He handed me back my highlighter.

We talked until my laundry dinged and I escaped back to the safety of my room. I only remember bits and pieces of what we said (which dining hall had the best taco bar, his favorite writer was Hemingway, I'd never been outside the country), but by the end of our conversation I couldn't walk straight, and my sweatshirt was drenched. In Luke's presence, I'd gotten a taste of what it felt like to be normal.

RACHEL FOUND ME staring at Luke's Facebook profile, my cursor blinking pathetically over the "Add Friend" button.

"Who's Luke Meyer?" she asked.

"No one."

I exited out of the browser and made my hands busy, pulling Post-it notes off the pad one by one and sticking them to the edges of my computer. Rachel took the pad and set it on the far end of the desk.

"Is that the guy with the pointed tooth?"

I sighed. She wasn't going to let it go.

"Yes," I said.

She raised an eyebrow at me. The last thing I wanted was Rachel's pity, but I'd made her look like an idiot in front of the guests, so I figured I owed her the truth.

"My ex. We broke up eight months ago."

"Oh," Rachel said. "I get it."

But she didn't, and before I could explain to her just how little she understood, our assistant manager Walter arrived.

"Good morning, ladies," he called out as he walked over to the front desk, wearing his signature starched, striped button-up with a pink tie.

He's the saddest creature in our hotel ecosystem—the middle manager who attended weekend webinars on how to "project power" and "radiate confidence." A week earlier I saw him on Tinder. All of his pictures were overexposed selfies of him in bed from different angles, and his bio read, "Just a normal guy looking for companionship."

I deleted the app after seeing his white chest peeking out from an equally white duvet. I don't know why I was on Tinder in the first place. I downloaded it after a bottle of wine, when I was drunk enough not to remember doing it but still conscious enough to list *Seinfeld* as my favorite television show and carrier pigeon as my preferred mode of communication. The next morning, I had twenty matches.

In my drunken state, I had used a moody black-and-white candid Luke had taken for my profile picture. It was from our trip to Cincinnati for Luke's friend's wedding, when he convinced me to leave our Airbnb in the rain and walk across the bridge that connected Ohio and Kentucky. Halfway across the river, Luke got tired of me taking photos of him and grabbed my camera. He knelt down to take a photo of my profile against the gray sky. The wind brought color to my cheeks.

"Your album cover," he said.

I studied the picture when we got back to the Airbnb and almost didn't recognize myself. In the photo, I look very sad and very Asian, like I'm being sold as a geisha and will eventually commit suicide to bring honor back to my family. In black and white, I have doll skin—no dry spot on my cheek, no pimples on my chin.

"Is this how I look to you?" I asked Luke then, our cold bodies nestled under a stranger's covers, but he was already asleep.

"Tuck your shirt in for me, would you, Vi?" Walter said now.

"Sure," I said without moving.

Walter ran his fingers across the desk as he walked to his office. Per Hillside policy, Walter has a camera in the back room to check for guests who come to the desk when there's no attendant on duty. Luckily there's a blind spot where we can pick wedgies and adjust bras without surveillance.

He paused and looked back at me. "Vi, would you come see me for a minute?"

"Just me?"

Rachel stared straight ahead at the computer. I thought I saw a hint of a smirk on her face, but I could've imagined it.

"Just you," he said and held the door open so I had to walk underneath his arm to get through.

Walter's office is bare and generic—white walls, a faux wood desk, paperwork sorted into manila folders. His placard doesn't even say his name, just "Assistant Manager" in peeling gold letters.

"How are you doing, Vi?" he asked.

"Can't complain."

We sat in unison. Walter crossed his legs and folded his hands, placing them on his knee in a way that couldn't be comfortable.

"Speaking of complaints, we've gotten a few about you in the past few weeks."

"Really?" I kept my face blank, innocent.

Walter unpretzeled himself and leaned his elbows on the desk.

"On their exit surveys, a few guests noted your curt manner. One mentioned that you gave him the wrong directions to his room."

"A misunderstanding."

"Look, I get it. You and me—we're the same. You're a Virgo, aren't you?"

"I was actually born in Dec—"

"We have to accept our limitations, we're not like the Rachels of this world."

Walter hadn't blinked once, and my own eyes watered from meeting his gaze.

"She's a charmer, an entertainer. She has natural charisma. Not us, we're not concerned with appearances or flash and glamour. That's okay, that's who we are. So, what can we offer guests?"

"I don't know."

"We're consistent, Vi. We show up when we're supposed to, we get the job done, and we don't ask questions."

Walter finally blinked, and a tear caught in the corner of his eye like a pearl. I looked down at my wrinkled, untucked button-up and the salsa stain on my dress pants.

"You can do better. We can do better," he said.

I said nothing, just nodded. Walter gave me a pamphlet on front desk etiquette, the same one I was given during orientation two years ago, and a map of the three-story hotel.

"These people count on us."

He dismissed me after pointing out the men's toilets on each floor. I wanted to rush out of his office but my forearms had fused to the uncomfortable metal and it took a minute to unstick myself.

"Good luck on Tinder, by the way," Walter said.

I reached for my purse without acknowledging that I heard him.

"Hey," Rachel said as I returned to my front desk spot. She had one hip popped up against the desk as she scrolled through her Facebook event invitations. She didn't ask about my Walter meeting.

"Want to go to a drag show with me tonight? It's at the Back Door. Might cheer you up."

This wasn't the first time Rachel had invited me out. I'm the one person at the hotel who doesn't like her, and my indifference makes me irresistible. Every other time Rachel had asked me to grab a drink, I pretended that I needed to care for my grandma or wash my hair or bake a loaf of bread for the homeless.

"Yes," I said today without hesitation.

CHAPTER TWO

Outside the Back Door, a safe distance from the blob, I scroll through my phone looking for answers. One 2013 poll named the blobfish the ugliest animal in the world, beating out the aquatic scrotum frog and pubic lice. Another news item corrects the "ugliest" misconception: it turns out that the infamous photo of the grumpy-looking goo is a dead blobfish. At its normal depth, the blobfish looks like any other bony fish. It's decompression damage that makes it ugly—the pressure difference when the fish is dragged up thousands of meters to the surface is two hundred times what a human would experience if they were blasted out of the airlock of a spaceship. The fish doesn't stand a chance; it unspools.

I step closer to the blob and watch its body slowly rise and fall. Definitely alive.

Growing up, my parents bought me pets on most of my birthdays. Later, Alex would tell me they felt bad that I had no friends and thought animals might help. Instead of playmates, I had a hedgehog, a corn snake, a red-eared slider turtle, a bearded dragon that my mom made my dad get rid of when I forgot to close the lid on the crickets he ate.

I still feel guilty about a few of my pets: I never cleaned the hedgehog's tank because I was scared of her spines, so she spent her days running in a wheel filled with her own poop. Slithers the corn snake, so beautiful with her glistening red and black scales, put up with being shoved into a Barbie car and made to zoom around with a shirtless Ken doll. Her diet consisted of a five-day-old pinky mouse that we bought from the pet store in a brown paper bag. As she got bigger so did the mice, upgraded from hairless pink things to furry young creatures. My dad was in charge of feedings, and eventually the scratches of the mice on the corners of the bag got to be too much for his conscience. We released the snake into the garden in late August. I made a "Goodbye Slithers" banner to hang above the back door as she ceremonially slithered across the threshold. My mom found her body three days later, picked apart by birds.

Now I use the toe of my sneaker to kick some glass away from the blob. It doesn't flinch. I'm early to the drag show, and there's no one to turn to and ask, *What do you think this is?* Surely someone better equipped to handle the situation will happen upon it eventually. I get up from my squat.

"I'll come back," I say as I slowly back away, as if the blob might startle if I move too suddenly. Its unblinking eyes follow me. It does nothing to stop me as I descend into the bar.

THE BACK DOOR is hidden underneath a farm-to-table restaurant, and the entrance is marked by a small down arrow hanging on the exterior wall. Only after descending a flight of concrete stairs and negotiating puddles of unidentifiable liquids are you greeted by a rainbow unicorn painted over rotting wood. Inside, the walls are black, and three disco balls throw light across a large open space that smells faintly like urine. It's a bar for townies, not college students.

Tonight the bar's empty except for Mary, a slim tattooed bartender with an undercut. She gives me a little wave as I walk in, and I nod back.

I've been coming to the Back Door once a week for the last few months. To avoid feeling awkward, I normally get there around midnight, when the stage is already full of sweaty strangers in muscle tees and the bass is so loud it vibrates my kneecaps. I don't have to talk to anyone—I can just dance and pretend the flashing lights mean I'm seconds away from being beamed up by aliens. I always wanted to go with Luke, but he didn't like dancing. He preferred breweries, where he would spend thirty minutes typing up reviews on Untappd, an app that lets you rate beers on hop flavor and mouthfeel.

I order a double gin and soda from Mary just as Rachel walks in. She immediately goes to the center of the dance floor and spins around like she's a Disney princess.

"I've never been here before," Rachel says to me as she approaches the bar, smiling and out of breath. "I love it."

Mary looks Rachel up and down, taking in her sorority girl ponytail, red lipstick, jean shorts. Rachel couldn't look more basic if she tried. For years the Back Door was the only gay bar in town, and they almost got shut down when the city found out about the genderless bathrooms. The employees and regulars are wary of interlopers.

"You've seen drag before, though, right?" I ask. "You're a theater kid."

Rachel shakes her head. "My mom never let me."

I sip my gin, let the alcohol hit the back of my throat, as Rachel takes in Mary's silence.

"I'm friends with Elliott Chin," Rachel says casually. "He's performing here tonight."

"I know Elliott," Mary replies.

Rachel senses weakness and continues. "We were best friends in high school. Used to binge-watch episodes of *The Real World* in my parents' basement. I can't believe he's going to law school. Growing up, we both wanted to be actors." Rachel's voice goes wistful. "He's really talented. He can become a different person when he wants to. It takes skill to inhabit another person's point of view like that, you know?"

I never met Elliott, but I did see him perform the scarecrow in Pinewood's production of *The Wizard of Oz*. My mom had dragged me to the play in an effort to get me to interact with kids my own age. Elliott was the only Asian actor in the production, a tall and lanky sixteen-year-old who danced around the stage with straw poking out of his sleeves. He played the part well, and I wondered afterward if he was double-jointed—his limbs moved so limply, as if independent of his body.

"This'll be the first time I've seen him in years." Rachel taps her pink nails on the bar. "I'm a little nervous."

I abandon my straw and take a gulp of my drink.

"Can I get you something?" Mary asks Rachel. She orders a vodka Red Bull, and I can tell Mary has softened because she doesn't roll her eyes.

"I've wanted to hang out with you for a while." Rachel turns to me as Mary stacks glasses in the background. "Why tonight?"

I shrug. "I needed a change."

I twist on my barstool and read the sign above the bathroom, which reads "Fuck Everyone" in glitter. I turn back to find Rachel swirling her vodka Red Bull like it's scotch.

"Tell me something real about you," I say.

I try to make the request seem playful, cute, rather than accusatory.

"My long-term boyfriend broke up with me too. Just a week ago," Rachel says, her eyes on the spinning disco ball.

"I'm sorry."

"It's okay. I'm just not used to being single."

"Now, tell me something about you," she says after a pause.

We're no longer alone—a few girls in their twenties have trickled into the bar, wearing leather vests and knee-high combat boots.

I stare hard at the silky shine of Rachel's ponytail. "I had trouble growing up . . . "

I need to finish the sentence, but I have nothing, no traumatic backstory to explain why I am the way I am. My parents loved me, I've never broken a bone. The only person I ever lost was Luke, and he's not dead, he's alive somewhere, unconnected from me. The sentence is already complete: I had trouble growing up. But I know I need to offer her something.

". . . Taiwanese." I say.

Rachel nods vigorously as I bite into the grit of lime rind on the rim of my drink. "Oh, totally," she says.

Nothing stops a conversation with a white person like the mention of race. Rachel and I drink in silence as club music comes on the speakers. We order another round before grabbing second-row seats for the show.

Ten minutes later the EDM beat cuts off, the house lights dim, and a spotlight appears on the stage.

"Elliott's the opener," Rachel whispers to me.

The opening xylophone chords of "Under the Sea" chime over the loudspeaker as a gloved hand holding a conch shell appears from behind the curtain. Elliott is revealed in pieces—

first the hand, then a smooth arm, a shoulder, a leg wearing neon-blue stilettos. A calf muscle glistens and shakes to the tempo of the music. Then Elliott, stage name Sea Enemy, shimmies out onto the stage like a snake shedding its skin. She wears a seashell bikini top and an iridescent mermaid tail. On her head is a wreath of fake seaweed, and under her arm, a stuffed Nemo fish. She looks beautiful, the Asian remake of Ariel I'd been waiting for since I was a kid. Rachel cups her hand to her mouth and *woos*.

Even as a drag show novice, I can tell Sea Enemy's a natural performer, her body movements fluid yet distinct and dependent on the lyrics, her mannerisms morphing between sincerity and teasing lust. As she mouths the lyrics, her gloved hand grazes the people in the front row, and she winks at Rachel, who whoops like she's trying to get her attention.

When Sea Enemy gets to the chorus and lip-synchs the word "wetter," the crowd goes wild. She licks her lips and gyrates on the stage, moving her butt close enough to the audience so that they can push dollar bills into the sequined waistband of her tail.

During the final verse, Sea Enemy jumps down from the stage and walks through the center aisle like it's a catwalk. Rachel pushes past the couple on the aisle to shove some dollar bills in Sea Enemy's seashells.

"I love you," she mouths. Elliott puts one of his glittering arms around her.

I stay in my seat, taking sips of my melting ice cubes. Like the rest of the audience, I'm smiling. The gin has loosened my shoulders, and Sea Enemy has transported me to a new world where even death and displacement are set to a Caribbean beat.

The rest of the show lacks the intensity of Sea Enemy's joy: a Cher impersonator, a decent Lady Gaga rendition of "Bad Romance," and a Michael Jackson dance-off.

"Wasn't Elliott great?" Rachel says after the show finishes. We stand up as the bartenders clear the chairs and sweep the floors to get ready for the DJ set.

"Exceeded expectation," I say.

"You have to stay and meet him," Rachel says before I can make an excuse to leave early.

She links arms with me and pulls me to the bar. There's at least fifteen people in front of us, and only Mary's serving.

"You know, ever since I was a kid, I wanted to be an actress. Always wanted to entertain people and make them happy." She pauses. "I'm the middle child, so I was always looking for attention. I performed *Romeo and Juliet* for an audience of stuffed animals in the third grade. Do you have siblings?"

"An older brother. He's a pediatric resident, and I'm a college dropout." I cheers her with my empty glass, drained even of ice cubes.

"To us," she says.

A tall skinny man who must be Elliott approaches Rachel from behind. Wearing a black T-shirt and skinny jeans, he looks unrecognizable except for the smudged blue eyeliner and gold shimmer on his arms.

"Rachel Wilson." He hugs her with one arm. "It's been forever. I'm surprised to see you."

"I got your Facebook invite and wanted to support you."

"Oh." He smiles with teeth as white as hers. They must be veneers, I decide. Do all actors have them? "I sent that to my entire friend list. You never know which closeted ex-football player secretly loves drag."

Rachel looks flustered. "Well, it's good to see you. This is my friend Vi—she works the front desk with me at the hotel. She's the best at heating up the cookies."

"The trade secret is the thirty-second microwave button."

"Did you survive Pinewood like us?" Elliott asks.

"No, Westside," I say. "I heard Pinewood was nicer. Fewer knife fights."

"It was hell for me. But not Rachel, she was our class princess."

Rachel shifts from one foot to the other. It's satisfying to witness her awkward tics, the lack of pretense in the way she digs her fingers into her arm. Something is going on between these two.

"Well, high school's over now. Let's drink," Elliott says, and, like magic, we turn back to the bar to find Mary waiting to take our orders.

The tension eases a bit after Rachel buys us a round of 100-proof peppermint schnapps shots.

"I feel like I'm back in the frat," Elliott said as he throws back the liquor. He orders an IPA on draft afterward.

A Chinese drag queen frat bro lawyer? I study Elliott closely as we grab a high-top next to the door. He's a mixture of contradictory traits, and I want to figure out what white midwestern pressures merged to create him. What a gift to be an actor.

"Elliott just graduated from Stanford," Rachel tells me. "He got a thirty-six on his ACT."

Rachel's doing her mom thing again, bragging about Elliott like he's her kid. I pretend to be impressed, even though I met three other dorks in my dorm who also got perfect ACTs, including Luke.

Elliott looks embarrassed. "I'm good at memorization. That's all those standardized tests are. How's the acting going?"

Rachel sips her drink. "It's okay. Not a ton of gigs but I've gotten pretty good at singing both parts of 'A Whole New World' for birthday parties."

Elliott laughs. "They let you play Jasmine? Do you color your skin?"

"Just a wig," she says. "I pull it off, trust me."

I say nothing. In seventh grade, I wanted to give myself blond highlights, so I bought the dye from CVS and hid it under my bed. My mom found the box a few days later when she was picking up my laundry and made me throw it out.

"You can't dye your pretty hair," she said, smoothing my frizzy black hair with her pale hands. "This is your culture."

It was easy for her to say. The truth is, I didn't know anything about what it meant to be Taiwanese or half Taiwanese or whatever, but I knew that hair wasn't culture, it was just dead cells. My mom was right not to let me get highlights, though. The blond and black would've made me look like a tiger.

"Do you still see Robby around?" Elliott asks.

"Not since he broke up with me the summer before college," Rachel says. "Why?"

"I think he's gay now. I matched with him on Grindr last night."

"You're kidding me." Rachel's brow furrows like she's trying to do mental math.

I notice that Elliott's barely touched his beer. I don't offer to leave, even though it's clear I'm not part of the conversation.

"It must be some joke he's playing on his friends," Rachel says. "We dated for years. I'd know if he was gay."

"If it's a joke, then he's really committed."

"What do you mean?"

"I mean, he sent me a dick pic." Elliott flicks through the camera roll on his phone and holds up a grainy sepia-filtered picture of an erect penis next to a Coke can. It's maybe six inches, with a vein throbbing down the middle. "Look familiar?"

Rachel averts her eyes, says she has to go to the bathroom, and almost knocks over her chair escaping from the table.

"That wasn't very nice," I say.

Elliott shrugs. The penis is still on the table between us. Even with Luke, I never felt optimistic enough to send the female equivalent of a dick pic. It requires a trusting nature.

"She'll be fine," he says.

I like Elliott despite myself. Somehow it's easy between us. We argue about the ending of *Lost* and which Chinese restaurant is the best (I'm a Golden Harbor regular, he insists Bo Bo China is underrated) for twenty minutes, until Rachel returns from the bathroom with a guy and a white miniature poodle.

"This is Derek," she says as she touches his arm.

It makes sense that Rachel would find the only straight guy in the bar. He's young and has a haircut that makes him look like the lead singer of a Christian rock band—buzzed on the sides and styled in the middle. His poodle stares at me from under his barstool.

"What's her name?" I ask.

"Talia."

"You gave her a human name?"

"She is human. Look."

Derek snaps his fingers, and the poodle's ears perk. He claps his hands, and she jumps on the barstool next to him. She barks at him until he pulls a treat from his back pocket, and then she jumps down.

"Good girl," he says.

"Brava!" says Rachel.

"She should do drag," Elliott says as he bends down to pet her. "She's got good stage presence."

"What do you do?" I ask Derek.

"I bought Bitcoin before it took off," he says.

Elliott raises his eyebrows. I bite my lip to keep from laughing.

"What do you want to do, Vi?" Rachel asks me. "I mean, you can't work at the front desk forever."

"Who says? Maybe I'll die at my post, and they'll install a plaque above that painting of a boat to commemorate my service to Hillside."

Derek chuckles while Rachel studies me, unsmiling, across the table.

"Be serious," she says.

"I don't know. Maybe I'll become an actress like you. How hard can it be? Pretending to be someone you're not."

"Harder than you think," Elliott says as he emerges from under the table. He's gotten white dog hair all over the front of his black jeans.

Rachel turns away from me and starts peppering Derek with first-date questions like, "Where are you from?" and "How often do you call your mom?"

I turn to Elliott and feign a yawn.

"Want to see something?" I say in his ear.

CHAPTER THREE

I lead Elliott to the entrance—across the bar, around the perimeter of the dance floor that has filled with crust punks, kids in neon crop tops, and one bachelorette party wearing matching pink shirts that read "One Penis Forever." I turn back to see Rachel and Derek where we left them, their heads bent toward one another in conversation, the poodle asleep under the table.

Elliott follows me up the stairs. Outside the promise of rain still hangs in the air, and I tilt my head to the murky sky. *Tipsy* is the perfect word for what I'm feeling: my pulse is in my feet and my body is a washing machine. The alley blacktop is still mostly empty, just a few smokers with their backs against the railing.

I find the blob where I left it next to the trash can.

"See?" I say to the blob. "I came back."

"Who are you talking to?" Elliott asks, arms crossed against his chest, skeptical.

"Come look at this."

He peers into the darkness.

"All I see are beer cans."

"No, here."

His gaze follows my finger to the blob's nebulous shape and small black stone eyes.

"What the fuck?"

I pull out my phone and show Elliott the blobfish Wikipedia page.

"You think this is it?" I ask.

He squints at my phone, at the blob, back again.

"I don't know. Shouldn't it be in water if it's a fish?"

I shrug.

"I'll be right back," he says and runs back down the stairs to the bar.

The blob and I wait for Elliott to return. I step backward into a puddle and the wet sinks into my toes through my canvas shoes. I hadn't thought beyond showing Elliott the blob, pointing to it and saying, *Isn't this thing crazy? Can you believe it exists?* I didn't want to save it; I just wanted another witness.

Elliott returns with a red Solo Cup of water. He pours it around the edges of the blob, and together we watch its edges ripple around the liquid.

"Weird," Elliott says. "Something about the eyes. They're sad, right?"

"I think you're reading too much into it," I say. "It seems okay."

I feel drunk and stupid. I put my hand to my cheek to check for Asian glow, but my face is numb. How did the night turn into me looking at a fish with a stranger and trying to figure out if its eyes look sad?

"I have to go," I say.

Elliott looks up, surprised.

"You're abandoning me to raise our blobfish alone?"

"Nice to meet you," I say.

I jog out of the alleyway, shifting left, then right, favoring my dry shoe. I read somewhere that running zigzag is how you're supposed to evade a bear attack.

IT'S A BAD habit—my sudden departures. As a kid, I watched *It's a Wonderful Life* and was jealous of George Bailey. I wanted a guardian angel to show me how shitty everyone's life would be if I'd never been born. I craved that kind of affirmation. My leavings were a test: Would anyone care if I disappeared? On a Girl Scout trip in third grade I wandered away from my troop on a hike, huddled up in an abandoned farmhouse, and started the timer on my watch. It wouldn't take them long, I thought, as I smeared mud drawings on rotted wood boards. It took them until the next morning to realize I was gone. They found me covered in a pile of wet leaves, chewing on a piece of bark.

As a ten-year-old, I snuck away from my mom at the grocery store and hid behind the milk refrigerator. As she went up and down the aisles, happily squeezing avocados and thumping melons, I imagined myself becoming a fridge creature, spending my days handing customers the dairy product of their choosing from behind the frosted glass. When she finally got to checkout, I heard my name on the intercom and felt a sick kind of relief. My mom rubbed my chilled arms and said, "Why do you do this?"

Despite my habit of disappearing, I'd never heard the phrase "Irish goodbye" before the night of Luke's department mixer. During cocktail hour, Luke was busy talking with his professors and I got caught in a conversation with his engineering friends, two identical twins named Brad and Lars. They were close with Luke—the three of them had survived their thermodynamics course by splitting up the problems and copying each other's answers. Now between caprese skewers, Brad and Lars rated the only two female engineering professors on a scale of one to ten.

"What's the criteria?" I asked.

"We rate face first. Then body," said Lars.

"Isn't the face a part of the body?" I asked.

They laughed, and I wondered if they ever played this game with Luke, if they rated me. I wouldn't score high in either category.

"Five for face," Brad declared about Dr. Clemens, the robotics specialist who'd let Luke retake an exam after he emailed her with some lie about how his grandma had just died. She was cute, a short brunette wearing plaid pants and chunky red glasses.

"Why?" I asked.

"She looks like a squirrel," Brad says.

"I need to pee," I said, and left out the back door.

It took Luke two hours to realize I was gone, long after I'd finished walking the eighteen blocks home in wedge heels. He called, and I didn't pick up. I have all of Luke's voicemails saved to my phone, but the others are mundane: should we do Mexican or Chinese for dinner, do we have eggs, will I come out for drinks after his lab. In this voicemail, his voice is soft and slurred.

"You and your fucking Irish goodbyes," he says.

I've googled the etymology of the idiom, and there's no definite answer as to its origin. One blog said the phrase came from a woman who had two Irish boyfriends, one after another, who both left her without explanation. Another theory was that during the 1845–52 potato famine, the Irish had to leave for America so quickly they didn't get a chance to say goodbye to anyone. Or, and this one seems most likely to me, it's just another xenophobic stereotype about how the Irish get drunk and leave before people realize how drunk they are.

I listen to Luke's voicemail again after I leave Elliott and the blobfish and return to my basement or "garden level" apartment. In reality, there's no garden—my half-submerged windows show the tops of grass, sidewalk, and pedestrians' shoes as they walk by. I don't mind the darkness; the real problem is that my apartment floods whenever it rains, and even after my landlord begrudgingly wet-vacs the standing water, the carpet smells like mildew and decay for months.

I smell it now as I lie in the fetal position in the center of my living room, drinking water from a mug that my dad gave me for Christmas. A little ceramic cow in the middle pokes its head out at me. I clutch my phone in my hand and press play.

"Are you testing me?" Luke whispers into the room. "You make me so tired."

I don't remember much about that night, but I must've made it up to him somehow because we dated for another two years. I might've told myself that I was being mysterious, that I needed to be unpredictable to keep Luke's interest, but the truth is, leaving was the only way to see if he'd come after me. I left him with strangers at my brother's annual New Year's Eve party, and he didn't notice until midnight. Once it took him thirty minutes to figure out that I'd hidden behind a concrete pillar to avoid getting into an Uber going downtown. I never made it through a full evening with Luke's friends, who talked for hours about sports and boobs and which engineering major made the most money.

"They're walking clichés," I said, and sometimes Luke agreed with me.

"You don't even know them," he said other times.

Even when it was just Luke and me, I still left. Later I would tell him, "I just needed air," or "I left the stove on," or "I was going to the bathroom and realized I forgot my wallet at home," or "I think I have a brain aneurysm and according to WebMD, I only have a month to live." It didn't matter what I said, my absences accumulated, and each time I left, it took longer for Luke to find me.

I take a gulp of water, and the cow in my mug is dry again.

"I'll see you tomorrow," he says before the message cuts out.

There's mercy in his voice—he gave me a promise that he knew I needed. Staring at my water-stained ceiling tiles, I think about how easy it would be to call him and ask him to repeat those words, in real time. *I'll see you tomorrow.*

I sit up, and the apartment spins. It wouldn't be easy though, I know this. Because there are other words between us, the ones he said to me eight months ago outside of Denny's, the world's dumbest place to have a breakup. I can't think about what he said, so I put on my still-damp shoes and stuff my phone and keys into my pocket. I open my door and step back outside.

IT'S FIVE IN the morning by the time I return to the alleyway outside of the Back Door. On the way back, I throw up water, peppermint schnapps, and gin on the base of a lamppost. The vomit stings my nose and throat, but the grass absorbs the clear liquid like it's dew. Bars close at three, and the streets are empty of partyers. No one sees me stumble, vomit, keep stumbling. I walk in the middle of the street and try to keep my sneakers aligned with the double lines. I lose my balance every ten steps or so.

I feel mostly sober by the time I return to the spot where I stood with Elliott six hours ago. My body's purged of toxins, and the lightening sky means night is almost over. I look next to the trash can; there's nothing but blacktop and a puddle of water where the blob used to be. I sit down beside the puddle and pull my knees into my chest. Did I imagine the swollen frown, the black bead eyes?

Elliott gave me his number while Rachel was in the bathroom, so I pull out my phone and text him.

did you take the blob home?

As I sit, it starts to mist. I watch the droplets gather on my sweatshirt, an oversized university hoodie that my dad gave me when I was accepted into the engineering college. I dropped out of the program in January, a semester before I would've graduated. My parents still think I'm going to go back, that I just left school so I could focus on applying to the Peace Corps. I told them I was going to go to Madagascar for a few years and bike around to local communities to help plant rice fields and advise on eco-friendly practices.

"You have a big heart," my mom said.

"I'll buy extra bug spray," my dad said.

"How are you going to learn another language? You barely speak English," Alex said.

For a month, I had fifteen Peace Corps website tabs open on my computer. I would look at the application for ten minutes, then turn on the three basic cable channels my TV gets and watch *The Big Bang Theory* reruns till I fell asleep.

I couldn't get past the first question on the first page: Why do you want to be a Peace Corps volunteer? I'm sure everyone wrote some version of the same cliché: I want to help people. But I couldn't bring myself to lie to the Peace Corps folks, who, based on the photos on the website, seemed like genuinely good people who did want to help. I didn't want to help. I wanted to escape, which didn't sound good on paper. When the Peace Corps deadline passed, I ceremonially got high and closed out all my tabs.

Now the mist turns into a light rain that dots my sweatshirt. I get up from the ground to leave. As I'm wiping the debris off my pants, I see the blobfish. It's moved maybe five feet away from its original position to a dry spot by the top of the stairs, under the building's overhang.

"There you are," I say, like it's the missing sock I've been looking for.

I crouch down close to it, closer than I've ever been, and let my hand hover over its body. Elliott was right—there's something sad about it. It's not like Talia the poodle, who could shake hands, spin, and play dead. It doesn't flinch when I lower my hand and let my finger pads graze the surface of its flesh, which isn't fishy but soft and dry.

"Where did you come from?" I whisper as I stroke the blob with two fingers.

Liam Johnson asked me the same question in freshman-year concert band. We both were percussionists and stood in the back behind the tubas for the whole hour, but we rarely spoke. He was out of my league, with his floppy emo hair, brown leather bracelet, and, according to Kylie, who had PE class with him, well-defined six-pack. I was nonexistent in high school. I had straight-cut bangs that covered half of my face and wore the same khaki cargo pants year-round. The only reason I was in band was because no one knew how to play any of the keyboard-based instruments, and I had been taking piano lessons since I was five.

"I come from here," I said, confused by the question.

"Yeah, but what are you?" he asked.

He wasn't trying to be hurtful. His innocent face betrayed no malice, and he wasn't laughing at me. The problem was that my parents sheltered me. They fed me Rice-A-Roni, bought me white Barbies, let me watch *The Amazing Race* snuggled between them until I fell asleep. My entire life I'd been hovering above my otherness like a kid in a dunk tank, and with one question, Bobby hit the target that dropped me in.

"My dad's from Taiwan," I said.

"Cool," Bobby said, and never spoke to me again.

The blob shakes beneath my fingertips as the rain starts to come down harder. Puddles form in the alleyway, and thunder rumbles in the distance like a motorcycle revving. I check the weather app on my phone, and it's 90 percent cloud with a lightning bolt for the next six hours. The rain could flood the street, spill into the overhang, drown the blob in muddy water.

"What do you want to do?" I ask.

The blob breathes, slow and steady. Before I can psych myself out, I scoop the thing off the blacktop and set it in the pouch of my hoodie. Instinctively, I rub my hands on my pants to wipe off slime residue, but there is none. The blob doesn't feel like slime at all; its exterior is smooth as baby skin.

CHAPTER FOUR

I wake up to the sound of my phone vibrating against the lamp on my bedside table. I feel like shit. My head's home to its very own marching band, and my mouth tastes like sour milk. I sit up without thinking and immediately regret it. I don't bother answering the phone—I know without looking that it's my mom reminding me about tonight's weekly family dinner. It's Alex's turn to pick the restaurant, and last time he chose a specialty steakhouse where you cook your own steak. I overcooked mine, and Alex took his off the grill after five minutes and ate half of it raw before my dad made him put it back on.

"Bet this is the first time you've ever cooked for yourself," he said to me with blood on his lip.

"Are you enjoying your *E. coli*?" I said in return, beef stuck between both of my canines.

My mom started family dinner after both Alex and I moved out so she could check up on us. "Who wouldn't want to spend every Saturday night with their parents?" she said, right after she'd finished helping me unpack things in my dorm room. She hung Christmas lights over my desk, and when she left, she squeezed my hand so hard my ring finger cracked.

I walk to the kitchen and chug a glass of tap water. I didn't take my contacts out before I went to sleep, so they've shriveled and hardened against my eyes during the night. They feel like pieces of glass on my eyeballs, and through them my apartment is sideways and blurry. I squint at my microwave: 11:42 a.m. In the bathroom, I grope through my medicine cabinet, find a few stray ibuprofens in the corner, their maroon coating chipping off, and swallow three pills dry. I walk back to my bedroom, grab my phone from the nightstand, and crawl into my twin bed, under the blue-and-white-striped sheets I've had since I was a kid, soft and pilled from repeated washing.

I have a missed call from my mom and a voicemail. I don't listen to it. There's a 9:00 a.m. text from Rachel: Hey girl! Last night was fun. I missed you leaving. Did you get home okay? Let's do that again soon xoxox. It's sweet enough to give me a cavity. I don't respond, just close my eyes and wait for the Advil to kick in. A few minutes after I fall back asleep, my phone vibrates.

It's a text message from Elliott: no I don't have the blobfish. I just gave it some more water lol it looked okay

"Fuck," I say.

I had forgotten everything—the blob, the flooding alleyway, the run home with its Jell-O body bouncing in my sweatshirt. I thought it must've been a dream or a gin hallucination. I stare at Elliott's text, read it again like it's written in code.

Finally, I get up. I move slowly toward the living room, trying not to make any noise. Luke and his parents, Montana born and bred, were avid hunters and taught me how to step silently, without crunching leaves or breaking twigs. The blinds are closed, but the afternoon sun streams through the cracks. In the middle of the room is the IKEA coffee table my parents gave me because of the chip in the corner. And there, basking in the light, is the blob. I watch the edges of its liquid-solid form ripple against the wood grain.

"Fuck," I say again.

I'm more scared of the blob today than I was last night. It looks bigger, its skin more beige than translucent, but it could be just a trick of the light. I drop to my knees and study the thing. I can't tell how it's feeling.

Last night I was worried about the blob drowning, but now, seeing the thing spread across my table like a giant booger, it looks unnatural. It can't be a land creature—it seems to have no legs or crawling ability, no way to move or find food. I get up, go to the kitchen, and fill the large bowl that I eat microwave popcorn out of with water.

"You can't be an alien, so you must be a fish," I say, and place the bowl on the side table next to the couch.

To pump myself up for the blob relocation, I clap my hands together and jump up and down. It was easier to touch the thing when I was drunk. After counting to five three different times, I finally scoop my hands under the blob's edges like I'm giving it a hug, lift it in the air, and toss it into the bowl. The blob doesn't sink in the water—it floats on top, like the fat you skim off soup. Nothing else changes. Its body is still spread, not crumpled or folded, and its mouth is above water, breathing in and out steadily. It leaves nothing behind on the table, no slime, not even the Doritos crumbs and stray Lucky Charms I left there. I can't tell if it ate them or if they're stuck to its skin. Either way, looking over my work, I consider it a job well done. The blob looks more like a pet in the bowl, contained and fishlike, something I can take care of.

My hangover returns as the adrenaline wears off, so I collapse on the couch and turn on an episode of *Chopped* that I've stopped midway through. The contestants have to make an appetizer out of Easter Peeps and horseradish. I open a box of Fruity Pebbles. The cereal kind of looks like colorful fish food, so I toss a piece into the blob's bowl just to see what happens. It lands on the blob's lips and quickly gets sucked up.

"Good job, Bob," I say.

I meant to say "blob," but I like the way "Bob" sounds. Pets should have names.

"Bob," I say again, cementing the name and gender. "Bob."

I fall asleep with my mouth open and cereal in my hand. When I wake up, Bob the blob is on my chest, eating Fruity Pebbles from my palm one by one.

I DRIVE TWENTY miles over the speed limit on my way to the restaurant my brother chose, a sushi place in a strip mall on the north side of town. At the red light, I rub my hands against my jeans and shiver. Its sixty degrees out, and kids in cutoffs and tank tops skateboard past the gray minivan my parents gave me when I graduated high school.

I didn't have time to process it as it happened: Bob sucking the cereal off my skin with bulbous lips. It didn't feel like a dog's lick, slobbery and wet, or a cat's sandpaper tongue. His suction on my skin was gentle and smooth, like a human kiss. As soon as I understood what he was doing, I jumped up, and he slid off my stomach and onto the middle couch cushion. My cell phone rang, and I picked it up without thinking. It was Alex.

"Where the fuck are you? They won't seat us unless our whole party is present."

I checked the time on my phone, quarter past six—I was already fifteen minutes late.

"What restaurant?" I asked, stuffing my wallet and keys into my purse and forcing my feet into my still-damp sneakers.

"Number One Sushi, across the street from the Best Buy on Prospect. Hurry up, I'm starving," he said and hung up.

I was almost to the door when I looked back at Bob, who had sunk into the crack between cushions, probably eating lint or old popcorn kernels. I could have left him there to rip apart my thrift-store furniture or do something worse, like multiply. I imagined returning home to find new blobs populating every surface of my apartment, a hundred sad marble eyes staring at me. I had no choice. As quickly as I could, I stuffed him in a Whole Foods paper bag, carried him outside, and buckled him into the passenger seat of my van. I would show him to my parents, those levelheaded mouse killers, and they would tell me what to do.

Now, pulling into the strip mall parking lot, I realize unleashing Bob in the restaurant might not be a good idea. He hasn't moved the entire van ride, and I'm not sure I've ever seen him move, not even when he crawled up the length of my body. I tighten his seat belt, park in the shade of a buckeye tree, and crack the windows.

"Don't do anything I wouldn't do," I say. "I'll be back soon."

From the outside, Number One Sushi looks like a mom-and-pop place, but inside it's slick, with mirrored walls, corner booths, ornamental fans. The AC is blasting, and the hairs on my forearm prickle. It's not busy, just a few couples and some college kids studying by the windows. My mom sits in the only chair in the waiting area, her purse in her lap, with my dad and brother standing on either side of her.

"About time," Alex says, and walks away to try to flag down a server.

"Are you all right?" my mom asks.

"I'm getting the sampler," my dad says.

"Sorry I'm late," I say.

They're not mad at me, just hungry and worried, and I want to explain the circumstances, the blob sitting in my van who I've just given a taste for sugary cereal, but Alex returns too quickly with a waitress. She seats us at a table big enough for a group of ten, and we leave an empty chair between each of us. The spatial distance is fitting—our family dinners are always disjointed.

In general, Alex's temper is difficult to predict. If he's in a good mood, he can charm my parents with stories about his residency—the kid with a speech impediment who calls him "the best dogtor in the world," or the little girl whose cancer he caught early in an annual physical. He always moves his hands in circles as he talks, like he's a magician practicing misdirection. I'm immune to Alex's gimmicks, although it's hard to sneer at photos of the handwritten notes he receives, the six-year-old patient who wrote "I LoVe Doc L" in shaky bubble letters. But if he's in a bad mood, Alex is a storm cloud of negativity, and I'm the lightning rod. It's too soon to tell which side of Alex is on display tonight, though he does seem quieter than usual.

Most weeks, my mother asks Alex and me questions like we're game show contestants. After thirty minutes of trying to draw out answers from us, she gives up and smiles wearily for the rest of dinner.

"It's nice to have the family together," she always says toward the end, picking apart her meal with fork and knife.

My dad mostly focuses on the food, chiming in occasionally with historical context from a podcast or facts from the continuing-education astronomy course he's taking at the university.

My parents are so different, it's difficult to believe that they ever found each other. They met in the Chicago suburbs, teenagers in the same honors US History class—my dad one of the only Asian kids at the well-off public school.

"How did you start talking?" I would always ask. "Who made the first move?"

But they'd just shrug off my inquiries, claim they couldn't remember. A few decades after my parents graduated, students from their high school made the paper for attempting to form a KKK club.

Maybe they connected because they both grew up working class—my mom's mother was a social worker, my dad's father worked ten-hour shifts at an electronics factory. But they don't talk about their upbringings. All I have are half-stories, blank spots in my family history. A Taiwanese great-uncle brain-washed by Japanese soldiers, never to be seen again. The rumor that my agong's father had two wives—a fact that was concealed so he would be allowed to marry in a Christian church. Only rarely will my dad mumble about being bullied, thrust into American schools with little English-language skills—a lamb to the slaughter.

When our waitress returns with our water, Alex, my dad, and I all order the sampler while my mom gets a vegetable stir-fry with sauce on the side. She gets sensitive when we joke about her white-woman taste buds.

"You're half white, too, you know?" she'll sniff.

Tonight she seems nervous and jittery, and I regret not listening to her voicemail. My dad fills the silence with moon facts. In his class, they're studying differential gravity and the moon's effect on the tides.

"Did you know the sun also produces tides?" he says, finishing up his monologue. I can tell he's just killing time until his food comes. "I hope you guys remember to never stop learning."

"But not all learning takes place in the classroom," my mom says and pats my hand.

My dad startles at the correction. He turns to me, and I watch the realization that I dropped out of college two years ago sweep across his face.

"Of course not," my dad says and wipes his glasses. "You know what I meant, Vi."

I nod and take a sip of water. The waitress brings us our meals, and my mom oohs and aahs over the colorful raw salmon rolls and sashimi that she would never order. I think of the blob shrinking and drying in the heat of the van. I'll tell them about Bob right after we eat. No one speaks as we break apart our wooden chopsticks.

IT TAKES THIRTY minutes for us to finish eating, or at least slow down. For once, I'm not hungry. I look up from my half-finished plate and study my family members instead. My role is usually to interject—a sarcastic one-liner to my brother, a platitude to my mom, a random fact I learned on *Cash Cab* to my dad. I play the role of pesky sister and dutiful daughter, and then I retreat. Today's different, though. Today I'm holding a creature hostage.

"I need your opinion on something," I say, breaking the after-meal stupor.

I expect Alex to say, "Again?" and roll his eyes to indicate that he thinks I'm helpless and spoiled. This is not the first time I've come to my parents with a problem. Like when I walked home from the dorm with a laundry basket soaked with my freshman roommate Jordan's pee. She had gotten blackout drunk and used my hamper as a toilet while I was pulling an all-nighter in the engineering library. My mom washed the pee-stained clothes while I watched TV and ate chicken salad. Or when Luke dumped me, and I spent days in my parents' basement, blasting Elliott Smith at top volume and walking on the slowest speed of the treadmill.

Alex doesn't bring up any of these incidents. Instead he turns to my mom and says, "Did you tell her?"

"Tell me what?" I ask.

My mom tilts her head at me sympathetically, the way you look at someone when you know they deserve the pain they're about to be in, but you still feel sorry for them.

"I tried to call you—," she starts.

"We sold the house," my dad says as he shreds his napkin. He won't look me in the eye.

"What?" I look from my dad to my mom to Alex.

The house in question is the only house I've ever lived in: a two-story Craftsman bungalow that they moved into when my mom was eight months pregnant with me. It was their reward for spending five hundred dollars on their wedding, clipping coupons, and buying secondhand furniture. My dad put a swing up on the big oak tree in the backyard, and my mom read romance novels in the garden. In the spring I collected rosebuds and killed Japanese beetles, an invasive species that made cookie-cutter holes in the rose leaves. Maybe I'm romanticizing the place. I can also see Alex sneaking out to smoke cigarettes, hiding the butts in my mom's hanging flower baskets. Me, upstairs in my attic room with the slanted walls that made me feel safe and suffocated, slamming my bedroom door over and over again. It was my home.

"It sold quickly. We closed in just under a month," my mom says.

"They got fifty over the asking price," Alex says.

"You knew about this a month ago?"

There's a long silence. I push my fingernails into the palm of my hand.

"We know you've got a lot going on. With Luke, applying for the Peace Corps. You've been preoccupied. We didn't know how you'd react," my mom says finally.

"Can I grab my stuff, at least?" I ask.

In the basement are stacks of notebooks from high school, in which I'd drawn comics and written manifestos and stories of what I thought I'd be like when I was older. I had to believe that things would get better. One day I'd have a ton of friends and be happily married to some blond man named Chet. I would host dinner parties in a beaded gold cocktail dress and swirl wine in my glass as I talked about Tolstoy.

"What stuff?" my mom says.

"My notebooks."

"I thought those were old course notes. They'd been in the basement forever."

I force air in and out through my nostrils. Blood rises to my cheeks.

"I threw them out," she says. "Everything's gone. The couple who bought the place have already moved in. They're both entomology professors—she studies mosquitoes, he studies flies. Isn't that cute?"

I close my eyes. I exhale through my mouth deeply and try to loosen the tightness in my chest.

"You're being dramatic, Vi," Alex says.

I open my eyes and see my brother leaning back in his chair with his arms crossed.

"How could you not tell me?"

"You didn't care when we told you Great-Aunt Fan died. You texted a crying face emoji. You didn't even call to check on Dad. Why would you care about this?"

I tug my hair out of my face and try to remember what I did when my dad texted us the news. It was a few weeks ago, on a Friday, so I was probably drunk, trying not to think about Luke. It hadn't sunk in that Great-Aunt Fan, the old woman who gave me White Rabbit milk candies at Christmas, was dead. I told myself I'd come back to the text thread, add a sincere condolence to accompany the emoji, something from the heart. But I never did.

"This has nothing to do with that," I say.

"Sure it does," Alex says. "You don't think about anyone but yourself."

"Fuck you," I say, and get up from my chair.

Alex smirks at me. My mom stares straight down at the napkin in her lap. She's embarrassed that I'm making a scene. I want to leave them with something more original, something that will make them feel as bad as I feel. A rock to sink to the depths of their stomachs. But I can't find the words, so I exit with my "fuck you" in the air and half-finished plate on the table.

I remember the blob just as I reach the van. I hesitate as I pop the door open. He's exactly where I left him.

"We don't need them," I tell Bob as I put the van into reverse and gun the engine.

CHAPTER FIVE

Bob and I spend the rest of the night on the couch, eating Cup Noodles with *Top Chef* on. One of the chefs immediately gets eliminated for tasting a sauce with his finger rather than a spoon.

"Padma Lakshmi doesn't come on as host until season two, but we have to start with season one for continuity," I explain.

The blob sits next to me now—him on the far right, me on the far left. The middle couch cushion is empty, a no-woman-or-blob barrier. It's our uneasy new agreement.

After I got home, I washed out the popcorn bowl with a generous heaping of dish soap as the blob sat silently in his take-out bag. I considered wadding up the plastic and throwing it in the garbage, but I couldn't have another pet death on my conscience. Another piece of evidence to support Alex's accusation.

I plopped the blob on the couch instead, on the cushion that already has a tear in it from when I tried to kill a house centipede with a butcher knife. Bob landed face down on the corduroy and righted himself so quickly, it looked like his body didn't even move, like his eyes just floated to the other side. A neat trick.

"Okay, so you're not a fish."

I leaned over him and put on my compromising voice.

"I respect that. I won't be submerging you in any more liquids. In return, I need you to stay where I put you. I can't have you moving around the apartment unsupervised and crawling on top of things. Understood?"

Bob said nothing. Maybe he was listening, though, because for the next eight hours, he didn't move. I stayed up till 6:00 a.m., watching cheftestants cry from exhaustion as they tried to make a five-course wedding meal for a hundred people in one day. I ended up falling asleep sitting up, with ice cream on my chin. Bob never twitched.

"It's bullshit that they moved without telling me," I say to him now as I scroll through my phone.

It's Sunday afternoon, and other than my mom texting *Are you okay, honey?* as I was driving home, no one has contacted me. No apology, no phone call. I can just imagine Alex at the table, scoffing at my dramatic exit.

Him saying, "You know how Vi is. She'll get over it. You coddle her."

On the television screen, one of the chefs uses another's pot of boiling water to blanch her asparagus.

"Are you kidding me?" the wronged chef yells as she runs to the pantry in search of another pot. Her face is red with anger, and sweat drips from her forehead to her chin and into her homemade ricotta. The rest of her words are a series of bleeps and "Jesus Christs."

"I'm not like that," I say to Bob. I can't tell if he believes me or not.

I never saw Luke get angry, or even worried, when we were together. It seemed like life was easy for him—he was a golden boy.

"You stress too much," he'd say and ruffle my hair like I was a dog. "It'll work out."

I always thought the easy way he existed in the world would rub off on me, but I was never as capable as him. Every winter he helped pull cars out of the snow with his truck and tow chain. He called the cable company when our internet went out. He was strong enough to wrap his arms around me and squeeze all the air out of my body. The world was meant for him.

"I can't be your only friend," he said once.

I was surprised. For the longest time I thought he hadn't noticed the difference between us. None of the friends I made stuck around for long. I was too intense, too sensitive. I pushed people away when I needed them the most. For Luke, I tried to be different.

"I'm friends with the barista at the vegan bakery."

"What's her name?"

I couldn't remember. I thought of her only as the tattooed girl who drew smiley faces on my bag of pink sprinkle donuts.

"The Homer Special," she called my order, and I laughed even though I'd never seen *The Simpsons.*

"I'm selective with friendships. A background and credit check are required. I have to hold interviews. What can I say? Sometimes they're more trouble than they're worth," I told him. He didn't laugh.

I throw a pepperoni from my Lunchable in Bob's direction, and it lands between his eyes. He sucks it down to his mouth and eats it.

"You're a friend," I say.

I swear he turns then, registers my compliment with a slight widening of his eyes.

"Good blob."

PAUL, THE NIGHT auditor, is used to me coming in for my shift with days-old smudged mascara and unbrushed hair. This Monday I surprise him with my early arrival, bright eyes, and lack of hangover.

"You're ten minutes early. Did you sleep at all?" Paul asks, yawning.

He's in his late forties, with a graying beard and a potbelly. Sometimes he shows me pictures of his wife Paula's cooking: lasagna, pork butt carnitas, chili with brisket. Hungover, I look at the blurry photos of heavy beige foods and sing "Paul and Paula" over and over again until he pretends to laugh. Like me, he knows about not sleeping. He knows that the hour between 2:00 and 3:00 a.m. is the worst because you both feel guilty for not sleeping and still plan to sleep—you tell yourself, *If I sleep now, I'll still get a solid five hours.* If you push past that hour, though, the dread alleviates. How beautiful it is to give in to sleeplessness. Insomnia's the reason Paul became a night auditor.

"I'd be up all night anyway," he said. "Might as well get paid for it."

"Got a full eight hours of beauty sleep," I say now.

"Well, look at you."

"My new roommate's a good influence on me."

"Roommate" is a bit of a stretch, but it's true that Bob's given me a reason to get up in the morning. A mouth to feed, a body with movements to monitor, a silent confidant. So far he's been happy to listen, sit on the right couch cushion, and eat cereal for three meals a day. I put a bowl of Froot Loops on the coffee table before I left for work.

"Woof," Paul says, and winks at me as he walks sleepily out of the hotel. He must assume "roommate" is a euphemism for getting laid.

WHEN RACHEL GETS in and doesn't hand me a Starbucks cup, I know she's mad at me.

"I forgot," she says. "There's free coffee in the breakroom."

I raise an eyebrow. She ignores me and starts checking off items on the clipboard. She looks a little worse for wear this morning—her usually ruthlessly straightened hair is frizzy, with flyaways curling around her temple. She's taken a stab at swabbing concealer under her eyes, but I can spot the angry red of a pimple on her left temple. It's disorienting seeing her without a full face of makeup—like a mascot without its head on.

For the next hour Rachel ignores me as I organize paper clips by color and scroll through Facebook baby announcements, memes, and my aunt's rants about Five Guys' customer service.

"So, I assume you got home okay?" Rachel asks finally.

"Friday?"

Rachel nods without looking at me. Her face is turned out toward the nonexistent customers. The only guests we've seen are a sunburned family of four who complained about the bacon being limp.

"We'll make a note of that," Rachel had told them, her voice sunny.

"Yup. I'm still alive," I tell her.

I know it's killing her not to say more. She can't stand not being liked because she's not used to it—being friendly and receiving friendliness is a given for her. Still, I remember Friday night. How Elliott knocked her sideways and almost made me feel sorry for her. Maybe fostering a blob is making me more maternal. Or maybe I really miss Starbucks coffee.

"Sorry. I should've said goodbye," I say.

"It's okay," she says, and smiles, and it's like sun bursting through clouds. No wonder everyone is in love with her.

A few hours later I'm home again, greeted by the television. I left the Food Network on for Bob—Bobby Flay was trying to prove that he could cook barbecue better than a man who learned from his grandfather and had been working the pit for twenty years.

"Honey, I'm home," I say.

I'm halfway to the bathroom, my pants already around my ankles, when I see John Cena on the TV, wearing a wrestling singlet and flexing his arms outside a boxing ring.

"Are you ready to see a fight?" he yells.

"WWF? I didn't even know I got this channel," I say.

I take my shoes and pants off to pee. I can't get out of the uniform fast enough—I hate polyester, the way it traps sweat and pinches my waistline. It's as I'm peeing that I realize. The blob changed the channel.

"Fuck."

I run to the living room without flushing or washing my hands. I'm wearing pink underwear that says "THURSDAY" on the butt, even though it's Monday. Bob is where I left him, flat as a pancake on the couch cushion, silent and still. The bowl of cereal on the coffee table is gone, licked clean.

"How did you do that?" I ask.

The wrestling crowd on the screen behind me cheers. The sound of fist hitting flesh gives me goose bumps. I pull the TV plug out of the socket and approach the blob.

"Tell me how you changed the channel."

It takes me a second to notice what's different about the blob. I turn on a light switch and crouch down to his level. His mouth looks normal, just how I left him—his lips puffy, like a model with a bee sting. I look for the black marbles of his eyes, the ones Elliott thought were so sad. But they're closed.

While I was at work, answering the phone, *Start your experience with Hillside Inn and Suites,* pouring cucumber water into the samovar, Bob grew eyelids.

EIGHT MONTHS EARLIER, I stood in the parking lot of Denny's, squinting against the noon sun.

"No rain," I said.

"No chance," Luke replied.

Weather, the great equalizer. We walked six feet apart as we entered the restaurant, our fingers swinging as we crossed the yellow parking lines and concrete dividers, not touching. Luke held the door open as I crossed the threshold, always the gentleman. The air conditioner swept my baby hairs up. I was the one who suggested Denny's as we lay in bed that morning, my eyes swollen from crying.

"I look like a Furby," I said to Luke, who wasn't looking. He was flat on his back with his eyes closed as he pretended to sleep, hands folded over one another like a dead soldier.

The night before, he told me he was tired of me. My leavings, my insecurities, my jittery need to please. I was tempted to beg. My life before Luke had been empty, an endless expanse of ocean, until he had bobbed to the surface like a life jacket. If he left, I'd be treading water again.

"I'm just trying to make you happy," I said.

For two years I'd gone on hikes, stumbled throughout cross-country skiing, pretended to laugh at the gross-out comedies he showed me. I tried to be the "chill girl" he said he wanted.

"I know," he said. "You're like one of those AI robots who keeps trying to autocorrect my words but never gets it right."

I sank to the floor and ran my fingers through the puke-yellow woven rug I'd bought at a thrift store. There's things you don't notice until you're on the ground—the cobwebs in the corners, the dead beetle under the couch.

"You're smothering me," Luke said.

"That's an easy fix," I said. My voice was high and loud, like the scrape of a bumper on blacktop. "We'll get rid of the pillows. I can't smother you without pillows."

I gathered the pillows and threw them into the middle of the room one by one—bed pillows, couch pillows, throw pillows—who knew we had so many? Pillows coated with Cheez-It crumbs, a leather cushion from his favorite chair, a fluffy white pillow his mother bought us as an apartment-warming present. Soon our scratched wood floor was covered with bedding, and Luke was gone, out the door, away from me.

"Death instruments," I whispered to the pillows.

I spread my arms and fell forward. I was maybe hoping that there was something sharp hiding beneath the fabric. Something that would maul me just a little, enough to make Luke come running back through the door. His face would collapse with emotions too tender to name, and he'd apologize for everything.

"I promise never to leave you alone again," he'd say.

But when I fell, it was just softness. It felt like falling onto a cloud.

At Denny's, a hostess gestured at a booth near the window with a view of the parking lot.

"We're training new hires today, so service might be a bit spotty," she said and handed us our laminated menus. Our waiter was a pimpled teenager named Jared whose hands shook as he poured our waters.

I ordered first—the Santa Fe skillet, an open-faced omelet topped with sausage, cheddar cheese, home fries, and two biscuits. Luke ordered fresh fruit and turkey sausage links.

I couldn't stop myself from laughing. Luke's a heavy eater with a fast metabolism. He once set off the dorm smoke alarm trying to deep-fry a cheeseburger. But for weeks he'd been subverting my expectations, watching premier league soccer when he prefers football, eating Raisin Bran instead of Cinnamon Toast Crunch. It was like he was trying to prove that I didn't really know him.

Luke ignored my laughter, just handed the menu back to the waiter and folded his straw paper into an accordion.

"He's watching his figure," I said to Jared, who walked away from the table as fast as he could.

"I hired a U-Haul," Luke said. "You don't need to help me move. Just stay at your parents' for a few days."

My parents were fond of Luke. My dad liked that he was in the engineering program, and he often spent our on-campus lunches praising Luke for not being a robot who spent his career following other people's plans rather than coming up with his own. My mom appreciated his old-school politeness. He complimented her on her cooking and didn't seem to mind when she dropped by unannounced with Kohl's bath towels she'd bought for 40 percent off.

"Why?" I asked.

"We don't like each other anymore," he said.

I shook my head.

"Everyone likes you."

Luke laughed. "You're not everyone."

It would've hurt less if he'd punched me in the solar plexus.

There was a white family of four in the corner booth—a baby with a pink barrette on her poof of hair. Over Luke's bent head, I could see her throwing her hands in the air. Her mouth was wide open, but she wasn't yet crying.

"I'm moving out tomorrow."

I reached out my hand to touch him. I felt like if I could just get him to look at me, he'd realize this whole thing was a joke. A misunderstanding.

"We can make this work," I said. "If you just give me a chance."

He kept staring down at the table and moved his hand from beneath mine.

"No, Vi."

I twisted my napkin in my lap. Where was Jared? I half stood in the booth and spotted him a few feet away, struggling with the corner booth family's food. An empty plastic glass hit the ground but made no sound.

I sat down. My face twisted, and my eyes filled. I felt my breath getting caught in the back of my throat and forced it down like swallowing a hiccup of air.

"Stop," Luke said under his breath.

"You stop," I said.

I went to the bathroom and sat on the toilet. I breathed in through my nose and out through my mouth and waited for the smell of waste and used tampons to calm me. Ten minutes later I faced myself in the mirror and wiped my Furby eyes. I practiced smiling at my alien reflection.

When I got back to our booth, our food was there, but Luke was gone. Out the window, I saw him walking across the parking lot to his truck. I ran past the family, past Jared, who called out to me that we hadn't paid yet, out the double doors. I caught Luke with his keys in the ignition.

"You can't leave," I said, my hands gripping the driver's-side door.

He rolled the window up so quickly I jerked my hand away to avoid getting my fingers clipped.

"I can," he said.

"I hope you get everything you want," he said through the crack he'd left open.

I watched him do a four-point turn to get out of the narrow lot and finally drive away. I went back inside and poked at my eggs until Jared came by and asked if I wanted a box.

"Three separate ones," I said.

I imagined Luke in our apartment, dividing up our things. Would he take one of the owl mugs from the set I'd bought for us? One of the matching lovebird potholders my aunt had quilted? Would he pack everything with care, using too much tape and tissue paper, or was he so eager to get done that he'd throw everything into the boxes and hope nothing broke? I suspected the latter. As I got up to leave, the pink-barrette baby started crying, and both parents got up to comfort her. They looked young, maybe late twenties.

"What do you need, sweetie?" they murmured to her in singsong voices.

She shrieked and flung a mash of eggs and sausage to the ground.

"Shut the fuck up," I said as I walked past.

IN MY APARTMENT, Bob blinks once, twice.

"Hello?" I say.

Suddenly self-conscious of my underwear, I pick up a blanket from the couch and tie it around my waist. Bob's open eyes are fixed on my face.

"My name is Vi," I say.

The blob's mouth moves, but no sound comes out.

"Vi," I say again. "And you're Bob."

I move my hand in front of Bob's face. Is this what it's like to have a newborn? His eyes follow my fingers from left to right. I scroll through my phone and consider calling my parents or Alex. Would they believe me? Not a chance. I press on Elliott's number instead and get his voicemail. I imagine he's screening calls, because his answering machine message sounds deliberately cool, just "Elliott Chin" spoken in a deep monotone.

"Hi Elliott. It's Vi, Rachel's friend from the other night. You remember that blob I showed you? I ended up taking it home."

I start to feel embarrassed, so I pace from front door to kitchen as I talk.

"It's growing."

I stop myself from saying "eyelids," because I know it'll make me sound crazy.

"It's growing really fast. Just wondered if you had any advice or anything. Okay, well, give me a call."

My cheeks are red as I toss my phone on the table.

STEPHANIE, MY BEST—ONLY—FRIEND in high school, got pregnant when we were sophomores. She was quiet, too. Her family immigrated from Thailand and lived in the trailer park off Washington Street. She spoke broken English and would listen to me talk for hours. Instead of going to Homecoming, we lied to our parents and spent the night studying at the university union, surrounded by undergrads who threw Frisbees through the cafe and napped on couches in front of the fish tanks.

Steph told me her secret while we sat under the bleachers playing MASH during PE. I got pissed because I kept getting shack and Mr. Jeffers, the creepy health teacher.

"This game's rigged," I said.

"I'm pregnant," she said.

"What?"

She took my hand and guided it to the flat stomach I'd always been jealous of.

"Baby," she said.

She was happy, almost in tears, as she rubbed her belly through her shirt.

"How?"

Slowly she told me about Doug Waalk, the fourth-seat tennis player who found her practicing clarinet in the band room and kissed her in the bass closet. She sat cross-legged and glowing, and I felt then the nastiness inside me. My chest tightened, and blood rushed to my face.

"You fucked him?"

She didn't understand me, but she could sense venom from my tone. She mumbled more about Doug, his blue eyes and gentle hands, the way they'd laughed together. I gave her the middle finger.

"Mad?"

"Mad," I confirmed. I got up from the gym floor and pulled on the drawstring of my gym shorts. "You're a slut."

I used the word because I knew she wouldn't know it. What I didn't know was that she would repeat it to herself the whole rest of the day, memorizing the shape of the word until she could go home and type it into her sister's iPhone. I turned and ran across the primary-color tape lines past the volleyball nets. Steph didn't follow me. She stayed beneath the bleachers cradling her belly and whispering to herself—she sat like this for the next two weeks of PE, until I tattled on her to Mr. Jeffers, who made her transfer from PE into pregnant-girl study hall. We never spoke again, but I saw her kid on Facebook, a smiley round-faced baby named Benji.

NOW I HAVE a growing creature of my own.

I don't know what to do, so I grab my wallet and walk to the corner store, where a sixtysomething cashier is listening to Taylor Swift. I buy a bag of chocolate pretzels and rip it open on my walk home.

"That's better," I say to myself.

When I get back to my apartment, the TV is on again. This time it's not WWF but UFC, Ultimate Fighting Championship. Alex loves UFC, and last Christmas he made my parents put the fights on in the background as we wrapped presents. This isn't fake wrestling, with gag tricks involving chair-throwing choreography. It's real hits and blood. The only rules are no groin kicks, fishhooks, or eye gouging.

I eat another handful of pretzels and study the blob. He looks like he hasn't moved. He's positioned exactly where I left him on the couch, but I know it's a lie. He must've plugged the TV back in and changed the channel—there's no other explanation.

"Why did you do this?" I ask.

I sit down on the middle couch cushion, the one right next to him. On the TV, a lightweight fighter pins another to the side of the cage and pulls him close to punch him in the ribs. There's intimacy in the close contact; it almost looks like an embrace.

Bob stares up at me and follows my movements. I'm surprised to find that I'm no longer scared of him. I carried this blob home in my sweatshirt. I'm responsible for him now.

"You see this?" I gesture to the two men, who've now split apart and are bouncing and jabbing in circles around the ring. "You don't want this."

I hover my hand over the blob and pet the air directly above him.

"This is what being a human is like. It's beating another human to the ground in order to survive."

Bob says nothing, but his mouth contorts into a round "o." My fingertips are directly above the blob's new eyelids. One of the fighters gets a fast right hook in, and his opponent's head snaps back. Blood wells from his upper lip. Bob's eyes have shifted from my face to the TV.

"You don't want this," I say. "You need to listen to me."

For a second, I consider action. I could push down my fingers and smooth out the blob's new eyelids. With one movement, I could unmold him and stop his growth, keep him a blob forever. What stops me is Luke's accusation, the one he left hanging between us when he left: the violence inherent in my love.

I move my hand away. I curl up beside the blob and fall asleep to the sound of flesh hitting flesh.

CHAPTER SIX

The summer I discovered romance novels and masturbation was the hottest on record—my dad spent hours rigging our sprinkler system, and still the grass browned. I was twelve and in the midst of what my mom called my "awkward phase," back when she didn't know that it would never end. Alex had just turned sixteen, and my dad gave him a beat-up blue-green Grand Am.

"Not because you deserve it," he said as he ceremoniously handed him the keys. "But because I'm tired of driving you around."

I barely saw Alex. He spent all his time in the basement watching ESPN or making out with his girlfriend, Kay, while blasting Coldplay to cover up their moans. My parents were too cheap to turn on the AC, so I was stuck sweating in my attic bedroom. I exclusively wore my Dad's XL T-shirts. I spent hours playing pool party with my Barbies, which involved soaking them in a ramen bowl filled with water. Alex never asked me to hang out with him, but once Kay called me after dinner and invited me to a party at his friend Matt's house.

"Come over, Vi," she said. She'd been dating my brother for six months, and I'd never heard her say my name before. I didn't know she knew what it was. "We're sneaking beers from Matt's dad's mini-fridge."

Her voice sounded murky, like she was talking underwater.

"I'm wearing a nightgown," I said.

I didn't tell her I'd been wearing it for two days, that sweat stains had blended with spaghetti sauce spills.

"That's okay," she said. "Just put something else on."

I heard Alex's laughter in the background. It was loud and mean, and I assumed he'd been listening in on our conversation and was laughing at me, his loser sister. Maybe Kay had called as a joke.

"I can't. Bye," I said, and hung up the phone. I cried snot bubbles into Spot, my stuffed dog that I was too old for, and after I was done, I wrote "Fuck Everyone" in block letters on the last page of my diary.

In general, my mom let me read everything I wasn't supposed to—true crime novels and violent Westerns. I tried the classics, too, even then drawn to important-sounding things I didn't understand. For a week straight, I fell asleep trying to read the first fifty pages of *Paradise Lost*. I copied out Hemingway quotes in my notebook, imagining that his minimalist thoughts on male impotence were fitting for my own life. *Isn't it pretty to think so?* I wrote in lime-green gel pens during algebra class. But that summer I asked my mom about the top shelf of her bookcase, the one filled with paperbacks that had titles like *Seducing Miss Harrington* or *A Rake for Christmas* written in pink and purple floral script.

"They're too adult," she said.

"I'm adult."

"You can't even reach them."

And she was right; even when I stood on my tiptoes and strained my body up, my fingertips only grazed the spine.

"See," my mom said.

When she went to the grocery store, I tried again. I pulled over one of the medieval dining room chairs that we never used, and ta-da! Dozens of romance novels with covers featuring half-naked men in tunics and corseted women with overflowing breasts were within reach. I picked three and rearranged the shelf so their absence would seem inconspicuous. I was an adult, after all.

The first one I read, *The Duke of Lyndon*, was a historical romance set in the early nineteenth century. The protagonist is quiet, virginal Elizabeth Binney, the eldest daughter of a drunk baron who, in his absence, takes care of her four sisters and sacrifices everything to make them happy. *Buy the gold ribbon, Shelly,* Elizabeth Binney says. *I'm not hungry for dinner anyway.* I was more interested in her love interest, a penniless orphan soldier inexplicably named Hunter who's so haunted by war atrocities that he must seduce innocent women to take his mind off "what he's seen." In the end, he's revealed to be nothing more than a wounded puppy. The dick who, beneath it all, has a heart of gold. He also, conveniently, discovers he's the heir to a dukedom.

From romance novels, I learned that anyone could have hidden royal blood or a secret inheritance. There was a chance this wasn't my real life. It was possible I was the victim of an elaborate case of mistaken identity, and I wasn't supposed to be stuck in this cluttered attic all alone. If I just met the right man, he would show me who I was supposed to be. I could change my name and take up a royal title (*Duchess Violet Barrington,* I wrote in the margins of the romances), and I'd be transformed into someone prettier, nobler, whiter.

Of course, I also learned about sex. I read and reread the scenes where Hunter suckles at Elizabeth's pale breasts or thrusts his throbbing shaft into her sheath. I didn't understand the logistics of the act or the exact meaning of the euphemisms, but I understood the seduction. The virgin's reluctance, the rake's control. I realized it felt good to put my fist to my crotch and rub, but the release made me feel ugly. This wasn't about "two bodies becoming one." It was just me there, sweaty and desperate.

"There's something wrong with me," I whispered to Spot after I masturbated. I confessed my sins like he was my priest.

One day, as I looked at Spot afterward, sitting there smugly, judging me, I got mad. I threw him against the wall as hard as I could. His button nose hit the plaster, but his body remained intact, so I picked him up and tugged at his limbs. I stopped when his front leg tore off.

I hid the romance novels under my bed and rotated them out three at a time. Over the course of that summer, I read every romance novel on my mom's bookshelf. The shame lined up inside of me like dominoes, and one day they fell.

"I've been reading your romances," I told my mom as she peeled carrots in the sink. "I skipped the dirty parts though," I lied.

"They're fun, aren't they?" she said, and flipped on the switch for the garbage disposal. She'd forgotten they were forbidden. I wanted to remind her, but I didn't know how to communicate the shame and longing that had been building in me. She flipped the switch off and started to snap off asparagus stems.

THE MORNING AFTER Bob grows eyelids, I wake up to sunlight and the sound of an old-timey sports announcer. I blink once, twice. The blob's where I left him, on the couch watching a black-and-white baseball game on ESPN Classic. On my third blink, I realize I'm fucked. It's light outside, which means I'm late for work, which means Paul, the night auditor, is probably pacing back and forth, cursing me. Or emailing Walter to get me fired. Or papier-mâchéing a life-size effigy of me to burn in the lobby. I grab my crumpled button-up and cram my feet into shoes without socks. On the way out, I grab my phone and keys.

I avoid looking at Bob as I stumble to the door. Last night I dreamed I was vomiting into the water off the side of an inner tube. A school of fish ate my sick. I'm afraid Bob's face will evoke that same nausea. I don't leave any cereal on the coffee table for him either. I want to forget about Bob.

On the ride to the hotel, I make myself breathe heavily. It's always better to look flustered when you're running late—I tousle my hair and turn the heat on in the minivan until my face goes red. I park and jog to the entrance to work up a little sweat. I'm surprised when I see Rachel at the desk.

"Where's Paul?" I ask.

"He left a few hours ago. I came in early."

I fight the urge to groan. Having to be grateful to Rachel is almost worse than getting fired.

"Did he call you?"

"No. I just came in."

I wait for her to explain why she came in three hours early on a random Tuesday. She doesn't.

"The pool's heating up, but it's nothing compared to you ladies," Rich the handyman says as he walks by. One of his classic cheesy one-liners. Usually Rachel responds but today she can only muster a half-smile.

"Only difference is, no one pees in me," I call out, and he grimaces.

An hour into my shift, Rachel's silence starts to freak me out. It's been slow so far, mostly just guests complaining about the breakfast buffet and checking out of their rooms. Frazzled moms drop their bent keycards on the desk and forget what their room number was ("I know it ended with an eight. . . .").

Ever since I asked Rachel if she had Chapstick and she went on for fifteen minutes about the pros and cons of different brands, my policy is to avoid asking her questions. But today her silence is distracting. I can barely finish my solitaire game.

"Are you okay?" is on its way out of my mouth when the sliding door opens and a guy walks in. It takes me a few seconds to realize it's the poodle boy from the bar, whose name I can't remember.

"Crap," Rachel says and ducks beneath the desk. I look down, and she's squatting next to a tangle of power cords. She puts her finger to her lips.

She knows I owe her this. A few months ago she covered for me when I hid from Tony, a regular guest who works as a construction foreman. I'd missed his wake-up call. I hadn't even been late that day, just inattentive and scrolling through my phone, looking at memes of the white guy blinking in disbelief. When I saw him approach, I pretended I needed to pee and ran to the back room. I watched on the security monitor as Tony yelled at Rachel until he was red in the face. She was "an idiot airhead who cost him thousands of dollars." Had I felt bad for letting her take the fall? I don't remember.

"It's Derek from the other night," the poodle boy says, unprompted. "Is Rachel here?"

"Home sick," I say.

I mime a cough, and poodle boy looks confused, his unlined forehead wrinkling like he's trying to do mental math.

"She seemed fine on Friday."

"Must've come down with something in her sleep."

"I really need to tell her something."

"What?"

The poodle boy looks embarrassed. How confusing it must be to wander through life believing that people aren't messing with you.

"I'd rather talk to Rachel directly."

I grab a rubber band from the desk and put my hair in a high ponytail.

"Look, I'm Rachel. I'm blond, and I love vodka cranberries. What do you need to tell me?"

Rachel grips my ankle, but the poodle boy appears convinced by my impersonation.

"I just wanted to tell her I had fun on Friday. She said we were going to hang out again, and I texted her, but she hasn't texted me back."

I can't help it—I cringe.

"Has that never happened to you before?" I tilt my head sideways at this delusional Bitcoin investor. The tips of his ears turn red.

"It has. I just felt like we really hit it off, you know? She listened when I talked. I felt like she got me. She understood. She saw, like, a better version of me."

"That's a good speech," I say, and I mean it. I half expect Rachel to crawl out from beneath the desk and jump into his scrawny arms. Instead she sinks her fingers farther into my ankle.

"I'll give her the message," I say.

"Thanks."

He walks slowly to the door.

"He's gone," I whisper when the sliding doors close, but Rachel doesn't get up.

I look under the desk to find she's given up on her squat and is just sitting on her butt among the cords and dust and crumbs.

"Are you okay?" I ask.

"No," she says.

I'M BOTH CURIOUS about Rachel's freak-out and hungry, so I multitask. I tell Walter we need a fifteen-minute break for a "womanly emergency" and take Rachel to the McDonald's across the street.

"My treat," I say.

I order a McChicken and medium fry. Rachel stares hard at the glowing menu for a good five minutes before finally ordering a snack wrap and coffee. The McDonald's is full of screaming kids, sleep-deprived parents, and elderly couples, so we go out to the parking lot and sit on the curb to eat.

"I wish they didn't have the calories on the board," Rachel says.

I'm already halfway through my sandwich. A limp piece of lettuce and a clump of mayo falls to the blacktop at my feet. Rachel hasn't touched hers. She sets it down.

"I know I shouldn't care, but the numbers are there. I want to pick something filling but not too many calories, because then I'll have to calculate how it affects subsequent meals. If I have a plain cheeseburger and fries, do I have to skip my after-dinner snack or spend twenty more minutes on the elliptical? What if I nix the fries?"

"Are you having a panic attack?" I ask and take another bite of my McChicken. The hospital's not far; I could probably drive there and back before Walter even notices.

"No," she says.

Rachel puts her thumb to one nostril and inhales. She holds her breath as she switches fingers to plug the other nostrils and then exhales.

"It's called alternating nostril breathing," she says. "A calming exercise."

She closes her eyes and switches nostrils. I watch a black ant approach her unbitten snack wrap. It inspects the wrap gingerly, first with its antennae, then with its hind legs. It moves away when it finds the tortilla impenetrable.

"Weird," I say as I crumple my wrapper. "So what happened with Derek?"

"Nothing really." She sighs. "I just know his type. I'm the one who 'gets him,' but he doesn't care about getting me. I'm just his container. It's exactly the same shit my ex used to do."

"Why did you tell him to text you?"

"I don't know," she says. "Why does anyone talk to anyone? I don't like to be alone."

The image comes to me unbidden: the blob alone in my apartment. Slowly starving. I stuff lukewarm french fries in my mouth.

"You know, in high school, I thought Elliott and I would be friends forever. I thought we had, like, this unbreakable bond. Now I'm just a joke to him." Rachel's laugh comes out brittle. "At least Derek likes me."

"A little too much," I say.

I thought she would laugh, but instead Rachel gets quiet again. I watch the drive-through line. It's long today, our hotel is right off the interstate, and everyone needs their Egg Mc-Muffin. A blond chick in a Hyundai honks at a soccer mom who tries to cut in line. A teenage McDonald's employee on his break practices his roundhouse kicks on garbage cans.

"Paul told me you have a new roommate," Rachel says finally.

"Paul has a big mouth."

"It must be nice. To have someone to come home to," she says.

I turn to look at her, but she's staring down at her feet. I never imagined I might have something that Rachel wants. I look at her hunched-over shadow in the store window, and start to sit up a bit straighter. If I were a better person, I would confess: *Don't be jealous. My roommate is a blob.*

Instead I say, "I have to run home. Will you tell Walter I forgot a tampon or something?"

"Sure," Rachel says.

"Thanks."

We get up. She throws her snack wrap in the trash uneaten on the way back to the hotel.

I drive twenty over the speed limit and get home in ten minutes. Bob's on his cushion, and the television's playing *Jeopardy!* reruns.

"I forgot to feed you," I say, like it was an accident.

I pour Froot Loops into an empty bowl and set it in front of the blob. He looks up at me and gurgles, a sound I've never heard before. He doesn't touch it, probably a shy eater.

I rarely see my apartment in the morning light—I don't wake up early enough on the weekend. Now I see it all: the abandoned coffee cups and moldy dishes piled under the coffee table. The dirty and clean clothes mixed in front of the bathroom door. The big orange chicken vindaloo stain on the fridge next to the picture of me and Luke.

"Now that we're roommates, you've got to start pulling your weight," I say to Bob as I pick dirty glasses up off the coffee table and throw them in the sink. "You could give me a hand, you know?"

I glance back at Bob to see if he's eaten, and instead I find that he's grown tall somehow. Protruding up from his amorphous body, below his eyes is a separate appendage, a column of beige flesh.

The glass I'm holding drops to the floor. It doesn't break, just bounces and spins slowly on the blue carpet. The column of blob molds itself into a circle. Five ligaments lengthen out from the center. I start to understand what's happening when the stumps grow knuckles, the suggestion of fingernails, lines that crisscross the circle.

"A hand," I say.

CHAPTER SEVEN

My first crush was Tyler, Alex's best friend, before he hit high school and got hot, back in middle school when he was a pudgy, pale boy who played goalie in youth soccer games because he couldn't run. He was thirteen, I was ten. Once after a game my mom insisted on a photo, and he picked me up by my armpits and swung me.

"Little monkey," he said in my ear. I didn't wash my pits for a week after that.

Our romance ended when I was walking home from school, singing Celine Dion's "My Heart Will Go On" at what I thought was a reasonable volume, and I heard Tyler yell, "Shut up, chink." He was walking at least two blocks behind with a few other boys in his grade. I didn't turn around—I just shut up and kept walking. I never figured out if he knew it was me.

It's not like I chase white boys exclusively, it's just that white people are always around. In middle school, Alex was in class with three other boys named Alex. To distinguish him, everyone, including the teachers, called him Asian Alex, or AA for short.

"Do you like your nickname?" I asked him once at dinner.

It must've been a Saturday—there was only ever one night Mom could get Dad out of his peeling blue-leather recliner, Alex out of the basement, and me out of the attic.

"You have a nickname?" my mom asked, smiling. She never thought about our race, never spoke it into the room, even when strangers asked if she was babysitting or if we were adopted. She'd smile too big and say, "Nope, these babies are my flesh and blood." It came from a place of love. She didn't like to be reminded that we were different from her.

"It's not a big deal. Just some of the guys call me AA." Alex kicked me under the table so hard I bit my lip.

"Why?" Dad asked.

"Because I'm like a double A battery. Always going."

The blood from my lip dripped into my mashed potatoes. I stirred it in quickly, my potatoes turning a faint shade of pink.

"Why didn't you tell the truth?" I asked Alex later.

"What?"

He liked to play dumb when I asked him a question. It was like he was allergic to giving answers or, it seems clearer to me now, he didn't want to admit that the answers didn't exist.

"Asian Alex," I said.

I was just trying to remind him of the conversation, but for some reason the name sounded like an accusation. It changed the way I looked at him too. Suddenly I saw, really saw, the Asianness of his eyes, his hair, his face shape.

"Shut up," he said and pushed me, almost gently, out of his room.

"You look more Asian than me anyway," he said as he closed the door.

I wonder if he knew those words would follow me around for years, ringing in my ears like little alarm bells when I looked in the mirror. Because he was right, after all. I did look more Asian than him.

THE FINGERS MOVE up and down, pushing slowly into the air like the blob's playing an invisible piano. I don't move. I let the water from my fallen glass seep between my toes as I watch the hand. It's like the scene in a movie when the naked girl gets surprised by a knife behind the shower curtain or a clown face beneath her bed. I want to be as horrified as the naked girl is when she sees the monster for the first time. Her eyes widen, her pink mouth makes a perfect circle, and she screams. There's no reason why I'm not screaming. I consider what it would look like, for a moment. I could run out of my apartment barefoot, find a kind-looking (handsome?) stranger on the street, and beg for their help. But the truth is, I'm not the naked girl. I'm Dr. Frankenstein—this is my creation.

Luke always liked horror movies. His favorite was *The Shining*. A wannabe writer travels to the Overlook Hotel for a winter with his wife and kid and goes mad.

"Is he possessed by a spirit? Or is that just what he's like?" I asked as Jack Nicholson's face contorted into a scary grin, his eyebrows arched into right angles.

"I don't know. That's what makes it scary," Luke said.

"I wish there was a real monster," I said after the movie ended. "Monsters are comforting compared to humans."

Maybe this explains why I don't run from the blob. Instead I sit down cross-legged on the damp carpet, and stare at the open hand. Nothing happens. It doesn't turn murderous and go for my throat or try to seduce me with its fingers. It doesn't move at all. It stays frozen at attention, like it's waiting for me.

"Give me a hand," I say again.

And like magic, the hand seems to grow bigger, pulsing slightly, like the eager student in class who's waiting to be called on.

"Fuck," I say.

I get up and pace. I'm supposed to go back to work, but how can I go back to directing guests to the ice machines when there's a person growing in my living room?

I text Rachel, can't come back today. tell Walter it's an emergency thx

She texts back immediately, are you okay???? I turn my ringer off and throw my phone in a pile of dirty laundry.

Part of me must've seen this coming—did I really think he was going to stop at eyelids? I sit back down in front of the blob.

"What do you want?" I whisper to the hand.

The hand doesn't move, but the blob gurgles. I've been so fixated by the new limb that I almost forgot that the blob has a face. Strangely, it looks the same, his body roughly the same size even with an adult hand protruding from his forehead.

"I can't understand you," I tell the blob.

He gurgles again, and I try to listen for tone. I want to know if he's happy or sad or confused or scared, but it's impossible. The sounds he makes are as indifferent as a babbling brook or a white noise machine. After a while, he goes silent and looks up at me with his black marble eyes. He's waiting for me to do something, to say the words that will transform him.

I know I could refuse. There's nothing stopping me from hiding him away, locking him in a closet that no one's allowed to enter. But I can't stomach the betrayal.

Still, I hesitate. I never learned the parts of the human body in school. In elementary school gym class, our PE teacher hung a skeleton on the wall with every bone labeled, and you got extra credit if you memorized them. One day Brian Mulvey stole the skeleton while the teacher was trying to teach us four-square rules and threw it behind the bleachers, which, due to a misreading of the instructions, were permanently screwed into the floor. When the teacher asked Brian why he did it, he just said, "I didn't like the way that guy was looking at me." There was no more extra credit after that.

I had other missed opportunities. In high school anatomy I was distracted by boys, so busy staring at Will's neck sweat that I cut an artery dissecting a fetal pig. In my college Integrated Biology class, Luke took all my online quizzes for me and made up mnemonic devices to help me memorize the Krebs cycle. I didn't pay attention to anything that would help me create a human from scratch. The only option is improvisation.

"Grow an arm," I say to the blob.

And he does. At first the thick column of blob flesh looks like a giant, flimsy noodle with a hand attached. I put my own hands up instinctively in case the thing bends or collapses, like the flesh equivalent of a Jenga tower. But it doesn't fall, just trembles under its own weight. In a few seconds the arm firms and grows bones or ligaments or whatever. A joint appears midway through the noodle, an elbow. The forearm near the hand gets thinner, and the shoulder fills out. It molds itself. In the end, it's recognizably an arm—milky white and hairless.

When you see a body part isolated, you realize how strange human limbs are. Suddenly my own arms feel like creatures independent from me. They tingle as my previously taken-for-granted blood rushes through them.

If I didn't know better, I might think Bob's arm belongs to a mannequin, or one of those realistic wax figurines. The arm's completely frozen, with a hand in the air, elbow bent slightly. The blob doesn't flinch when I put my hand near his wrist.

AFTER "GROW AN arm," I don't give any more commands, although I do plot the logical progression in my head: torso, head, arm, legs. Hopefully too much detail isn't required. I could walk the blob through face, nose, ears, mouth, but I'm clueless about hip joints and genitals. It only took him a few minutes to grow an arm, and at this rate, I could make myself a person by sunrise.

I don't know why my first thought is to continue, to Build-A-Bear myself a friend. I should be calling 911 or the National Science Foundation so they can send over a blobologist to run tests on the thing. But I don't. Bob's quiet too, his fingers twitching every so often, like a dog running in its sleep.

The phone rings. I answer it without looking at the caller ID first. I'm afraid to take my eyes off Bob. Before I even say hello, a man's voice is in my ear.

"Hey, sorry I missed your call. I'd make up an excuse as to why I didn't answer, but honestly I forgot people even used phones to make calls. I thought everyone just texted or sent each other passive-aggressive TikToks."

"What?" I look down quickly at the name on the screen. "Elliott?"

I feel slow, high.

"Present," he says.

"I called about the blob," I say as I recall my embarrassing voicemail. The panic I felt when I first saw the blob's eyelids.

"Yeah. I still can't believe you picked that thing up and carried it home. How's the little fella doing?"

"Um . . . well . . ." I start to back away from the couch. I don't want to let the blob out of my sight line, but I also don't want him to overhear our conversation. What if I suggest getting rid of him, and he gets pissed? What if I accidentally say something figurative—"Lean on me," or "You're the bomb"— and he suffocates me or explodes? It occurs to me, as I sit and stare at him, that "Give me a hand" could've turned out much worse.

I prop my door open and sit on the threshold outside, next to the water drain. I get shitty reception in my basement apartment. Even here, I can see the blob hand peeking from above the couch's armrest like a buoy.

"He's growing," I say finally.

"I mean, that's what animals do, right?"

"It's hard to explain." I pick at the leaves and sticks that have accumulated against my door. Last night, I wanted to tell Elliott about the blob's eyelids. After all, he's the one who first saw the blob's sadness. He must've recognized, somehow, that the creature was special. I figured if anyone would know what to do next, it would be Elliott. Now I'm not so sure.

Over the phone, I hear police sirens and children laughing. "Where are you?"

"In the park. I had to get away from my family. Their love is suffocating me. Have you ever felt your spirit leave your body and float above you?"

"No."

"Well, I get tired of watching myself go through the motions."

"Oh."

"Which reminds me, could you help me with something?"

"With what?"

I chew my nails, my eyes on the blob hand. Favors make me nervous.

"My parents don't know I'm gay. And they're having a big dinner on Monday to celebrate me getting into law school."

My pity for him being closeted is tempered somewhat by the reminder that he's a successful lawyer-in-training.

"They supported me through college, so I want to give them something back. What better gift than to give their favorite son a girlfriend? And you're perfect beard material."

"What?"

I think of Elliott at the bar, filling out a black T-shirt and skinny jeans with the type of easy confidence that attracts all genders. He could have any fake girlfriend he wanted. "Why me? Why not Rachel? She's an actress."

"I could lie and say you're my soulmate, but the truth is, you're the only Asian chick I know in this town. Well, half, but half is good enough."

Something in my chest aches. When has half ever been good enough?

"And I'll pay," he says. "A hundred bucks."

"Yeah, okay," I say, even though I hate parties. I hate small talk. I hate "meeting the parents."

"But will you come take a look at the blob afterward?" I ask.

"No problem. I majored in blob health in college."

I give him my address, he says he'll pick me up at six sharp on Monday, and then he hangs up without saying goodbye. I dust the leaves off my butt and return to my seat in front of the blob.

"We'll hold out till Monday," I whisper to the blob.

I put my hand up to his and extend my index finger. For the first time, I touch my finger to his. Not until I've done it do I realize I'm reenacting the scene from *ET.* Bob's finger feels normal, human. He even has a fingerprint.

"Not extra," I say as I put my hand down. "Just terrestrial."

I turn on the TV, and a sitcom laugh track fills my apartment.

CHAPTER EIGHT

It was not long after my first crush yelled, "Shut up, chink," that I developed my second crush. I was eleven, and he was a white boy named Cole. He was my age but hadn't grown since the third grade. He wore his brown hair just a little too long and was constantly brushing it out of his eyes or tucking it behind his ears. Somehow this gesture made him seem deep, artistic, emotional. He wasn't like the other boys in our grade. Too short to play basketball, he spent recess on his stomach in the shade of a buckeye trading *Yu-Gi-Oh!* cards.

During recess, I played games with the other unpopular girls: hand-clap games, string games, four square, and, the most elemental game of all, tag. The brick wall next to the butterfly garden was "safe," so you couldn't be tagged if you were touching it. As soon as your fingertips or foot left the wall, you were fair game. We were a tribe formed by exclusion, loosely connected weirdos, but within the group I had one true ally: Lottie Davis. Lottie always won at tag. She was faster than me, faster than every girl in our class and most of the boys.

Other than Stephanie, who I met in high school, Lottie was my only childhood friend. She was the daughter of two new-age hippies—her mother a night nurse at the hospital, her father an out-of-work artist who would inexplicably disappear for weeks at a time. They were vegetarians who refused to kill the ants that invaded their tiny apartment's kitchen or wear shoes outside, except in winter. They lived in a run-down apartment complex three blocks from my house, and to get there you had to walk through an alleyway strewed with broken beer bottles, cigarette butts, and, once, a used condom. My mom made Lottie clean her feet with Wet Ones before she was allowed in our house.

After a few months of pining after Cole, including a bold move where I borrowed his pencil during World Cultures and never returned it, I invited myself over for a sleepover at Lottie's place to tell her about my crush. Beforehand, I cut out a photo of him from the middle school yearbook and glued it to a picture my mom had taken of me on Christmas Eve in a snowflake nightgown—I wanted Lottie to be able to visualize us together. I didn't know how she would react. Unlike the other girls, Lottie never spoke about boys or crushes. I never heard her curse or slam doors or cry for no reason. Besides her dirty feet, Lottie was an angel.

I waited until nighttime, until her mom slipped out of the apartment in her scrubs and locked the door behind her. We were already tucked in. We always slept in the living room under scratchy handmade wool blankets, the kitchen light glowing dim behind us. Lottie's eyes were closed, so I kicked her awake and pulled out my Frankensteined photo.

"Look at us," I said, and showed her the picture. "See. We look good together."

We didn't. Cole was tiny, and I looked giant in comparison. Not to mention I still had my baby fat, geeky glasses, and a thick helmet of bangs that were always greasy but at least covered up the bushy eyebrows I hated. In contrast, Lottie was thin, all collarbones and wiry bicep muscles. Not only was she the fastest girl in our grade, she was the only one who could do twenty pull-ups. She belonged in a YA novel about teen superheroes, although, like me, she would've preferred Hobbiton.

"You look cute," she said, her voice sleepy and soft. "Did you know he lives six doors down?"

I did know this, but I feigned surprise. I had done some recon during my month of pining. After school I waited under the monkey bars for him to finish trading cards and throwing wood chips at squirrels, and then I followed him home. Maybe that's when I fell in love, when I saw him walk up the stairs of the familiar dingy half-shingled building. Part of me knew, from the chipping paint and the arguments I heard through thin walls, that Lottie and Cole understood things I didn't.

"He invited me over a couple times," Lottie said. "He has duct tape swords."

"Can he invite you over again? And can I come?" I asked, maybe too quickly.

Lottie went silent, and I couldn't tell if she was hesitating or falling asleep.

"Okay," she said finally.

It took a few days of nonstop Cole talk until Lottie broke down and asked him to play after school. He said yes, and the three of us walked home in a row, me in the middle. Cole wore a short-sleeved blue button-down with white sleeves, identical to the one Ash Ketchum wore in *Pokémon*. I don't remember what we talked about, maybe art class or science homework—it was hard to pay attention with the blood rushing to my head and the chapped lips I kept biting.

We set down our backpacks in Cole's patio area. Every apartment in the complex was allocated a small square of outdoor space, some grass and maybe a tree. Beyond that was half a dozen pines separating their complex from the next one. Maybe he was putting on a show for us that afternoon, but Cole was fearless—jumping through the neighbors' patios, zigzagging to avoid sticks and trees and one patch of poison ivy. The game was simple: Lottie and I were merchants carrying precious cargo (small rocks and a Snapple bottle cap stuffed in Lottie's pocket) from one side of the apartment complex to the other, and Cole was the pirate trying to stop us.

Immediately Lottie picked up a duct tape sword and started running through the patios, with Cole following her. They both had a natural physicality that I didn't. I couldn't stop thinking about how my T-shirt kept riding up, exposing my stomach rolls to open air.

When we got tired of running, we lay down on a stranger's patio. Cole threw leaves in Lottie's hair, and she picked them out one by one.

"Do you think there's an afterlife?" I asked Cole.

I wanted to dig deep into his mind, get to know the very contours of his soul.

"I dunno," he responded.

We were catching our breaths when we heard the strangers' blinds move. When they opened, there was a middle-aged man wearing nothing but plaid pajama bottoms. His neck and chest were covered with thick curly hairs.

"Hey, you," he mouthed. He pointed his finger at us, and it hit the glass of the sliding door.

We got up and ran, over flowerpots and firepits, jumped logs, startled a fat rabbit. Of course, it was me who hit a tree root and ate shit just as we reached Lottie's patio. My ankle twisted unnaturally, and I started crying before I knew I was hurt. Lottie was still running; she hadn't seen me fall. Cole crouched down next to me, and it was just like a romance novel—him brushing his hair out of his face as he moved my ankle in ways that caused unbearable pain, asking, "Does that hurt?" In my diary, I replayed his dirt-encrusted fingers on my ankle, the fabric of his shirt against my bare skin.

"It was so intimate," I said to Lottie afterward as she popped all the ice cubes out of her mom's freezer trays to make a cold pack.

"It was so intimate," I whispered to myself in the mirror for weeks.

What I didn't replay was the way Cole looked at Lottie like she was Pikachu. What I didn't see was Cole tucking a strand of Lottie's blond hair deep into his pocket.

I UPGRADE BOB from Fruity Pebbles to precooked hot dogs a week past the expiration date.

"Help yourself," I say, and put the plastic package on the coffee table in front of the hand. By the time I'm ready to leave for work, two hot dogs are missing.

"Still a shy eater," I say and pet Bob's forearm.

On the way out the door, I wave. I'm only slightly startled when the hand waves back.

It's 5:45 a.m. and dark outside. I usually blast 2000s pop-punk bands on my way to work. Partly for nostalgia, partly to wake myself up. Today I choose silence. It's been two days since the blob grew eyelids, four days since I took him home. And I know now that I have the power to mold Bob into anything or anyone I want. Luke's face comes into my mind unbidden; I force it back into my unconscious. I reach for the old thermos in the cup holder and take a gulp of a week-old gin-and-sweet-tea concoction I made on my way to the Back Door. I consider spitting it out but swallow instead.

I get to the hotel on time, and Paul gives me only a minimal amount of shit for sleeping in yesterday.

"Don't let boy problems distract you, or you're gonna have man problems," he says and slaps his belly, laughing.

I have three hours alone at the desk, and for once I don't open up solitaire. I look around the hotel instead and study it like a stranger. I want to know how Bob might see the blue-and-gold-patterned carpet, the spider plants in the lobby with their greedy offshoots reaching for the windows. As the sun comes up over the pool and reflects orange and red in the water (Rich is late and hasn't yet begun the draining and cleaning process), I think about the guests asleep in their beds. How little I know about their lives. The truth is, I've never even been inside one of the hotel rooms—just glimpsed them in passing as I delivered towels or toiletries. During my first week, Rachel asked me if I ever got curious about the guests. We had just finished checking in a mother and daughter who were both openly crying, tears and snot running down their faces. Rachel offered them tissues as she listed off our business center hours.

"I just want to know what happened," Rachel said after they shuffled away, sniffling, to the elevator. "Don't you?"

I didn't at the time. Now, I wonder.

When Rachel walks in today, she offers a half-hearted "Morning" and throws her bag down. The only thing she asks is if I've heard from Elliott.

"Yeah. I'm actually supposed to be his beard on Monday for some family thing."

"No shit?" Rachel says as she shreds an old to-do list into squares.

It's slow, a Wednesday stream of regulars, a few construction workers. They usually stop to flirt with Rachel, but today they see her frown and keep walking.

Walter comes in next, chest first, like a male peacock looking for a mate. He's probably the least interesting person in the hotel, but I watch him anyway. He's wearing a pink button-down and a matching pink tie. What is he thinking as he zigzags across the lobby floor, picking up old napkins and empty water cups? Rachel is checking her phone under the desk so guests can't see; she hasn't looked up in ten minutes. Cell phone usage is prohibited, according to the Hillside handbook, but everyone breaks the rule. I leave her behind the desk and approach Walter in the lobby.

"Do you need something, Vi?" he asks. His voice is tight. I wonder if he's heard any of the things I've said about him behind his back to Claudia, the head housekeeper. When it's slow, I fold towels with her, and we laugh about the fake southern accent Walter puts on when he talks to guests. "Y'all have a good stay," he'll say when he passes through the lobby.

"No, I just thought I'd help," I say now.

His gelled hair doesn't move as he bends to pick up a clump of mud on the floor. Walter's only a few years older than me and Rachel. He went to Pinewood, Rachel's high school, but she has no memory of him. "I feel so bad," she said when Walter brought up sitting behind her at some anti-meth assembly. "Oh no," he said. "I wouldn't have seen me either."

Now he says, "If you're trying to make up for your absence yesterday, it's okay." He smacks his hands against the chair pillows.

"Rachel told me about your womanly issues. I've factored four woman days into the calendar."

"Glad to hear it," I say as I pick up a dusty, foot-long CVS receipt from under the couch.

"Nice find," says Walter.

I follow him into the breakfast area and watch him sweep muffin crumbs into his cupped hand. There's tenderness in the gesture. It reminds me of something my mom would've done for Alex and me when we were kids.

"You really care about this place," I say.

I mean it as a compliment, but I must sound surprised because Walter stiffens.

"I care about giving guests the quality experience they deserve," he says.

It's a phrase right out of the employee handbook. But it sounds more sincere when Walter's on his knees, crawling under the buffet table to retrieve a loose apple. I sit on one of the tables, kicking my feet aimlessly, as Walter retrieves his prize.

"Well," I say. "You're doing a good job."

"Wish I could say the same," Walter says as he straightens the chafing trays.

AT ELEVEN THE entire staff meets in the breakfast area for our daily "huddle," where Walter pretends he's a football coach and hurls "game plans" at us. Rachel and I forward the front desk phone to a cordless handheld so we can take calls, and sit in the back to keep an eye out for guests. I load up on whatever food the guests haven't eaten: today it's rubbery eggs and cold sausage links. Rachel eyes my plate, and I wonder if she's calculating the calories in her head.

Walter's first point of business is our "prostitute problem," and I can almost hear Claudia and the other housekeepers rolling their eyes. They like sex workers because they tip well.

"How to spot a prostitute? Number one: provocative clothing." Walter puts a finger up as he paces back and forth in front of the juice machine. "Number two: folks paying in cash."

"They need to do their job somewhere," Rachel interrupts. Walter stops pacing, and everyone turns in their chairs to stare at us. Rachel never speaks in meetings unless it's to play peacekeeper. She usually just waves her hands around, saying, "You both have good points."

"Their 'jobs' are illegal," Walter says with exaggerated air quotes. "What would you do if one of their pimps accosted you, Rachel? This is a family-friendly hotel, and their presence completely taints our image."

Rachel shakes her head and presses her lips together so tightly they turn white. I stare at the cordless phone in my hand and will it to ring. Thankfully, the meeting ends quickly.

When we get back to the desk, Rachel turns her frustration on me.

"Why didn't you back me up? Walter was being shitty."

"About the prostitutes?" I shrug. "I don't know. I didn't think it was a big thing."

"That's your problem." She pulls out another piece of scrap paper and shreds it vertically into scraps. "You don't care about people."

I'm too surprised to be offended. I stare at Rachel, but she's consumed by her shredding and won't look me in the eye. I can't tell how serious she is, so I decide, for once, to give her the benefit of the doubt.

"Not true," I say slowly, putting on my calming spa voice. "I care about Bob."

"Who?"

"My roommate."

"You just met the guy," Rachel snorts. "And I don't know why Elliott asked you to be his beard. You don't even know him."

The last thing I want is to fight with Rachel over Elliott. Again, I will the phone to ring, the sliding doors to open, Walter to walk over and order me to pick fuzz off the towels. But no one comes, and Rachel continues.

"I was the first one he came out to. We'd just gone to the movie theater to see *The Social Network*. Mark Zuckerberg getting questioned by Rashida Jones, you've probably seen it."

I saw it years ago; the only part I remember is the opening scene where Rooney Mara breaks up with Zuckerberg and calls him an asshole. It was the mic drop moment, the utterly satisfying comeuppance of the narcissist that can only happen in films, never in real life.

"So, afterward, Elliott drove me home, and before I could get out of the car, he grabbed my wrist. I thought maybe he was going to kiss me or something. But no, he just held my hand. He told me he was gay, and I said, *That seems hard*. I didn't know what to say. I didn't know any gay people, and am I wrong? It does seem hard."

Rachel rotates the long strips of paper and starts tearing them perpendicularly, making squares with torn edges.

"After I said that, he got quiet. I knew I'd done something wrong. So I tried to kiss him, just to see. I thought I was helping. Maybe I could change his mind or at least confirm it. I loved him, Vi."

I nod. I can see why she wanted Elliott. He's effortless in a way that's only achieved by expending an incredible amount of effort.

Rachel goes on to describe how Elliott pulled away and drove off, left her standing alone on the curb. And when she texted him, he texted back recriminations, accused her of being homophobic, which was, Rachel insisted, the furthest thing from who she was. Then, in the weeks after, he ignored her in the hallways at school, left her texts on "Read," and only signed her senior yearbook with a scribbled signature—no personal note, no Xs or Os, not even a "Have a good summer!"

As Rachel recounts Elliott's slights, the paper squares get smaller and smaller, and I think about Elliott showing her the dick pic at the Back Door. It makes sense now. He wasn't just trying to hurt her; he was trying to insist that she see what she didn't want to see, to recognize difference when it stared her in the face.

I don't know why it bothers me that she's painting herself as the victim. Like it's spiteful that Elliott won't forgive her. Good intentions and white tears are supposed to absolve everything, after all. The unfairness of it breaks through my ennui.

"You can't deal with someone not liking you," I say.

"That's not true."

"You did the same thing with me. You basically made us matching BFF necklaces once you realized I was a challenge."

"I wasn't doing that for me. I was doing that for you," Rachel says. The words ring strangely through the empty lobby. She's finally looking at me. "No one I know from Westside remembers you. You have no friends, and you're rude to the guests. All you do is play solitaire and mutter to yourself. I feel sorry for you."

I turn away. I know she's telling the truth. I've been fooling myself, thinking Rachel's pursuit was motivated by anything but pity. I'm just an awkward loner for her to save and rehabilitate.

Would she still feel sorry for me if I pulled her blond hair out by the roots? If I told her she's vapid and fake, and her voice reminds me of Alvin and the Chipmunks? I could laugh in her face, and if I laughed long enough, maybe Walter and the house-keepers would join in.

What happens is the phone rings and I pick it up.

"Start your experience with Hillside Inn and Suites. How may I help you?"

Rachel and I say nothing to each other for the rest of my shift. When I get home, I'm greeted by Bob's hand-waving, and suddenly everything becomes clear.

CHAPTER NINE

I didn't transform into a beauty in sixth grade, although I wished for it. I wasn't an idiot, I didn't think it would happen by magic. I just thought maybe puberty would hit and stretch the rolls of fat on my stomach, clear my acne. Plastic surgery was my backup plan—I watched episodes of *The Swan* in the basement after my parents went to sleep. Each week two ugly women received a beautifying team: a coach, trainer, therapist, cosmetic surgeons, and a dentist. The ugly women weren't uniformly overweight or asymmetrical; sometimes I couldn't even pinpoint what was wrong with them. They were just ineffably, undeniably ugly. Over the course of the show, each contestant received banal motivational speeches and extensive plastic surgery. In the end, a panel of critics judged their transformation from ugly to pretty, and the prettiest swan went forward to compete against the other prettiests.

My parents only got the tiny TV in the basement, so my dad's parents, my ama and agong, could watch the Weather Channel in bed when they came to visit. They lived three hours away, were hard of hearing, and spoke mainly Taiwanese. Still they bought me gifts, kissed my cheeks, hugged me tightly.

"Pray every night," my ama told me. "And your wishes will come true."

It seemed unlikely that my prayers would be answered, but what did I have to lose? Maybe Jesus was a hot Santa Claus or something. And maybe praying would help me understand my grandparents better. Bridge the gap between us, the languages we couldn't speak. And so for a month straight, I prayed.

"Ignore what Ama said about that praying stuff," my dad said one night when he saw me kneeling at the foot of my bed. My hands were pressed together, my eyes closed, as I prayed fervently for bigger boobs.

No one heard me when I crept downstairs to watch the TV. I kept the lights off. I didn't just watch *The Swan*; I watched MTV, VH1, and whatever cartoons were on Adult Swim. One night *American Pie* was on, and I rubbed myself as Jason Biggs dipped his fingers into a warm apple pie. In the blackness, it was easy to pretend that my hand didn't belong to me. That it was a disembodied stranger groping me in the dark.

After a year of my crush, I still wasn't ready to give up on Cole. It got harder to pretend that he wasn't interested in Lottie, though. He made her daisy chains at recess. He crumpled up the perforated edges of his notebook paper and stuffed them down her shirt in geometry. He chased her during tag, even though he never caught her. In line for gym class, he whispered in her ear, and she laughed.

"What were you talking about?" I asked Lottie later, and she insisted that it was nothing.

At lunch he pointed the arrow of his milk cartoon at Lottie, which everyone knew was a signal. Cole ate hot lunch every day while I brought a bag lunch packed neatly by my mom with a turkey sandwich, grapes, rainbow Goldfish, and cookies. Some days, when I had enough pocket change for hot lunch, I would throw the whole thing away without looking and buy lukewarm pizza squares instead. Lottie's mom packed her weird bland shit, like nut crackers and hummus and cucumbers marinated in oil. Cole never spoke of his mom. We'd only ever seen his dad, a short, muscular man with tattoos covering his right arm.

"He's been to jail," Cole bragged once.

We didn't know if this was true.

"I wish I could get hot lunch every day like Cole," I told Lottie.

"He gets free lunch," she said.

"How do you know that?"

"He told me," she said, like it was the simplest thing in the world. It hadn't occurred to me yet that boys were capable of offering up information. All I knew was that they shared a connection that I had no access to. It hurt like a splinter I kept stepping on.

The truth was, Lottie wasn't just skinny and blond and white; she was also nicer than me. She was patient when things didn't go her way, she forgave easily. I held grudges, didn't like being told what to do. My mom still tells horror stories about trying to teach me piano. Every time she pointed out that I played a wrong note, I would kick the pedals and slam flat fingers into the keys. It was that stubbornness that wouldn't let me let go of Cole. If romance novels had taught me one thing, it was that love conquers all. Period.

On the swings in the spring of sixth grade, Lottie told me that Cole had asked her to be his girlfriend.

"Do you like him?" I asked.

I had gotten on the swings first, but it only took her a few pumps of her legs to get higher in the air than me. She had a crescent-shaped scar on her left hand from when she'd jumped off and fallen onto a particularly pointy wood chip. She always said she didn't mind the scar, that it helped her tell left from right.

"No. I promise."

I wasn't reassured. I knew that even if Lottie turned him down, Cole would still push coins and dandelions through the slats in her locker door and let her cut in line at the water fountain. My stomach turned sour. I pumped my legs harder and faster, but no matter what I did, I couldn't reach Lottie's height. That night I listened to Celine Dion's "My Heart Will Go On" on repeat and plotted ways to make Cole fall out of love with Lottie.

My plan was, of course, stupid. I outlined it in my spiral notebook and even gave it a code name: REVERSE SWAN. The plan was to make Lottie unlikable. If ugly could turn pretty, then pretty could go ugly. I tore pages out of my notebook, used my left hand to disguise my handwriting, and allowed my meanness to blossom.

I wrote: LOTTIE DOESN'T SHAVE HER ARMPITS. I wrote: LOTTIE DOESN'T WASH HER FEET. I wrote: LOTTIE SMELLS LIKE POOP. I wrote: LOTTIE EATS RABBIT FOOD. I wrote: LOTTIE HAS MAN ARMS. I wrote: LOTTIE HAS BAD BREATH. I wrote: LOTTIE SLEEPS ON THE FLOOR.

I got to school early and slipped the notes in Cole's locker. I'd folded them only twice, so they'd look more official. What I hadn't counted on was the breeze from the double doors as kids walked in. As soon as Cole opened his locker, the notes fluttered out across the hallway. Matt T. picked one up, Heather Clark another. They read and giggled and showed the notes to other kids, who whispered the secrets to others. It was Angela Harris who finally approached Lottie and showed her one of the notes. I've always wondered which one gave me away. Was I the only one who knew Lottie slept on the living room floor some nights? That one day her mother woke her up too late to brush her teeth? Maybe. Or maybe she just knew me better than I thought. Understood that I had the capability to wound that she lacked.

I still remember the look she gave me before she turned back to her locker and gathered her books, before she walked to class while the school laughed at her, before she found out someone had written "SMELLY FEET" on her desk in black Sharpie. It wasn't anger or even hurt. It said simply: *I see you.*

WHEN I GET home, I print out screenshots of male movie stars: Ryan Gosling, young George Clooney, Leonardo Dicaprio in *Titanic*, Hugh Grant in *Four Weddings and a Funeral.* I lay out the pictures on my coffee table and feel fourteen years old again, collaging hot guys to the wall so I could practice kissing. I only stopped when I wore a hole in Jess from *Gilmore Girls's* face. I don't notice that all the pictures are white dudes until I'm done. But Bob's hand is already white, and who am I to tell him he can't be a white man? Who wouldn't want to wield as much privilege as they can? Maybe as a white man, he can storm into the hotel and demand Walter give me a raise.

I decide to write down my commands before I start. I've watched enough movies to know I have to phrase things carefully, without wiggle room, to avoid unforeseen consequences. I find my laptop in my bedroom under a pile of dirty leggings. I open up a blank Word doc and type, "Grow a neck," and then my phone rings. It's my mom. I think about ignoring it, but I know she'll just keep calling.

"Happy Wednesday, Vi," she says.

I can hear the smile in her voice. I picture her in the worn pink armchair by the window that still bears scratches from Mocha, our fat family tabby who died five years ago. It's the same spot where my mom does her crossword puzzles every morning. For a moment, I forget why I'm mad at her. And then I remember—she's not sitting by the window. They don't live there anymore.

"Hi Mom."

"I just wanted to make sure you're okay," she says. "You never texted me back."

"I'm okay," I say.

"I know you expect an apology."

"You sold the house without telling me."

I hear the petulance in my voice. It's surprising, even to me, how I revert back to a kid when I talk to her. All I need to complete the transformation is boy-band lyrics written in Sharpie on my wrist.

"And I'm sorry that we felt we needed to," my mom says. "But my therapist recommended that I set boundaries. I can't let your reactions rule my decisions anymore."

"You're seeing a therapist?"

I'm surprised. Out of the four of us, my mom has always been the patient one. She waits out our storms, allows herself to be the shore that we crash against.

"Yes. It's been good for me. It might be good for you too."

I walk back into the living room and glance at the blob hand and the shirtless pictures of famous men in front of me.

Who needs therapy when I have Bob? And maybe my mom would be relieved if she knew I was planning to build my own man. After all, she's made no secret of her desire for grandkids. She has stacks of children's books lining the guest room and plush new stuffed animals still wrapped in plastic, waiting. She's given up interrogating Alex on his love life. Ever since Kay dumped him after high school, he's been tight-lipped on his relationships.

"I'm married to my work," he says, and it's cliché, but my mom can't argue. He's a pediatric resident. I have no such excuse.

On the other hand, maybe Bob would horrify my mom. She's a romance purist at her core—the only man she's ever dated is my dad.

At one of our family dinners, I let my mom swipe left and right on Tinder guys.

"I feel like I'm spying on these men," she said after accidentally super-liking a forty-year-old pharmacist.

"It's a dating app. They consented."

"It's unnatural," she said and handed my phone back.

Now, she says, "I want you to come over for family dinner. Saturday at our new place. It's important to me."

"I don't know your address," I say, and hear her sigh.

"I'll text it to you. Just come, okay?"

"Sure," I say, and hang up without saying goodbye. It feels good to be petty.

I don't know what to type when I return to my laptop. I contemplate googling human skeletons or one-day Amazon Prime shipping an anatomy textbook, but something about talking to my mom makes me reckless. She thinks she knows the shape of my fucked-upness, but she's wrong. She doesn't know I've gone to the Back Door alone and fallen down drunk on the floor of the unisex stall, my hair draped in a suspicious puddle. She doesn't know about the patches of ice I purposefully swerved into after Luke dumped me, my hands hovering over the steering wheel like it was a body I was trying to heal. It makes me tired, sitting on the floor biting the skin off my lips and feeling sorry for myself. So I decide to wing it.

"Grow a neck," I say.

The skin around the blob's shoulder lengthens and thickens upward. In front of my eyes, a red and veiny column of flesh grows. If my mom had ever seen a neck without a head before, she wouldn't call online dating unnatural. The neck is large and imposing. When it stops growing, it's clear that it's the neck of a bodybuilder—Bob's been watching too much UFC.

I hold an old picture of Leonardo DiCaprio up to the blob's eyes. I point to his boyish neck and say, "Thinner."

Bob's a good mimic. At my command, the extra flesh from his neck melts back into his body. The blob sculpts his neck into something delicate, refined. I laugh, breathless, when the blob stops moving. I put my finger to the new, untouched skin just below where his jaw would be.

"Beautiful," I whisper.

Next, a left arm and shoulder to match his right. It takes Bob a bit longer this time to stretch and lengthen: shoulder, forearm, hands, fingers. I can't tell if the act of creation is filling me with wonder, or if it's just adrenaline and fear buzzing in my ears.

"Now, grow a head," I say.

Even to me, this command sounds unclear and difficult. The skin on the blob's neck ripples.

"Look," I say, and hold up the picture of young George Clooney in *ER*. I binged the whole series in high school—I found the medical jargon comforting. I would fall asleep to the beep of a pretend EKG machine and wake up from a sex dream about Dr. Doug Ross.

The blob's body tenses as he struggles to grow. His arms and neck flex, and tendons poke out of his skin like he's lifting weights. The flesh around the neck pushes upward, but it won't stretch. I've exhausted his elasticity.

"It's okay," I say.

I reach for Bob's limp hand and hold it in mine.

"Rest," I say.

IN THE MORNING, I make a ham and cheese sandwich for my headless man and place it on the coffee table. It takes me a second to realize that the blob's eyes and mouth have migrated north in the night. They're no longer part of the puddle of flesh below his arms—they've moved up his neck, closer to his invisible head.

"Hi," I say.

The neck eyes blink at me, and I blink back. His hand twitches, but he doesn't reach for the sandwich while I'm there. Before I go to work, I switch the TV to Comedy Central—it seems important that Bob develop a sense of humor beyond nineties sitcoms.

Work is slow, boring. During the late-morning lull, I shop on-line for Bob, using my mom's Kohl's account. I put black V-necks, gray joggers, boxer briefs, and size-twelve white canvas sneakers into my virtual shopping cart. It's exciting to dress a man. Luke mostly wore flannels and the same pair of jeans every day. An ex-girlfriend had told him jeans don't need to be washed.

"Dirt is like seasoning for jeans," he said when I complained that he smelled like old eggs.

After adding two hundred dollars to my mom's credit card, I google the human head. I suspect my command yesterday ("Grow a head") was too vague. According to Wikipedia, the human head has twenty-two bones and twelve pairs of cranial nerves, and that's not even taking into account the complexity of the brain. I feel like an idiot, so I bookmark some YouTube videos to watch with Bob tonight before trying again. I don't want him to end up with the wrong number of nerves or a melted face. Halfway through my shift, Walter comes out to tell me Rachel called in sick.

"We need you to stay." He leans against the desk, a Hillside Inn pen sticking out of his mouth, like a cowboy with a piece of hay.

"Well." I try to think of an excuse and draw a blank. I can't tell him that I have to go home and help my blob grow a head.

"I don't want to hear it. Rachel covered for you on Tuesday," he says when I start to protest. "And we only need you until five p.m."

"Fine."

"You two are really taking advantage of your woman days," Walter says. "Only three left."

"You know women's periods sync up when they spend time together. It's called menstrual synchrony."

He rolls his eyes. "I'm not falling for that."

An hour later, a Facebook notification dings on my screen: a message from someone I'm not friends with. Luke? I look around to see if anyone's watching me. There's no one—no Rachel, no Walter, no guests loitering around. I don't know why I'm afraid someone will see anyway. What could his words make me do: Cry? Laugh? Disintegrate into dust?

It's not from Luke. It's from Stephanie, my high school friend who got pregnant. The girl I called a slut. I forgot that

I had messaged her eight months ago, right after Luke left. I was drunk when I wrote the message and now I wince at the earnestness.

> Stephanie, It's been a long time. I had a dream about you last night. We were hiding from Mr. Jeffers. Remember his snaggle tooth? Remember the cologne he wore that smelled like rotten cinnamon? Remember how he pulled Kayla's gym shorts down because he said they were too short? We were hiding in those big rolled up wrestling mats. I don't remember the rest of the dream. I know it sounds stupid but I wish we were there now. Telling secrets and reading into our futures. I miss you, Steph. You look so happy now.

I don't remember the dream I describe in the Facebook message. It sounds fake, like something I made up to justify getting in contact after so many years. The truth is, I do dream about her regularly. My dreams aren't nostalgic or sepia-tinted, though—in one recurring dream, Stephanie bleeds out from a miscarriage on the high school steps. In another, we meet at a café, and Stephanie shows me her blue-black bruises on her stomach and whispers, "My husband." In another, Stephanie gets into a car crash. Every dream involves Stephanie getting hurt and me doing nothing but watching.

Her response: Hello Vi! I am doing so well. I have a job now working with my husband, Doug, you remember him? It's like my MASH dream came true! We own a dental practice together (www.cleanersmiles.com). Feel free to refer friends. You get a $20 discount for every referral. I also have an Etsy store (www.etsy.com/shop/StephSews) where I needlepoint landscapes. I just got back from a trip to Thailand! Thanks for checking in!

I'm impressed by her English. When I knew her, her sentences were broken and halting. She dropped articles and conjugated verbs incorrectly, and whenever she raised her hand in class, there was a collective eye roll.

I click on her Etsy store and find needlepoint prairies, sunsets, and ocean vistas, intricately embroidered onto miniature hoops. I like her most recent creation the best—a bay landscape with basket boats and mountainous outcroppings. She's somehow managed to capture the mist hitting the rocks and the shifting colors of the ocean. The caption says, "Inspired by my trip home to Thailand." It's $150. I consider buying it. Steph used to know everything about me; maybe I could know something of her now. I close out the window instead.

During work, all I can think about is getting home, but when five comes, I'm not ready. I kill time driving in circles around the strip mall parking lot, passing Big Lots and Shoe Carnival and the Dollar Tree. I only head home when I notice a police car tailing me as I zigzag across parking spaces.

When I get there, I throw my keys on the side table and hear the ice machine turn on in the kitchen. The blob's still sitting on the couch where I left him.

"Hi," I say.

The neck stiffens and turns, and suddenly I'm staring at a human face. Brown hair, thick eyebrows, green eyes. He has a nose, ears, mouth, the whole thing. He doesn't look like any one movie star but rather a conglomeration of movie stars. If you met him, you'd be convinced you knew him from somewhere or had seen him in something.

"Hi," says Bob.

He smiles at me. His teeth are straight and white.

CHAPTER TEN

I called Lottie the day after I stuffed Cole's locker full of notes. I had her number memorized—I still do. I called again and again, and no one picked up, so I rode to her house on my rusted Razor scooter. At the rocky alleyway to her apartment building, I got off and jogged, dodging trash and glass. I knocked on Lottie's door, but there was no answer.

"She's not home," said Cole.

I hadn't seen him sitting on the curb. I tried to air out my pit stains as he walked over, hands in his pockets.

"Her mom took her camping for a few days. I guess she called the principal about the notes." Cole spun a yo-yo as he spoke, and it made me nervous. He was playing it cool, but I wondered if he knew I was guilty, and instead of confronting me, he was playing the good cop, trying to get me to confess.

"I don't know why anyone would do that to her," he said. "Lottie's nice to everyone."

It was true. The only person I'd ever seen Lottie talk back to was her mom. One night when Lottie's mom was exhausted from an overnight shift, she forgot about dinner and let the mac and cheese burn.

"Can't you concentrate for once?" Lottie yelled as she threw water at the smoking pot.

Her mom just sat down on the wet kitchen floor and put her head in her hands. I couldn't tell if she was sleeping or crying.

"Not everyone," I said.

Cole looked up, surprised.

"No one can be nice to everyone all the time. That's not possible."

Cole shrugged. He didn't look convinced.

I kept calling Lottie's apartment every day for a week, until my mom sat me down at the dining room table after school and told me that Lottie and her mom had moved away. Her mom had left her dad; he had been abusing her. Did I know what abuse was? she asked. My mom had gotten me a glass of ice water and forgotten a coaster. As she rubbed my arm, I watched the condensation drip and puddle on the wood table.

"Yes."

"Did he ever hurt you?" my mom asked.

No, of course he hadn't, and I was sheltered enough that I didn't even recognize the signs. The expletives and crashes from upstairs that made Lottie go still when I was over for a sleepover had no impact on me. I just kept molding Lottie's colored clay into spiders and sea turtles. When her mom came downstairs with bruises or puffy eyes, neither Lottie nor I looked.

"No," I said, and my mom hugged me like I was a victim. She told me Lottie and her mom were living on a houseboat off the coast of Florida, where they had relatives to support them.

"Lottie will be safe now," my mom said. "I know she wanted to say goodbye, but it happened fast."

I knew she was lying about Lottie wanting to talk to me. It was too big of a coincidence, my betrayal coinciding so neatly with their move. It was my fault, my stupid plan that set off a chain reaction resulting in Lottie floating on the ocean nine hundred miles away.

"They don't have phones yet, but she'll write to you. Maybe she'll send you a sand dollar," my mom said.

Lottie never sent me a sand dollar, and I never figured out her phone number, although I tried a few Florida numbers at random. She had no AOL Instant Messaging, no email, and even years later, no Facebook or Twitter. My mom couldn't figure out why she never reached out, but I knew. I was almost proud of her.

I tried to forget about her until one day, three months after Lottie disappeared, my dad called to me from the den.

"Vi, one of your friends was just on the porch scurrying around."

"Who?"

"I don't know. Short, brown hair, T-shirt with some Pokémon thing on it."

I ran barefoot onto the porch, my warm feet melting the early March frost. "March comes in like a lion," my mom said repeatedly to us as kids. It wasn't until we grew up that we realized she'd dropped the last half of the saying.

Cole was gone by the time I got out there, leaving only muddy shoe prints on our sidewalk. What had he been doing on my porch? I shivered as I searched for a hidden note or a ring or some object that would prove that it had been worth it. What I found on our porch steps was a baby bird the size of a half-dollar, purple and pink flesh with a delicate hint of a beak. I nudged its body with my toe and it didn't twitch. I bent close to watch for signs of movement. Its chest was still, no breath.

"Are you dead?" I asked the bird. It didn't respond.

After five minutes of crouching in the cold, I used a leaf to carry the body from our steps to the grass in front of the bushes. I laid it there. I went back inside, upstairs to my bedroom, and wept.

For the rest of middle school, I avoided Cole, and in high school I barely spoke to anyone. Cole got into drugs and Black Sabbath; he wore baggy black cargo pants covered with safety pins. Sometimes I wondered if he ever thought about Lottie. Maybe we'd both lost the same thing.

I never figured out what the dead baby bird meant. I thought it was a punishment for the mean things I said about Lottie. Cole knew what I was capable of, and he wanted to scare me. Other times, I wondered if it was something more tender than that. Maybe he thought I could've saved the thing. Maybe he imagined me pressing my lips against the tiny beak and breathing life back into its small body. My real punishment is not knowing.

IT TAKES A few hours to acclimate to the good-looking head in my apartment. I realize quickly that his vocabulary is limited to the words "Hi" and "Yes." Beyond that, he just smiles, and enthusiastically nods. He also blinks too much, which makes him look like a web browser refreshing itself. I want to talk to him, to fill the silence of my apartment with words, but I can't think of anything intelligent to say. So I just start repeating self-evident facts.

"You grew a head," I say.

"You're alive," I say.

"You don't have any legs," I say.

Maybe it was a mistake, making him so handsome. Looking at Bob's perfect face, his sharp jawline and poreless skin, is like staring into the sun. So instead I study his bottom half, where muscle dissolves into blob. He looks like a melted Ken doll. He has no torso, no pecs—his body ends just below the collarbone. His arms rest stiffly on the couch, elbows bent at right angles, as if at any moment he could pull himself up and out of the hole he's gotten himself stuck in.

Bob nods. "Hi," he says.

I don't sleep that night. I sit with Bob on the couch, and we watch old episodes of *Project Runway*. I'm afraid of making the wrong move, the same feeling I had when Luke and I first met. On our third date, Luke fell asleep on my shoulder while watching *Top Gun*, one of his favorite movies, and I let my arm go numb because I thought any movement might wake him up. I was terrified that when he opened his eyes, he'd realize the whole date was a mistake.

I figure at least the show will give Bob a sense of how beautiful people move. It's something he'll need to learn. We start with the first episode of an old season, so there's twenty designers, whose aesthetics range from bubblegum chic to minimalist black.

The unconventional materials challenges are my favorite. Dashing fashion mentor Tim Gunn leads the designers into a junkyard or a Tractor Supply Company store or a flower shop, and they have to make a high-fashion look out of dried mealworms and guitar picks. Unlike normal challenges, the goal is not just to make something beautiful but to transform the grotesque and the ordinary into something transcendent and unrecognizable.

At the end of the third episode, I feel Bob twitching next to me. When I turn, I see his mouth moving. He's lip-syncing along with the words being spoken on-screen.

"I'm sorry. You're out," Bob mouths along with supermodel host Heidi Klum as she sends home the designer who tried to make a dress out of a vinyl whale he won at Coney Island.

"Good job," I say to Bob.

I imagine being able to have a full conversation with him one day, and the prospect fills me with a weird mix of excitement and dread. He's so pure. Anything I do or say could taint him.

"Hi," he says, and smiles.

I CALL OUT of work at 5:40 a.m., twenty minutes before my shift's supposed to start.

"Don't do this," Paul grumbles into the phone before he's even heard my excuse.

"It's an emergency," I say from the toilet. I'm still nervous that Bob might overhear a command. Through the crack in the bathroom door, I monitor the back of his head. "My friend's in crisis."

"I'm not covering for you."

"Go home," I say. "Rachel comes in at nine. The desk will be okay for a few hours."

I hang up before he can respond.

I return to the couch, but I'm too nervous to sleep. The hours of watching TV have worn on me. During our tenth viewing of the animated gecko commercial in which he pretends to forget his lines, I turn it off. Bob looks at me.

"Hi," he says.

He's stopped his rapid blinking and, for a full minute, we stare at each other. His eyes are so bright they look photoshopped, shifting from green to gold, and his floppy chestnut hair is reminiscent of Hugh Grant in his rom-com heyday. I think of the blob's old eyes, black and depthless. "Sad eyes," Elliott had said. They don't look sad anymore.

After a few minutes, Bob turns his gaze from me to the apartment. It's filthy—recycling bin overflowing, dirty plates stacked on top of my dresser, a graveyard of discarded clothes piled on top of the table I never eat at. When it was just me living here, it seemed fitting, but an otherworldly creature doesn't deserve to live in a shithole.

I'm generally bad at the everyday things other people handle no problem: dishes, writing a check, parallel parking. Even perpendicular parking. I still remember my dad, the one and only time he volunteered to teach me how to drive, white-knuckling the cup holder and side door, pumping his foot on an imaginary brake as I clipped the curb. My dad never gets mad, so it made sense that his words, not yelled but muttered as though he was talking to himself, got stuck in my head like a song on an infinite loop.

"Are you stupid?" he said. *Am I stupid?*

It took Luke a few months to realize I never washed a single pan, and when I did, it took me fifteen minutes.

But something about Bob—his face, his beauty, his innocence—makes me feel hopeful. We watched a few episodes of *Tidying Up with Marie Kondo* so I feel somewhat qualified to find "what sparks joy."

"Okay," I say as he keeps nodding and smiling at me. "We can do this."

I leave Bob on the couch and drive to CVS to buy supplies: garbage bags, bleach, paper towels, disinfectant wipes. The cashier is young, the red kiss of pimples and razor burn on his cheeks.

"Throwing a party?" he asks.

"A baptism," I say as I watch him bag up sponges and soap. "You're invited."

He doesn't respond, just frowns and hands me the bags.

One of Marie Kondo's rules is to "do it all in one go," and as I start cleaning, I realize she's right—if I stop, I'll never get started again. I'll melt back into a lazy, self-medicating mess. I clean like my life depends on it.

I find things I thought I'd lost. My fancy bra, covered in dust behind my TV stand—I brush it off and change into it immediately. On the coffee table under the dirty dishes and clothes are hundreds of pages I printed out about the Peace Corps: brochures, information packets, application tips. I toss them all in a garbage bag. I find the phone number of a pay-what-you-can psych clinic that Alex gave me. I couldn't tell if he was joking or being sincere when he slipped it in my purse, but for some reason I haven't thrown it away. Today I do.

"I'm starting fresh," I tell Bob.

"Yes," he says.

To prove it to him, I throw away a small box of mementos: first-date movie stubs, a Valentine's Day card from my mom, that pencil I stole from Cole back in middle school.

I don't have to scrub my oven, because I've never used it. In contrast, the fridge is littered with take-out containers and unidentifiable meals in Tupperware that I made weeks earlier. I don't bother to salvage the containers, I toss everything. I find the leftover Denny's boxes from the last time I saw Luke stashed behind expired condiments and sickly-smelling lunch meat. I take the boxes out and turn back to Bob.

"Want to see something gross?" I ask.

"Yes," he says and nods.

I open the box, and it's a burst of smell, color, texture. A fuzzy white-and-blue mold blooms on the pancakes, and their edges and middle ripple; it looks like they're trying to inch their way out of the box. The syrupy sausages are strangely intact, and the eggs look okay too, just slightly grayer in their old age.

Bob smiles and reaches for the spoiled food.

"Stop. This'll make you sick," I say, and throw the boxes away.

DURING MY APARTMENT sweep, I find a full-length mirror forgotten in the back of my closet, covered by a pile of old course notes. My mom must've given it to me when I moved in. I clean off the dust with some Windex and paper towels. The satisfying action of wiping and crumpling is addicting; I'm already on my fifth roll.

I study myself in the mirror. I don't know if it's fair to say I let myself go, as I never really held myself together in the first place. Strangely, I haven't felt self-conscious in front of Bob. I can tell he's not judging me—after all, as a blob, he saw me belly out, eating Lays by the fistful. Still, I want to try to show him a better version of myself.

I start with what I can control. I go to the bathroom and look for a razor. I can only find a disposable one, with two blades covered in rust, so I leave Bob for the second time and drive back to CVS. I load my basket up with shaving cream, five-blade razors, facial hair bleach, Spanx, mascara, concealer, antiperspirant, and gas relief pills. Somehow I get the same teenage cashier. It's already 5:00 p.m.; this must be the end of his shift. He pretends not to remember me.

"Did you find everything all right?" he asks.

"Sure did," I say. "The baptism continues."

I'm not sure if I'm trying to weird him out or if sleep deprivation is starting to get to me. Either way, this time the boy's prepared. He picks up the gas relief pills before he scans them and examines the box.

"Good luck," he says, and holds my gaze.

When I get home, I shave everything—armpits, legs, pubes, nipples. I pluck my eyebrows, bleach my mustache, and haphazardly slap on some makeup. I find some old lavender glitter body lotion in the back of my medicine cabinet that I've had since high school. I slather it on too, and soon I'm sparkly and slick as an eel. I pull on a long velvet black dress that I wore to a New Year's Eve party years ago, another thing hidden in the back of my closet. The dress is flattering, with cap sleeves to cover my arm fat and loose fabric around the belly.

When I'm done, I open the door of my bedroom a crack and peek at Bob. It's been a while since I cared what anyone thought I looked like. After Luke and I broke up, I wore sweatpants and stained T-shirts 24/7. I once asked him why he thought they were called sweatpants, not cozy pants or comfort pants. That's intentional rudeness, I contended.

"Well, you do sweat in them, don't you?" he said.

I didn't engage with him on that point, instead telling him the story of when I was little and thought I could lose weight by sweating. I covered myself in blankets, turned off the attic's AC unit, and sweated for hours.

"At some point, I couldn't take it anymore. I went downstairs and chugged three glasses of water."

"You could've hurt yourself doing that," Luke said.

"No one noticed, and I never told anyone. I wasn't ashamed that I did it. I was ashamed that I stopped. I didn't want it bad enough."

Luke didn't respond. Maybe he'd stopped listening or gone back to scrolling through his phone.

I step out into the living room, and Bob looks up.

"What do you think?" I ask and do a little twirl.

"Pretty," he says.

"A new word." I laugh, almost cry.

I put an arm around Bob's shoulder for a half hug. He smiles, and I can't tell if it's because he's always smiling or because he likes the feeling of the embrace.

In my dress, I make Bob a peanut butter and jelly sandwich, and we watch *Jeopardy!* I prop my feet up on the coffee table and put my hands behind my head like the husband in one of those fifties sitcoms. I'm exhausted from all my self-improvement.

Bob has rearranged the settings on the TV—somehow the blue looks more blue, red more red. Trebek's gray hair glows.

"According to superstition, if this body part burns, people are talking about you."

A frizzy-haired schoolteacher buzzes in.

"What is your ear?" she and I say in unison.

Bob turns and smiles at me. His muscles have grown a bit more defined, but no new body parts have sprouted while I've been cleaning. His strong collarbone still melts into a beige blob body.

"Hi," he says.

"Hi," I say.

A commercial for hair dye starts, and I pick up the remote and mute the TV.

"Nice . . . day?" Bob asks.

He looks pleased with his expanded vocabulary.

"What else have you learned?" I ask, and Bob shrugs. Another new gesture. It unnerves me slightly, but I try not to let it show.

"It was okay."

Bob nods, keeps watching *Jeopardy!*

After the show ends, I turn off the TV, and though I'm tempted, I don't go to the bedroom to strip out of my dress, scrub the makeup off my face. I feel a tickle on my inner thigh. It's Bob, running a fingertip across my skin.

"Leg," he says. He replaces his finger with a palm. He touches me, and I can't help it, I shiver. Gently, he touches the raised mark of an old mosquito bite that never healed and the scars on my knees I was too drunk to remember getting. He's transfixed by my banged-up legs, pets them like they're sacred.

"If I made you legs, would you leave?" I ask.

Bob stops smiling and furrows his brow. It's the face he makes when he can't understand me. I don't push him for an answer or explain what I mean, and together we sit in a dark silence.

"I like you, Bob," I say finally.

Even though I don't mean it like that, I can't help feeling like I'm in a bad teen melodrama confessing my love to a boy who's just come out of a coma.

"I like you," Bob says back, and suddenly I don't care how stupid I look or how misguided this situation is. Someone likes me.

CHAPTER ELEVEN

I wake up to a knock on my door. It's not quite banging, but it's loud enough to let me know that whoever is knocking has been knocking for a while.

"Fuck," I say and rub my eyes, instinctively putting my feet on the ground and heading toward the door. I turn back when I realize I haven't seen Bob. I fell asleep on the couch with my head on his shoulder, but now he's not there.

"Fuck," I say again, this time with feeling.

I don't have time to find him, I need to make the banging stop.

I don't have a peephole, so I just lean into the door and pray that it's good news. A pizza I don't remember ordering, or a lawyer telling me a long-lost relative died and left me a million dollars. Please don't be the police calling me in for questioning about a blob man who's roaming the streets and terrorizing the public.

I open the door, and it's Rachel. She's sweaty, just wearing leggings and a sports bra with her hair in a slinky ponytail, her headphones slung around her neck. I make a note to tell her she should get sponsored by Adidas or something, become one of those Instagram fitness models.

"Vi, you're here," she says, visible relief crossing her face as she pushes past me into the apartment.

"Now's not a good time," I say.

I realize, belatedly, that I slept in my black velvet gown. My mouth tastes sour.

"I covered for you yesterday with Walter, but you need to come back, or you're going to get fired."

I roll my eyes. We both know Walter isn't going to fire me over this, it's just an excuse she's using to invite herself over.

"I know we had an argument. I'm sorry," she says. "I don't know what's going on with me. Maybe my iron levels are low or something."

"Sure."

"I didn't mean what I said," she says. I don't believe her.

I hear rustling behind me, and watch Rachel's face change from a mask of concern to shock. I turn around to find Bob back on the couch. While I slept, he lengthened and grew the upper half of a torso—he has pecs and dark pink nipples, his body still hairless, like a mall mannequin. His chest is so exquisitely molded that it's difficult for me to look at. Thankfully, from this angle, Rachel can't tell he has no legs.

"Hi," he says to me.

"Hi," he says to Rachel.

Once I've regained control of my body, I run over to Bob and throw an afghan over his chest and nonexistent legs.

"Sorry," I say to Rachel. "He's European."

Rachel's face is red, and I can't tell if it's from her exercising or from seeing Bob.

"I'm Bob," he says.

"Rachel," she says.

Without saying goodbye, she turns and runs.

"HOW DID YOU get off the couch?" I ask Bob.

The afghan slides off his chest, disrupting the illusion that he's sitting, which answers my question for me. He still has no legs but there's also nothing left of his original blob form. He stands on my couch cushions with stumpy ankles and normal-size feet that have grown directly under his torso. His tiny bottom half looks cartoonish and absurd—like a Goomba, one of the brown mushrooms from *Super Mario*.

"Why run?" Bob asks.

It takes me a second to realize he's talking about Rachel.

"She was scared," I say.

I'm scared too. Bob's changing quickly, without waiting for my commands. I don't know what I'll do when he turns into a man who, I suspect, will want to do things like go outside and talk to people.

The clothes I bought Bob from Kohl's haven't arrived yet, so I dig up an old Christmas gift from my ama: an oversized powder-blue hoodie dress that says "It's a love story" in pink cursive on the front.

I shove the hoodie over his head and pull, like a mother with a toddler.

"You need to get dressed. People don't walk around naked."

My phone rings, and I pick it up automatically.

"Vi, it's your mom. I texted you our address, and you never responded. Did you not get my text?"

I check my texts as Bob struggles to pull his big arms through the armholes. When he finally does, he looks up at me and smiles. The hoodie falls just above his feet.

"Yes, I'll be there."

As my mom gives me overly detailed directions to a house just a mile away from where they used to live, Bob jumps down from the couch and begins testing the limits of his new feet. He runs full speed, his short ankles pumping him along from the back of the kitchen to the front door, flat-footed. His feet slap the linoleum tile and make the glasses clink together.

"When should I get there?" I ask.

"Six sharp."

I glance at my watch as my mom describes the menu: fresh herbs from the garden and a lemon roasted chicken. Bob attempts a cartwheel, a somersault, a handstand. He's muscular but graceless and top-heavy—I watch him elbow the wall and head-butt the sofa.

"Hey," I whisper. "Be careful."

"Who are you talking to?"

I forgot about my mom's freakish sense of hearing.

"No one," I say.

My mom drops it and starts talking about the tomato plants she's planning for this season and how she might have to put a fence up to keep the squirrels and rabbits away. Bob attempts a one-handed push-up, loses his balance, and falls. I think I see his arm bend weirdly, the bone buckling unnaturally. I drop the phone and start to move toward him, but he bounces back up before I reach him, his perfect arm uninjured. He smiles like, "Did I fool you?" and I know then I can't leave him on his own for the night. He's going to have to come with me.

"Your dad suggested chicken wire, but that might look a bit too austere," my mom is saying when I pick the phone back up.

"Actually I was talking to someone. My friend Bob is here," I say. "Do you think he could come for dinner?"

There's a pause, and I know my mom is wondering if Bob is a random hookup I'm going to use as a distraction or, worse, a punishment.

"Are you two an item?" she asks.

"No. Yes. Unclear," I say. My mom sighs like she's heard this from me before, even though she hasn't. I usually go to great lengths to keep her away from my one-night stands.

"Look, he's European and he has no friends. He barely speaks English."

"Where did you meet him?"

"The hotel."

I'm pleased that my story doesn't sound like total bullshit. It could've happened—Bob, the sexy foreigner, walks into a Midwest Hillside Inn and Suites, takes one look at my chubby arms, bad attitude, and wrinkled periwinkle uniform, and sweeps me off my feet. It's like the plot of a novel.

After a long pause, my mom agrees.

"Does he have any dietary restriction or allergies?"

I glance at Bob. He's trying to jump up to the kitchen counter but failing to get more than a few inches off the ground.

"I have no idea," I say.

After I hang up the phone, I approach Bob slowly. He's lying flat on his back now, kicking his feet up in the air. I take his foot in my hand to still his motions and get him to focus on me. It's weird to hold a man's foot, even weirder when the foot is uncreased and uncalloused, baby soft.

"You need to grow legs," I say. "Now."

He looks confused, gestures at my thighs and then his ankle-feet.

"No legs," he says.

I realize it's because of last night's conversation—he kept himself legless to please me. It's romantic in a grotesque way. I could keep him a half-man forever if I wanted.

I let go of his foot. "I changed my mind. You need to grow legs."

"Okay," he says.

Nothing happens.

"So now you're shy?"

I go to the store to give him space and get him some real clothes. If he goes out dressed in my sweatshirt, he'll get arrested for public indecency, legs or no legs. Before I leave, I lock the windows and doors, hoping that he doesn't realize how easy it would be for him to unlock them and clamber out into the world.

"I'll be right back," I say. "Don't go anywhere, okay? And grow some legs, please."

I drive quickly, throw random men's jeans and long-sleeves in a cart, and run to the check-out. A gum-chewing girl rings me up, pets the plaid shirts I'm buying, and says "Pretty."

When I get home, I hesitate on the threshold. It would've been selfish to keep Bob dependent on me. He can't stay my pet forever. But as long as the door stays closed, I don't have to face whatever changes are coming.

I WALK IN to find Bob standing naked in the kitchen. I take in the entirety of him—his muscular tree-trunk legs, washboard abs, hips, and an above-average but not excessively large dick. I'm surprised that it's circumcised, and wonder who he used as a model. He's unselfconscious, exhibiting none of the hangups indicative of natural-born humans. It's clear that he doesn't know what to do with his hands, though. They're weirdly locked and raised away from his sides, like he's a child pretending to be an airplane.

"Here." I toss the shopping bag of clothes at him. He doesn't catch it, and the bag falls to the ground.

"Pick something out," I say, and head for the bathroom.

I strip out of my own sweaty clothes. I'm exhausted from the effort it takes to worry about someone else. I briefly wonder if this is what my mother feels like, but stop before I come to a realization about myself I might not like. I step into the shower and let the spray hit my face, turn the knob so the water's uncomfortably hot, and try to scrub off last night's makeup.

It's not like my parents taught me to be selfish. If anything, they're too polite—my dad can't sit in the middle seat at a movie theater because if he had to pee he'd spend fifteen minutes apologizing to each person he passed for disrupting their experience. Maybe they were learning to be more selfish with the new house. Maybe that's what my mother was learning in therapy. Maybe throwing away my childhood memories was part of their fresh start.

My parents were basically kids when they started having kids: twenty-two when they had Alex, twenty-six when I came along.

"Why so young?" I asked my mom once when I was still in high school. We were in the car driving to an extended family birthday party. My mom couldn't find an oldies country station because our antenna was broken, so there was no music and we had to fill up the silence by talking to each other.

I expected my mom to say something about how she always wanted kids or couldn't wait to start a family, some Hallmark-card bullshit.

"It wasn't really a decision. It's what everyone did. It was programmed into us," she said instead. Part of me wanted to ask her if she'd redo it if she could, but I wasn't sure I was ready for the answer.

Now I dry off and listen for sounds of Bob in the other room. Silence. I jimmy into skinny jeans that barely buckle and an itchy sweater I've only worn once. I open the door to the living room, and Bob's standing in front of the fridge, dressed in jeans and a plaid shirt that's too tight in the shoulders. For the second time that day, I gasp. Maybe even more so than when he grew a torso, he looks human.

"Food?" he says, and gestures to the fridge.

"Something small. We're going to my parents tonight for dinner."

I make him a fried egg sandwich with tomato, and he eats it in three bites. I cross my fingers that he doesn't hulk out and burst the seams of his shirt at the dinner table.

Although my parents always invited him to Saturday-night dinners, Luke only came a few times. He would make up some excuse about working late hours in the lab, but I knew he was drinking at Murphy's, the local Irish pub, with his engineering bros or playing video games. I never pushed the issue. I didn't want to come off too needy. Conversely, I endured multiple phone calls a month with his mother, who reminded me during every conversation that Luke was coming home to Montana, to her, after college. With or without me.

Bob has no mother, no father, no family baggage to unpack. He just has me.

"What words do you know?" I ask.

"Many," he says, spitting breadcrumbs at me as he speaks.

"Can you tell me where you came from? What you are?"

I probably should've asked these questions earlier, but the truth is, I don't care about the science behind Bob. I don't stay up at night wondering if he's an alien sent here to kill us all or something. But it occurs to me now that maybe, before I bring him to meet my family, I should ask.

"I'm Bob," he says.

I stare at his chiseled jaw and nod.

"Good enough for me."

I get Bob buckled into the passenger seat of the van thirty minutes early, even though my parents' new house is only ten minutes away. It doesn't matter where you go, everything in this town is ten minutes away. I start driving, keeping one eye on Bob. He's like a little kid—everything about my shitty old van is interesting and new. He stares at the coins and old french fries at the bottom of my cup holder. He flips through my radio presets and settles on a station playing Foreigner. He rolls the windows down, then up, then down, sticks his head out into the open air, and lets his tongue loll, like a dog he must've seen in a commercial.

The closer we get to the address, the more nervous I feel. It might be too soon to expose him to the pressures and expectations of other people. I imagine him collapsing like an overcooked soufflé, deconstructing into something even less than a blob, just a trickle of liquid on my parents' new floor. I bite my fingernails, and Bob sticks his tongue out at me.

My parents' new house is smaller than the old one, but it has a larger lot, set away from the road and shielded from neighbors by big pine trees. All it needs is smoke billowing out of the chimney, and it could be a cottage in a fairy tale. Alex's practical Subaru is already in the driveway. I wonder how early he got here.

"Are you ready?" I ask Bob. He nods. It feels natural to take his hand. Together we walk up the drive.

CHAPTER TWELVE

My mom opens the door before we knock; she must've been watching us from the window. She pulls me in for a tight hug, and I close my eyes at the familiarity of her slender shoulders.

"You look good, Vi," she whispers in my ear. I know it's a lie, but it's comforting nonetheless.

"And good to meet you," she says as she turns to Bob. If she's surprised by how handsome he is, she does a good job of hiding it.

Bob smiles and mimics the hug I gave my mom.

"Come in," she says, makes a sweeping arm gesture, like she's welcoming us into a palace. We step into the smell of roasting vegetables and a balsam and cedar Yankee Candle. I realize belatedly that I should've brought something: wine, a baguette, some handcrafted soap—it is a housewarming, after all.

The doorways of the new house are rounded, with dark exposed wood trim.

"I feel like I'm in a hobbit hole," I say. It's a compliment, and my mom smiles with real warmth.

My parents' taste has always been a hodgepodge of gifts and antiques and things from their college years that they never threw out. It's strange to see those items displaced from their natural habitat of twenty years. Out of that context, the suit of armor my dad garbage-picked from the side of the road isn't just a bargain hunter's impulse; it's something he chose to keep, to lug from one house to the next.

My mom leads us into the living room, where my dad and Alex are standing around, talking about the uptick of hate crimes in town. They stop talking when we enter, and I catch Alex's eyebrows rising when he sees Bob, this handsome white movie star who's a good six inches taller than him. Bob follows when I tug on his hand, and I wonder if I can hang on to him all night, maneuver him with my fingers like a puppet. After I introduce Bob to Alex and my dad, we settle onto a leather loveseat. My parents don't drink, but surely Alex brought some wine or beer. I already know I'm not going to make it through this night without alcohol.

"So, Bob, what do you do?" my mom asks.

"He's a student," I say.

"Of what?" my dad asks, suddenly interested. He's perched on the arm of the couch next to my mom. I should've known better than to lie about Bob being a student to my dad, the lifelong learner who's taken ten classes and audited another five since he retired two years ago.

"Atmospheric science. He's got his head in the clouds."

Alex rolls his eyes. I do think there's something romantic about people who study storms. I took two courses in meteorology and weather systems before I realized how dull it is. As a kid, I would go outside with a point-and-shoot camera and click, click, click, trying to capture lightning on film, until one day I did and it looked like nothing, just a blurry squiggle in the darkness.

I carried a camera with me everywhere until I was about fourteen, and announced to the family that I wanted to be a photographer.

My dad winced. "That's not really a career. How about something in the sciences?"

"Nice house," Bob says now.

I squeeze his hand in approval. Perhaps I underestimated Bob's limited vocabulary and the power of nodding and smiling.

My mom explains that she found the house through a friend in her combination Pilates-yoga class, and they were able to put in an offer before it was officially on the market.

"You know I always wanted a bigger yard to start a wildflower garden," my mom says to me, and I nod, even though I didn't know this.

"These houses have so much character," my dad says. He tells us about the old-fashioned laundry chute from the master bedroom to the laundry room, the pocket shutters common in the nineteenth century, and the claw-foot bathtub that weighs over four hundred pounds.

It's hard not to say anything about our old house. The playground my dad built in the backyard that rotted to pieces. The pet graves littered throughout the garden beds. The garage where my parents stored the canoe they were given as a wedding present and never once used. All of that gone now.

I don't bring it up because the truth is, my parents look happy. They seem closer in every way possible, as if the downsizing of their house has physically pushed them together.

"Where are you from?" Alex asks Bob.

Alex is in a good mood today—he's scowling less than usual, and he's wearing the gray sweater I got him last Christmas. When he opened it, he said "A sweater" in his best deadpan, and even I laughed.

Bob puts both hands on his chest and says "Bob."

Everyone smiles politely, including Bob, and Alex repeats the question, this time with hand gestures. I watch Bob's forehead furrow.

"Um . . . ," I jump in. I struggle to think of a country that doesn't have an accent. I've always been shit at geography, lost bar trivia once because I didn't know what state the Alamo was in. "Denmark, I think?"

"I've always wanted to visit Denmark. How do you like it?" asks my dad.

I'm somewhat surprised at my family being so inquisitive and attentive to Bob as a guest. Have they always been this thoughtful? It would make my life easier if they were cold and disinterested.

Before I can interject with some made-up facts about Denmark, Bob starts talking. "In 1944 this island country officially declared itself independent from Denmark."

I look at Bob sideways. This is the most words I've ever heard him speak.

"What is Iceland?" my dad replies, smiling.

"That is correct," Bob says.

"He's been watching too much *Jeopardy!* It's helping him learn English."

My dad looks intrigued, ready to ask follow-up questions.

"Oh man, I'm hungry," I blurt out loudly.

"What else is new?" Alex says. He softens the words with a smile.

THE DINING ROOM is filled with gentle light from the stained-glass lamps my dad collects, tea candles, and Japanese lanterns hanging in the corners.

"It feels like Christmas," I say, and my mom smiles weakly at me.

We find our seats at the large wood table, my dad at the head. I pull on Bob's hand to let him know he's supposed to sit. I make a mental note to tell him to blink more when we get home—his stare causes other people to stare, and my dad's eyes are watering from the effort.

Dinner is roasted tomatoes, brussels sprouts, and fingerling potatoes with a whole chicken. Just like on Thanksgiving, my dad carves, making slow, precise cuts into the bird for a good fifteen minutes while we all try to pretend we're not starving.

I don't know why I thought a change of location would save us; my dad keeps talking as he cuts. He read somewhere that Denmark is consistently ranked one of the world's happiest countries.

"It's easy to be happy when you have health care," Alex says as he spears a tomato onto his fork.

"And great bike routes," my mom says.

My dad goes on about the free college tuition and childcare, every now and then looking to Bob to validate his Denmark facts. Bob nods with his brow furrowed, as if listening carefully. I decide this is as good a time as any to make a run for the kitchen and the promise of alcohol. I've never been thirstier in my life.

The kitchen is predictably gorgeous—I wouldn't have thought white cabinets and dark wood countertops would look good together, but somehow it works. I scan the fridge for alcohol and find only Mike's Hard Lemonade.

"Fuck it," I say. I twist the cap off. I stick another under my arm for later and turn back for the dining room to find Alex in the doorway. I resist the urge to curse again.

"Go ahead, judge me," I say.

"Judge you? That doesn't sound like me."

I move toward the doorway, but Alex doesn't move. Although we've never been close, I know Alex like I know myself—his mood swings and sarcasm, his insecurity, his pride—whether we want to admit it or not, we are two sides of the same coin. That's how I know something's not right: he looks hesitant, off-kilter.

"Everything okay?" I ask.

He doesn't talk about it much, but I know that being a pediatric resident is hard. The death gets under his skin. For every success story he brags to our parents about, there's five kids who never get better.

"An inevitability," he might say in his colder moments.

"I'm sorry," he says now. "For what I said last week at dinner. I was out of line."

The bottle stuffed in my armpit almost drops to the floor. Alex never apologizes. Neither do I—it's a point of connection between us, we share a grudging respect for our mutual stubbornness. So I don't know what to make of this. Maybe Mom told him to apologize. Maybe he's putting on a show because Bob's here.

"Mom didn't tell me to say this," Alex says, reading my mind. He looks down and shuffles his feet. "I was too hard on you."

I feel myself starting to cry, so I stare at the ceiling. There's no more mysterious yellow stains, just a clean expanse of white. We never have real conversations, so we're bad at it, like two actors who've forgotten their lines.

"I'm sorry too," I say, although I don't know exactly what I'm apologizing for. My general selfishness? My inability to tell my brother that, despite all evidence to the contrary, I do want to know him? For now, a general "sorry" feels like enough.

Alex nods, turns, and walks out to the dining room. I chug the rest of the lemonade, and when I get back to the table, the malt liquor is churning in my stomach.

My dad has finished carving the chicken and exhausted his knowledge of Denmark. In silence, we pass the dishes around the table, and Bob mimics us as we spoon things onto plates.

"To family," my mom says when we all have full plates. We clink our water glasses ceremonially. To an outsider, we must look like an idyllic sitcom family, eating chicken dinner in our cozy cottage.

Within five minutes Bob's plate is finished, and he's reaching for more chicken. I'm relieved that at least he's using a knife and fork—thank god for all the *Top Chef* I made him watch.

"Do you not feed him?" Alex asks me.

"He does intermittent fasting," I say, and pop the cap off my second bottle.

My dad nods, looks like he wants to say something about the science behind fasting, but thankfully his mouth's full.

"I'm glad you like the meal," my mom says.

"Thank you," Bob says, his mouth full, chewing loudly.

My mom sits back in her chair, satisfied. For her, appreciation is the biggest compliment. And the food does taste particularly good; the crisp lemony chicken skin and garlic parmesan potatoes melt on my tongue. Has she always been such a good cook?

"What do you think of the house, Vi?" my mom asks.

Everyone except Bob turns to look at me. I know this is a trap, a way for my mom to assuage her guilt over selling the house and throwing away the journals I'd abandoned in her basement for the last decade. I thought my mom and dad would stay in that house forever.

"I like it," I say.

I see the tension leave her shoulders

"This family. A happy place," Bob says after finishing his second helping.

My parents' faces look flushed, even though they're just drinking water. I put my hand on Bob's thigh, and he smiles at me.

CHAPTER THIRTEEN

After we finish our desserts of chocolate cake and candied orange slices, my mom pulls me into the kitchen to help her clean up.

"I never help clean up," I say and hop on the counter.

"That's because you don't scrub," she says.

I watch my mom take off her watch and run the hot water till it's steaming.

"Bob's nice," she says, elbow deep in soap bubbles and chicken grease.

"He is."

"Not like Luke."

I turn and stare at her profile. It's a universally agreed-upon fact that Luke is nice. He's stop-and-say-hello-to-every-stranger-on-the-street nice.

My mom hands me a dish to dry. "I know it was hard for you to see, but Luke had a lot of flaws."

"Like what?"

"Remember your cousin's wedding?"

"Bits and pieces."

What I remember most clearly is the open bar and the five gin and sodas I drank.

"You were dancing and spilled your drink on your dress. I remember you laughed, and Luke didn't. He looked embarrassed."

I shrug. At the time, I thought we were just doing a comedy bit—Luke played the straight man and pretended to be annoyed by my quirks when really he was charmed. I'd never considered that there was another possibility.

"Is Alex dating anyone?" I ask to change the subject.

"He doesn't tell me anything," my mom says.

She takes the bait, though, goes on about how young and responsible Alex is.

"And his job's so important," she says.

I'm half listening, half watching Bob from the doorway. I'm not nervous that he'll be discovered anymore. Seeing him sitting with his feet crossed at the ankles in my mom's old pink wing chair, it would be impossible for anyone to believe that a week ago he was a blob.

"He's a catch, if only he'd put himself out there."

"I'm going to see how Bob is," I interrupt, leaving my mom to the dishes.

In the other room, Alex and my dad are arguing about a new Michael Jordan documentary.

"If Jordan wasn't so competitive, they never would've won so many championships," Alex says.

From his seat, Bob nods.

"See, Bob agrees," Alex says.

"Nope. He pushed his teammates too hard," my dad says.

Bob nods again, and Alex laughs. "You can't have it both ways, Bob."

"He's diplomatic," I cut in.

We leave quickly after that, my mom loading our arms up with plastic containers filled with leftovers. Everyone walks us to the door.

"Come again soon," my mom says.

"You're always welcome," my dad says.

"Good to see you," Alex says.

It feels almost perfect. I squeeze Bob's hand as we walk down the steps to the van and think, *This, this, this.*

"Did you have fun?" I ask on the ride home.

Bob smiles and nods.

"They liked you, I can tell."

"I like them," he says.

My mind goes back to the other night, Bob's palm on my thigh. Does he like me specifically, or does he like everyone? Or maybe he's just a good mimic. I look over and realize Bob's still smiling. He's been smiling the whole dinner; his mouth muscles must be aching.

"Stop smiling," I say, and he does. His face collapses into a frown, his brow furrowing. I'm relieved that he still listens to me. We ride the rest of the way home in silence.

As soon as we walk into my apartment, I feel bone-deep, soul tired. I leave Bob on the couch, go to my room, and change into silk pajamas that my cousin gave me one Christmas, a bridesmaid's gift that was too big for her. I climb into bed and feel comfortably heavy.

"Come here," I call to Bob.

He comes to my bedside and squats so we're face-to-face. Up close, I see not just his milky skin but the dark circles under his eyes. I must've been too distracted by his handsomeness to notice his exhaustion. I've never seen him sleep.

"Are you tired?"

Bob nods.

"Do you know how to sleep?"

"No."

Of course not—sitcoms never show their characters sleeping. I pat the other side of the queen-size bed I bought used from a rich coworker at the animal science lab. "I want you to have one nice thing," she said when I picked it up and handed her ninety bucks. She's right, though, the mattress is nicer than anything I could've afforded.

"Come here," I say.

Usually it's hard for me to fall asleep next to someone. Toward the end with Luke, I stayed awake the whole night, jacked up on adrenaline and fear that he would leave me. I would watch him curl away from me, smaller and smaller, like a turtle retreating into its shell.

Bob's different. He gets under the comforter and immediately starfishes, stretches his long, muscular limbs out to all four corners of the bed. I nudge his body to the left side.

"Close your eyes," I say. Only the desk lamp is on, so I can still see Bob's silhouette. "Now relax. Think of simple things. A meadow, grass, an episode of *Seinfeld*."

I stare at the cobweb shadows in the corner of my ceiling. Bob doesn't snore like Luke. He breathes steadily, the rhythm like my mom's grandfather clock. In my mind, I erect an invisible barrier between us. I won't do anything to take advantage of him. He needs to sleep, that's all, and his warmth, his weight, next to me is just a necessary evil.

I WAKE UP to Bob's muscular limbs wrapped around me like a koala scaling a eucalyptus tree. I allow myself a minute to enjoy the uncomfortable position, my neck crooked awkwardly in his elbow crease, before rolling out from underneath him.

I was dreaming about Luke. When we were dating, he was always trying to get me to go outside. He took me on a four-hour bike ride on a trail so bumpy I puked on a fern midway through. A few weeks later we foraged for mushrooms in a valley infested with mosquitoes. I couldn't believe he was dating me, so I did everything he suggested.

In the dream, we were at the university arboretum where he once fingered me on a bench in front of the butterfly garden. In the dream, he rode a bike as I jogged alongside him.

"What are we doing?" I asked.

"I love you," he said. "But I'm married."

I kept jogging, not to stay close to him but to see if I could catch a glimpse of a wedding band. I wanted to know if he was lying.

Now I get up and watch Bob sleep.

"You're real," I whisper, but I don't know if I'm trying to convince him or me.

I open the blinds and let in the late afternoon sunlight to see if it wakes him. It doesn't.

It's Sunday, and there's nothing to do, no work to dread, no social obligations to ruin with my presence. I've never understood what to do with Sundays—I'm tempted to find religion just so I have somewhere to go. I leave Bob in bed and wander to the kitchen, looking for food. I threw away all the spoiled groceries, so my fridge is populated only by leftovers from last night's dinner, shredded cheddar cheese, almost expired orange juice, and gin.

My phone dings, and it's a text from my mom: thx for coming!!! with three purple heart emojis. She's also attached a photo she took of me and Bob at dinner when we weren't looking. I have a double chin, a forkful of chicken halfway to my mouth; meanwhile Bob's smiling like a movie star greeting his adoring fans. I zoom in on his eyes. Is he looking at me or at the table in general? I can't decide, but I save the photo anyway. I pace the length of my apartment, once, twice.

I'm staring at my spice rack when Bob walks in. He's naked from the waist up, the elastic in Luke's old boxers stretched out so they hang low on his hips. His six-pack looks unhuman—I realize I've never seen one in real life, only in movies. The shadows and divots, the rippling muscle definition, is straight out of an ad for preworkout. It takes me a second to realize that Bob's still not smiling.

"When I said to stop smiling, I didn't mean forever."

Silence.

"You just don't have to do it all the time."

"Yes."

"Like you don't have to pretend to be happy if you're not, just because you think it might make other people happy to see you happy. You don't exist for the sole purpose of making other people happy."

Bob's mouth looks confused now, his lips pressed together too tight, frozen in a half smile, half frown.

"Food?" he asks.

I reopen the fridge and heat up the leftovers from last night, less appetizing now that the chicken skin's not crispy and the vegetables are smushed together and dull. The silence between us is awkward. What do normal people say to each other on Sunday mornings? Should we be discussing sports or talking about office gossip? I'm at a loss. I put the leftovers in front of Bob, grab the handle of gin from the fridge, and pour myself a shot. I risk adding the questionable orange juice—it's worth it to pretend this is a normal breakfast drink. Bob doesn't seem to notice. He eats and eats as I sip on my gin-mosa and feel the familiar buzz enter my bloodstream.

I was a sophomore in college when I had my first drink. Alex ruined the thrill of high school intoxication by being stupid enough to get caught drunk on rum with a blunt in his pocket. My mom cried and my dad bought a breathalyzer, and no one invited me to any parties in high school anyway.

My first drink was during a friend setup orchestrated by Luke with a curly redhead anthropology major named Jayla.

"I think you'll really hit it off," he said, although I suspect he was just annoyed by my lack of friends.

That's how I ended up on a scratchy rug Jayla told me was handwoven by single mothers in India, doing shots of strawberry Burnett's vodka.

"Luke is such a good guy," she said as she poured alcohol into shot glasses.

"He is."

I tipped the shot back and let the liquid pool in my mouth, the sickening strawberry hiding none of the cheap vodka's burn. It tasted like rancid cough syrup. Jayla threw her head back and swallowed quick. This clearly was not her first shot.

"Not bad," I said when I could breathe again. Jayla let out a squeal of approval at my watering eyes and poured another round.

After the third shot, Jayla let slip that she'd kissed Luke at a party the previous semester.

"It doesn't count, though. He hadn't met you yet, and I was high on shrooms."

I didn't react, though I could tell Jayla wanted me to. I could have been mad at Luke or maybe embarrassed that the only girl he could get to hang out with me on a Friday night was a former hookup. I wasn't. I took another shot. I was drunk but not too drunk—everything was pleasantly hazy, and the voice in my head that told me how inadequate I was had quieted. I took another shot.

"It's okay," I told Jayla. I hugged her to my chest, and she inhaled. We stayed like that for a while. "We can both love him."

After eight shots, I was still lucid and upright. I marveled at my tolerance. I told Jayla to take a strand of my hair for DNA sequencing; surely I would be studied and my genes would be used to help others who were struggling with alcohol consumption. At four in the morning, she asked me, politely, to leave her apartment.

Only a few weeks later, when I threw up after a biochemistry meet-and-greet, did I realize that Jayla had been pouring me half shots. My tolerance was the same as any other pudgy teenager's. I couldn't be mad at her though. She had still given me a superpower—the ability to shut off my inner monologue long enough to speak, make jokes, even win a round of darts. Alcohol made me into something more than the extra in the background.

I POUR A half shot of gin and juice into a glass and push it toward Bob.

"Do you want to try some?" I tip my drink toward him. He sniffs the air above it like a sommelier. "It's gin. Alcohol."

"Alcohol," he repeats.

"You've probably seen it on TV. People drink it to loosen up and do things they don't have the courage to do sober."

Bob touches the glass to his perfect lips, sips, and immediately gags. The cocktail dribbles out of his mouth onto his perfect chin, and I laugh. He shakes his head as if to shake the taste out of it and sticks his tongue out. Without thinking, I pinch the pink muscle between my index finger and thumb.

"Aaaah," Bob says, and opens his mouth wider, like he's at the dentist.

"Sorry."

I pull my hand away. I pour another half shot into Bob's glass.

"Here. Drink," I say.

By noon we're drunk, lying flat on the floor with the gin and juice between us. I roll my head left and then right, digging the fibers of the carpet into my scalp.

"What bad words do you know?" I ask.

I've already asked him most of the questions I could think of. When I asked him to tell me a story, he recounted scene by scene the episode of *Seinfeld* where they get lost in a parking garage.

"Bitch, ass, dirty, pussy."

"How did you learn pussy?"

Bob points to the remote control. "One eighty-six."

I pick up the remote and type in the number. It's a pay-per-view porn channel where apparently Bob purchased an adult film entitled *Hot for Teacher* for $12.99.

"You're kidding."

Bob doesn't respond, shows no sense of shame or guilt. It's already paid for, so I push play, and together we watch a blond woman in pigtails wearing a Catholic schoolgirl outfit walk into an empty classroom. A disclaimer flashes at the bottom of the screen: ALL PERFORMERS ARE OVER EIGHTEEN YEARS OF AGE. The teacher's at his desk, shuffling his papers around. He's hot and old, but not too old.

"You know this is fake, right?" I say.

On the screen, the schoolgirl explains that she's here during her lunch hour to complain about her midterm grade. "My parents will kill me," she whines, biting her bottom lip.

As the teacher looks for her paper, the schoolgirl leans forward and undoes three buttons on her shirt to show off her giant boobs.

"And those are fake too," I say.

Bob lifts his own shirt, flashes his sculpted abs and chest, and points to his own nipple.

"Fake?"

"No." I pull his shirt down, and something comes over me. I want to touch him, so I do. My hands move over his body, his face, his shoulders. "Not fake."

Now the schoolgirl is sitting on the teacher's desk. She hikes up her skirt and shows her transparent pink panties to the camera as the teacher remains oblivious. He's bent over, looking in drawer after drawer for her lost exam.

I'm lying on my side, my hands still on Bob, when something moves. I look down and see a bulge sticking up from Bob's pants. He scoots away from me, his brow furrowed in confusion or concern, I can't tell which. With his hands, he pushes down on his erection and watches it bob back up like a bath toy.

The first time I saw Luke's dick, I only managed a glimpse of it, in the pitch-black on the top bunk of my dorm room, before Luke jammed it into the back of my throat and I tried not to choke.

"Am I hurting you?" he asked when I couldn't answer. The musky smell of his ball sack lingered on the ends of my hair the day after.

Luke had watched a lot of porn growing up, not the gentle kind with natural light and two performers committed to worshipping one another's bodies. He watched slam, bam, no-thank-you-ma'am porn full of high-pitched squeals and grunting. I can't blame the bad sex all on him though. I could've told him that I didn't like it when he pinched my nipples hard between his fingers, or when he pulled my hair back while I blew him, or when he thrust into me bone-dry. I didn't. It was easier to fake-moan and writhe and pretend until it was over.

"Look," I say, and point to the TV, where the schoolgirl has taken off the reluctant teacher's belt and unzipped his fly.

The camera closes up on her hands, massaging the teacher's impressively big member. Bob looks from the TV to his own crotch. I watch the schoolgirl lean over and suck on the teacher's dick. Bob takes out his almost comically big erection and kneads it in his hand like dough. Part of me wants to watch, but instead I get up and avert my eyes. I feel nauseous, the gin burning a hole in my empty stomach. I turn off the TV just as the teacher pulls the schoolgirl's lips from his dick and starts to energetically fuck her on his desk.

"Enough," I say, but Bob doesn't stop. He's still flat on his back, pulling on his dick, biting his lip in pleasure.

"Stop," I order.

Bob looks up at me with his hand on his dick and groans just like the teacher on the screen. A deep low rumble. I feel the acid of the orange juice in the back of my throat, a warning for what's to come. I run to the bathroom and vomit an orange rainbow into the toilet bowl. I cough and gag and spit until I'm emptied of liquid. Through the bathroom door, I hear Bob moaning in what could be pleasure or could be pain.

CHAPTER FOURTEEN

On Monday morning, I walk into the hotel at 5:57 a.m. Paul greets me with a grunt.

"Look who showed up."

He sounds a little disgruntled, like maybe he missed our Friday-morning chat.

"I couldn't stay away from this place if I tried," I say. My smile doesn't reach my eyes.

Paul raises his eyebrows as he clears the desk of his coffee and crossword.

"Apparently not."

Alone at the desk, I wonder if Bob's awake yet. I tried to wake him before I left. I poked and shook him, and he just mumbled and turned away, swatted at my fingers like they were spider legs. I wrote him a note, even though I wasn't sure he'd be able to read it. *Went to work. Be back by 3 p.m. Don't leave the apartment.* I didn't know whether to put "Love" above my name, so I just drew a heart beside it and immediately felt like an idiot.

The hotel looks the same, down to the grime on the coffee maker and the generic geometric paintings next to the elevators. I have the urge to tear them off the wall and throw them in the pool. I square my shoulders. All I have to do is make it through the next eight hours, and then I can go home to Bob, my real life.

A harried middle-aged man walks up to the desk at 8:00 a.m. A woman, presumably his wife, sits on one of the couches with their bags, trying to rock the screaming kid in the carrier.

"I'm sorry to bother you," he says. It must look like I'm typing furiously. From his vantage point he can't see that I'm playing Tetris, stacking up blocks on the left side of the screen and biding my time till I get the I-Block to clear all the lines. "Is there any way we can check in early?"

I pause the game. "Let me check."

No rooms have been marked as clean yet, so I radio the head of housekeeping.

"Look who's graced us with her presence," she crackles through the walkie-talkie before listing off some in-progress rooms.

"Gotcha," I say. "We'll get something figured out for you. In the meantime, have a seat."

I watch as he returns to his wife. She's bouncing the crying baby, whispering "It's going to be okay," and fake smiling. Finally she cradles the baby's head in the crook of her arm, like it's a football. This technique works for a few minutes, until someone comes in and the cold draft from the sliding door sets the baby off again. The woman hands the infant to her husband, who's had his eyes closed for the last ten minutes. How he could sleep through the crying is beyond me.

"Any word on that room?" the woman asks.

"No," I say without looking up. The Tetris blocks are coming faster, too fast, until finally I get an I-Block. I push the space bar and watch the lines disappear. It's so satisfying, I don't notice that the woman has leaned over the desk and is watching my screen. My score goes up and up. I pause the game.

"Are you kidding me?" she asks.

"Sorry."

"Can you check on the room?"

I take my walkie-talkie to the back room and radio the head of housekeeping.

"Give me a room, any room, a dirty room. I don't care anymore."

She gives me a number, and I go back out and make keycards.

"Here." I shove the keys at her. "Happy?"

She closes her eyes for a long second. The baby's screams have started to trail off; they're more like shout-coughs now.

"Never been happier," she says. "You?"

AT 8:45 A.M., Rachel walks through the sliding doors. Right away, I can tell she's reverted to her girl-next-door persona. Her ponytail is high, with no flyaways in sight, her natural blush and nude lip applied meticulously.

"Vi," she crows from across the room. "I'm so happy to see you."

She runs around the desk and hugs me with deceptively muscular arms.

"Do you lift weights?" I ask after I've disentangled my face from her flowery-smelling hair.

"Just yoga and Pilates," she says with a wave of her hand.

I go back to my computer screen, where I've been scrolling through Instagram, clicking on videos of cats jumping in and out of boxes. Rachel keeps standing there, looking at me expectantly, like she's waiting for me to say something. Finally it clicks; the last time she saw me, she also saw Bob.

"Sorry about my roommate."

"It's okay." Rachel finally sets her bag down and logs into her computer.

Just when we've almost settled into a companionable morning silence, Rachel blurts out, "I went on another date with Derek."

"The poodle guy? I thought you hated him."

"It's nice to have someone," she says.

"I don't know." I think about the woman I just checked in— her screaming baby and sleeping husband. "Being alone isn't bad."

"I never pictured you with someone like Bob."

I feel my blood rising, but I keep my voice level. "What does that mean?"

Rachel gives me a deer-in-the-headlights look.

"No, no," she says finally. "He's just very buff. I didn't know you were into gym rats."

I nod begrudgingly. We both know what she meant. Hot men aren't supposed to date chubby, socially challenged introverts. They are meant to get married and procreate with the Rachels of the world. Our coupling is messing with the natural order of things.

The rest of my shift is uneventful—travel-weary guests come and go, wheeling suitcases and hefting overnight bags over their shoulders. They gravitate toward Rachel's line like she's handing out free candy or something. At least watching the guests gives me the illusion of travel and movement. It makes me feel like I'm not just standing still.

There's only an hour left in my shift, and I can already taste the McChicken I'm going to order for the ride home, when the sliding doors open and Bob walks in.

"Shit," I say.

I run out from behind the desk and catch Bob by the elbow. I try to spin him around back to the entrance, but he has a low center of gravity and doesn't budge.

"How did you get here?" I hiss under my breath, but he doesn't seem to hear me. He continues his march toward the front desk, unfazed.

At least he's not naked. He's wearing the jeans I bought him and an XL sleep shirt that he must've dug out of the depths of my closet that says OK, BUT FIRST COFFEE in block letters. He waves to Rachel as he approaches.

"Good to see you again," Rachel says, but she looks uncomfortable.

"Sorry I scared you," Bob says.

"Oh no, of course not." She looks down at her desk as if something vital has come up on our daily checklist. "It's okay. I'm happy for you two."

She sounds like she's being held at gunpoint, but Bob doesn't notice. "I'm happy too," he says.

There's something delicious about this moment, so I let it linger without intervening. I almost wish I could leave them there in this awkward silence: Bob nodding and smiling as Rachel stews. Instead I pull on Bob's hand, hard.

"Good to see you again," he yells to Rachel as I drag him toward the empty breakfast room. She nods weakly.

"What are you doing?" I ask. "I told you to stay in the apartment."

Bob shifts from one foot to the other. His shoes are coated in mud, and little clumps of dirt break off onto the carpet as he moves. He must've walked along the interstate in the knee-high prickly grasses.

"On TV, people leave. They go places."

Bob moves his hands back and forth as he talks. His whole body is swaying—I've never seen him look this unsure before.

"How many people honked at you?" I ask.

"Five."

"How did you know I worked here?"

He tilts his head, confused. "You told me."

I don't know how this could be true. Then it comes back to me, how I complained during *Top Chef* about my commute, the traffic and unnecessary five-way stop on Riverside. I didn't tell this to human Bob. I told blob Bob.

I glance at my watch. I still have forty-five minutes of standing behind a desk to do. I take Bob's hand and lead him to the uncomfortable yellow sofa.

"Can you sit?" I ask.

Bob points to the pool. No guests have been in it yet, and even I have to admit that the blue water, untouched by dirty diapers and used Band-Aids, looks tempting.

"Can I swim?"

"No. Sit. Stay." The words come out sharper than I intended. If anyone overheard me, they would think I was angry at a labradoodle.

Bob follows my orders, but his smile's gone. He sits on the very edge of the sofa with his back to the front desk, staring through the glass window at the empty pool.

"Is he okay?" Rachel asks when I get back to the desk.

"He's fine."

For the next ten minutes, he sits still and silent as a statue.

WHEN I WAS a kid, my mom was always trying to get me into a pool. She thought I needed a break from my obsession with romance novels and taking blurry photographs. It started with swim lessons, something my dad decreed a "basic survival skill," though except for flying from Taiwan to the US when he was eight, he had spent his life landlocked, surrounded by cornfields.

The pool was just a ten-minute walk from our house, but it wasn't really designed for kids. There were no inner tube slides, no sprinkler systems disguised as dolphin spouts, no designated kiddie pools, no lazy river. It was just a big rectangular swimming pool from three feet to nine feet deep, with two diving boards off the deep end.

Part of the problem was that I didn't have any friends at swim lessons. Even at twelve, during my last year of water torture, none of the suburban kids went to my public school—they went to Uni, the gifted school for professors' kids, or Judah Christian, the private school where Bible verses were played over the loudspeaker. So before the lesson I wound up standing alone, pulling at the crotch of my bathing suit, as the other kids splashed around playing a game I didn't know the rules of, some Marco Polo variant. Sometimes I tried to work up the nerve to interrupt, but much as in double dutch, I didn't have the rhythm or the courage necessary to jump in.

On the last day of my last year of swim lessons, our instructor Lenny decided it'd be fun to have a surprise swim competition. Lenny was a friend of my brother's, a fifteen-year-old wannabe punk drummer who came to the pool with Blink-182 lyrics written on his forearm in black Sharpie. I was so in love with him, I couldn't find a way to say more than five words in a row without mumbling.

"You've been waiting all summer for this moment," he boomed in his best WWF announcer voice. "Swim Force Olympics."

Everyone laughed and clapped and yelled except me. I could feel my skin pruning in dread. We swam to the deep end together to begin the competition. I sank down, dawdling, scanning the bottom of the pool for an escape hatch. All I found was a few pennies and a yellow hair scrunchie.

First up was treading water.

"Remember to use your core. Keep your body steady," Lenny yelled as we pedaled our legs like we were riding water bikes.

I only lasted a minute treading water before I swam to the wall. Lenny stood outside the pool, dripping chlorine on the concrete.

"You're done?" Lenny said.

"Yeah," I said. I felt like crying so I dunked my head under water and blew bubbles.

"Okay," he said. "Not bad, Vi."

Redhead Sally, the budding basketball star who was a foot taller than all the boys in our class, won.

"Could've gone another three minutes easy," she gloated as Lenny bowed to her from outside the pool.

"My queen," he said like he was a court jester.

Next was diving for rings. This was my only hope at not coming in last. Finally being chubbier than the other girls might come in handy. I had to be better at sinking than them. Lenny threw in ten colored rings, and it was a free-for-all. The water churned like we were sharks after chum. I sank but not as quickly as I'd expected, and bubbles engulfed my vision. I couldn't wear glasses underwater, and my parents were too cheap to get prescription goggles. I came up with nothing, my hands clasping water like loose pebbles. Kaleb won, and wore the rings around his upper arm like bands of honor.

"On to our last challenge," Lenny yelled from the ladder. "Holding your breath. No sabotage. Everyone give each other space."

We spread out across the pool. I hung out in the shallow end, right around the four-foot mark, while the jock boys, led by Mark H., took over the deep end.

"This challenge is mine," Mark H. yelled, and pounded his chest like an orangutan.

I was just glad this waking nightmare was almost over. I was already imagining sitting in the back seat of my mom's minivan on the way home, knowing that I'd never have to go to swim lessons again. I just needed to lose one more time.

"Ready, set, go!" Lenny yelled.

I took a breath (not deep enough, surely) and sank. I crossed my legs and sat at the bottom of the pool. My hair looked like tentacles drifting around my face. It was peaceful. Maybe I could stay like this, I thought. Immediately after that thought, the fear came crawling at my throat, and I was pushing up, up, away.

I came up first, gasping like I'd just been born. Everyone else was still submerged, scattered around the pool, little pods of bodies and burning lungs.

"Go back down," Lenny said softly.

"What?"

"Just do it. Quick."

I did as Lenny said. I took a deeper breath this time, felt my belly expand against my hands, and sank back down to the bottom of the pool. I sat cross-legged again and closed my eyes. I tried to sleep, to let go of fear. Would it be so bad to drown here? Lenny was up there above me, with his blue eyes and inked arms. He'd save me. The thought was so comforting, I almost forgot the burning in the back of my throat.

When I reemerged, everyone was there. Smiling at me. The sun was shining.

"You won." Lenny danced around the edge of the pool, his bare feet slapping against the concrete. "Go Vi!"

"Cheating dog," Mark H. yelled, his palms slapping the water so droplets jumped high and glittering against the blue sky.

CHAPTER FIFTEEN

I retreat to the back room for the last thirty minutes of my shift. It's Walter's day off, so I sit at his desk and spin around in his black leather chair. I root around his drawers for hidden chocolate, but he must've eaten his stash already; all I find is loose paper clips and rusted pennies.

Bob's hunched-over form in the lobby is too sad to look at. How have I turned into a mean mom who won't let her blob swim? He isn't even supposed to be here. On Walter's computer, I google padlocks and email myself links to gates used to contain farm animals.

My phone dings, and it's Elliott texting me a GIF of two squirrels waltzing.

Don't forget you're my date tonight!

What should I wear to this thing? I text back.

Whatever makes you feel beautiful. He adds a star emoji.

I roll my eyes.

Two minutes before my shift is over, I go back out to the lobby. It's deserted. No guests, no Rachel at the desk, no Bob sulking on the couch.

I glance through the glass walls to the pool area, and there they are.

Bob stands shirtless in the pool, cupping water in his hand and letting it fall. Rachel sits by the edge, her feet dangling in the water. She's taken off her black pumps and rolled up her dress pants, and she's laughing at something Bob's saying, which seems impossible to me. He's only been human for a few days. How can he be funny?

I grab a keycard from behind the desk and swipe myself in. As soon as Bob sees me, he dives underwater.

"What's going on?" I ask Rachel.

She gives me a weak smile and takes her feet out of the water. I feel like the wife who's just walked in on her husband fucking the secretary.

"Bob said he's never been in a pool," Rachel says. "Can you believe that?"

Bob still hasn't surfaced, but I see his legs kicking underwater. Air bubbles float to the surface.

"He doesn't know how to swim."

"Really?" she says as we both watch Bob's shape glide gracefully along the bottom of the pool like a stingray.

"Anyway, this isn't allowed." I cross my arms over my chest.

I can tell that Rachel wants to laugh. She's probably thinking of all the times I got bored and took forty-minute breaks to throw rocks at road markers on the side of the highway. Whenever Rachel asked where I went, I told her I was on a walkabout. Now suddenly I'm a rule follower.

"Walter's off today," Rachel says. "And I forwarded calls to the portable phone. I still have a clear view of the desk if any guests come in."

I shrug, purse my lips—there's no arguing with that. Bob finally surfaces. By now he's been underwater for a good three minutes, and I expect him to come up sputtering and contrite.

I'm even trying to remember the rhythm of "Staying Alive" from the CPR class I took in health class, so I can keep my chest compressions on tempo. But no, Bob surfaces gracefully, like he's in a *Baywatch* episode, water streaming down his face in slow-mo.

"Hi," he says.

"I told you not to swim."

Rachel raises her eyebrows. I know I sound ridiculous, but I don't care. I move closer to where Bob has resurfaced and crouch by the edge of the pool so Rachel can't hear us.

"The pool is nice," Bob says.

He cups the pool water in his hand and holds it up to me like an offering.

"You have no idea how many kids have peed in that," I say. "Come on, get out."

"No."

"What do you mean, no?"

"I want to stay." He leans back in the water and floats to the center of the pool.

"Bob," I yell, trying to make my voice sound friendly, like maybe we're play-fighting or teasing or something. "It's time to go home."

Rachel has put her feet back in the water and is pretending not to watch us, staring straight ahead at the pool maintenance shack.

Bob says nothing. He floats on his back in what Lenny called the dead man's float. I crouch, my fingers gripping the edge of the pool. I feel myself slipping before I fall in. My body tips, my sneakers squeak on the tile, and I don't stop it. Fuck.

I somersault into the water, my head tucked into my chest, and for a second I don't know which way is up. All I can see is bubbles and murky reflections of light. I swallow chlorine water and kick my legs. I surface sputtering.

"Are you all right?" Rachel yells. I can make out her blurry figure, standing now, waving her hands like she's signaling for help.

"I'm fine," I choke out.

I swim toward the center, where Bob's still floating, his Zen posture unaffected by my fall. I cut through the water quickly. I kick out into breaststroke, my arms and legs obeying me, though I haven't swum in a decade.

"Let's go," I say when I reach Bob, grabbing his arm and pulling him so he's vertical in the water. "Now."

He's bigger and stronger than me; he could pull me to the bottom of the pool by my hair if he wanted, but some semblance of blob obedience must remain. He goes limp when I touch him, unresisting as I tow him to the shallow end and push him up the metal stairs.

"Walk," I whisper-yell, like my mom used to do when I fidgeted during Christmas church service.

Bob walks across the tile and toward the door. He looks back at Rachel and waves goodbye.

I don't turn back to look. I push us through the lobby, where we drip puddles on the floor, and out the sliding doors, my toes squishing in my sneakers.

IN THE PARKING lot, Bob and I shake the water off our bodies like dogs. It's a cloudy May day, 65 degrees, with a breeze that would've felt nice if we weren't soaked. I blink until my contacts realign and the world comes into focus again. It's a good thing the parking lot's deserted, because Bob's basically naked. Shirtless, he tries to wipe dry his stretched-out wet boxer shorts. I slide the backseat door open and am about to tell him to get in when I see Rachel running toward us, holding my sleep shirt and the tennis shoes I bought Bob at Walmart. Apparently he hasn't figured out the necessity of socks yet.

"I thought you might need these," she says, and hands him the clothes.

"Thank you," he says.

She's staring at his six-pack, and I can't blame her. Water droplets roll off his perfectly engineered abs. I get in the driver's seat and feel the wetness of my work pants sink into the beige nylon.

"We have to get going," I say. "Bob. Get in."

I want to be patient, benevolent even, but it's difficult when I can feel my skin wrinkling. Bob gets in and waves to Rachel, all sad and dramatic, like he's leaving for war. I gun it out of the parking spot, and he slides like an air hockey puck until he hits the armrest.

"Put your seat belt on," I say, and he does.

"Where are we going?"

"To the apartment."

"I'm not going," Bob says.

"What do you mean?" My ears hurt, and I don't know if it's because I got water in them or if there's just too much blood rushing through my body. "You're not going?"

Bob shakes his head.

"Why?"

"Other places," he says. "I want to go."

"You want to go other places?"

I sound like an idiotic parrot, but I don't know what else to say. We hit a red light, and as I slow to a stop, in my rearview mirror I see Bob pulling on the door handle. What he doesn't know is that the back-seat child lock has been stuck in the on position for years.

"Out," he says.

I look both ways; it's a slow intersection, so I take a chance and run the red light. The van hurtles forward at forty miles an hour, and still Bob keeps trying to escape. He pulls, twists, yanks on the handle.

"Don't," I say. "Not while I'm driving."

The door doesn't budge, but he's strong, and the handle might break off in his hand. I feel sick, coffee and pool water swirling in my stomach.

"Stop," I say. "Stop."

Bob bangs on the door. I pull over into the Busey Bank parking lot and dry-heave onto the blacktop. A middle-aged bank teller smoking outside stares as I run to the manicured bushes to gag and spit phlegm on the foliage.

All I want is to go home, turn on the TV, and for a few hours forget that I'm alive. In my apartment there are no responsibilities, no guests with screaming babies, none of Rachel's white-girl problems. I have no family, no ex-boyfriend, no past. Nothing and no one can hurt me. I thought Bob understood that when he was a blob. For a while, he seemed happy enough to eat and breathe and exist—the perfect companion. I should've anticipated that molding him into a man would trigger something deeper, some sort of existential awakening. Now he's just like everyone else. He has needs and desires beyond me, an internal life that I have no access to. He could leave without me ever knowing why.

Ten minutes later, I walk back to the van. The teller on her smoke break has gone back into the bank, and in the back seat, Bob has gone still and silent. When I open the back door, he crawls out cautiously. He's put his shirt and shoes back on, and he looks significantly dryer and more presentable than me. I wipe spit from the corner of my mouth.

Things have changed between us. I can feel the tension in the air as Bob shuffles his feet. Compromise is the only way forward now.

"Here's what we're going to do," I say as I try to wring out my still-wet hair. "There's a coffee shop two blocks from here. We're going to go there, sit down, and talk about this."

Bob nods and gives a small smile. He lets me take his hand and lead him away as I try to forget about my apartment and the parallel universe in which I'm watching TV beneath my down comforter.

I HAVEN'T BEEN to Kopi Café since high school, but it looks the same: a small space that manages not to feel cramped by virtue of its natural wood and big windows. The regulars are mostly hipsters wearing thrifted overalls and graduate students who never look up from their MacBooks.

I pass the barista, who's reading a sci-fi paperback, and lead Bob to a small table in the back. It's the worst spot in the café, right next to the bathroom, with a strong smell of disinfectant from the cleaning closet.

"Perfect," I say.

I fold my hands on my lap, try to visualize my clothes dry, and breathe in and out the way my mom's favorite online yoga instructor taught us. Bob looks everywhere except at me—he studies the thirtysomethings sipping cappuccinos, the couple with matching bangs who sit on the same side of their window booth and share sips of a frozen coffee drink. Bob used to spend all night staring at me. I never thought I'd miss it.

"Bob?" I say, and he turns to me slowly. "Let's talk."

He nods.

"What's going on with you? You're escaping and swimming and not listening to me. Are you sick or something?"

"No," Bob says. He spreads his hands across the table like he's playing poker and he's decided to go all in. "I'm a slave. Slavery is illegal."

"Where did you learn about slavery?"

"PBS."

I sit back in my chair and chuckle. I cross my legs, even though my wet thighs chafe.

"You're not a slave. You're an alien that I found next to a trash can." Bob flinches at the word *trash*, and I wonder if he remembers lying on the ground outside the Back Door, surrounded by litter, in an alleyway filling with rain. Did he hear Elliott and me standing above him, trying to figure out whether he looked sad or not?

"And anyway, you're white," I say.

"I can't do anything. I can't go anywhere. I'm trapped."

His blue eyes seem to get bigger, and I almost fall for his act. His lips, modeled off an old picture of Brad Pitt, look solemn and sad.

"You've only been alone in the apartment for a day. I've been stuck in that basement for six months."

Bob's brow furrows. It's easy to debate someone who's only been alive for a week. Easier than it was to fight with Luke when he insisted on playing the devil's advocate about politics. He would interrupt me when I was making a point and then act horrified when I shouted over him. We once got a note from our neighbor that just read: "Please stop."

"You choose," Bob says finally. "I don't."

I don't have a quippy comeback for that one. I look down at my hands. I'm starting to feel cold, the wet of my clothes sinking deeper into my skin.

"I'm going to get a coffee. Do you want anything?"

Bob shakes his head, and I get up abruptly, head for the counter. The line's long, and by the time I get to the front, Bob's chatting with some hippie chick with long brown-hair who must've caught sight of him on her way to the bathroom and decided movie star handsomeness was worth a UTI.

The barista clears her throat, looks at me expectantly. I haven't ordered yet.

"Medium black coffee to go," I say, and she rifles through cabinets, looking for more cups and cardboard sleeves.

I look back to see if the hippie girl is gone, but they're both gone. The table's empty. Bob must've snuck out the side entrance.

"Fuck," I say.

I run to the window and see him sprinting down the street toward the bridge that leads to campus. I grab my purse, abandon my coffee on the counter.

"Are you okay?" the barista asks, but I don't have time to answer. I stumble out of the café, onto the sidewalk, and start running. I have to catch Bob.

CHAPTER SIXTEEN

After just three blocks I start wheezing, and my legs cramp up. When I realize I'm not going to catch Bob, I stop running and bend over. A kid riding his bike by me whistles.

"Keep going," he yells. I flip him off, and he pedals away, laughing.

I walk back slowly to the bank parking lot and lean against the van as my breathing steadies. The sun's come out now, and it's a bit warmer. I feel my wet clothes drying slowly, like a muffin in an Easy-Bake Oven. After five minutes, I get in. The radio's blaring the Ed Sheeran song about being in love with the shape of someone.

I'm tempted to drive back to my apartment and forget about Bob. I could let him disappear and pretend he isn't real, just a hallucination, a story I told myself to keep going. Once upon a time I met a blob. But already I know I won't be able to forget him. And I can't leave him alone in the world. He doesn't yet know the worst of what people can do.

I drive out of the parking lot and across the bridge. I haven't been to campus since Luke and I broke up. I'm surprised to find it different from how I left it. Construction has started on new high-rise apartment buildings, and my favorite Chinese place, the one where the owner knew Luke and me by name and always gave me chopsticks and Luke a fork without asking, has shut down.

At the light across from the student union, college kids wearing backpacks and leggings walk en masse through the intersection like a herd of cattle. One girl has an old-school film camera hung around her neck. I look for Bob but can't find him. The light turns green, and the car behind me beeps. I lurch forward like I'm jerking myself awake. A block from the engineering library, I park in a faculty-only parking lot because I don't have change. As I get out of the van, I cross my fingers that I don't get towed.

I pass the lab where I spent so many hours trying and failing to get the right results in organic chemistry. Classes are in session, and I'm surrounded by students a few years younger than me, carrying books and moving with purpose to their next courses. They have plans beyond just waking up, going to work, shoveling a microwaved bean burrito in their mouths. They're trying to be things like doctors, accountants, actuarial scientists.

Even when I was in college, I wasn't good with "purpose." I picked the science path and took difficult courses to fulfill my destiny of becoming a quiet, antisocial Asian nerd. In high school, that worked for me. The night before calculus exams I spent hours cramming formulas and equations into my head, and when my teacher posted grades on the door before class, there I was at the top of the list. Even then, my parents knew I wasn't like Alex, a natural math and science whiz kid, destined to be a doctor since birth. I was the one who overcame natural deficiencies by "working hard."

College was when the Jenga blocks fell. I forgot everything, or maybe I had never learned anything in the first place. In physics especially, I floundered. It required logic and application of concepts, not rote memorization, and all I had were broken fragments of knowledge. My foundation was full of holes. The only classes I ever excelled at were my photography electives, and even I knew becoming a professional photographer wasn't realistic. I never told my parents about the Ds, the probation letter I got from the dean of the engineering college before I dropped out. I couldn't stand to hear the disappointment in their voices or, even worse, the lack of surprise.

Now I crisscross the main quad, scanning the sunbathers and Frisbee throwers, the English majors reading poetry under the oak trees. No sign of Bob. I walk past the auditorium and the knockoff *Thinker* statue, past the underground undergrad library where the tops of trees stick out of the middle of its sunken court-yard. I'm about to turn back when I see Bob, running around the agricultural quad in my T-shirt.

I cross the street without looking both ways and swerve to avoid getting hit by a cyclist. When I reach Bob, I have tunnel vision and an adrenaline rush. It takes me a second to realize that he's not alone. Spread out in a loose circle around him are six or seven frat bros, all wearing the same uniform—backward baseball caps, boat shoes, and muscle tees with Greek letters. I'd imagined rescuing him from a squad of evil scientists, but somehow this is worse.

"Vi," Bob says.

I take it as a good sign that he doesn't look altogether un-happy to see me. At least he doesn't run in the opposite direction. He just squints at me, like I'm someone he only met once that he's trying to remember.

"Vi," he says.

"Bob. Who are your friends?"

He says nothing, just nods at the word *friends*. I swallow my follow-up question, which is, roughly: How the hell does a blob make friends in five minutes?

"Do you want to play?" the curly-haired boy to Bob's left asks me. He's holding a Frisbee stamped with a beer company logo.

"No, I don't catch," I say.

But he's already launched the plastic through the air, and I'm the target. I raise my hands to my face, not bothering to pretend I'm trying to catch the disc, and brace myself for impact. Maybe during the surgery to get my face undented, they'll fix my deviated septum.

A few seconds before it reaches me, Bob plucks the Frisbee from the air.

"Nice catch, bro," yells curly-haired boy.

Bob grins. He's having fun impressing these boys. I swallow my resentment. I should be happy that he's happy.

"Thanks," I say to him. "Can I watch?"

He nods. I sit down in the grass as Bob and the frat bros throw the disc across the circle, hard and fast.

SITTING ON THE sidelines watching men play sports isn't new for me. In high school I watched Alex's varsity soccer games with my parents, shivering in the bleachers with my hands in my pockets as my dad paced the sidelines, yelling out advice, and my mom cheered too loud next to me. To pass the time, I took photos of Alex with my dad's camera setup on a tripod. With Luke, I often fell asleep on the couch while he played *WWF WrestleMania* on PlayStation. Now it's Bob throwing a Frisbee around with frat bros, running and leaping after the disc like the golden retriever in *Air Bud*.

I lie back in the grass as the sun comes out again to warm my skin. I used to sit on this quad often when I worked at my job with the pigs in the animal science laboratory.

I almost cried in my interview for the job when Jared, the interviewer, accused me of not having enough lab experience. They were all graduate students—PhD candidates in behavioral science, and one lab guy who was a biologist.

"I can't gain experience if no one gives me a chance," I said, my voice trembling like an opera singer.

I wonder if that's why they hired me. Probably they just didn't get many applications. Who else wanted to clean up pig feces at ten o'clock at night and take rectal temperatures at six in the morning?

One day on the quad, ants found the half-eaten granola bar in my backpack and made a home between the pages of my chemistry textbook. They were small ants, harmless. I didn't notice they had infested my backpack until I got to work and saw a few of them scurrying out. Disoriented by their new surroundings, they followed each other in a line for a minute before scattering on the blue carpet. I wished they'd stuck together.

I left my backpack there in the office and went about my duties, scrubbing food dishes and cleaning up after piglets. Half of the batch were sick with the pig equivalent of the common cold; the other half were the control group, perfectly healthy. The healthy piglets were easier, more energetic, but I was a sucker for the sick ones and always stayed longer in their room to give them extra scritches and wipe their butts clean of liquid feces.

When I got back to the office, Jared greeted me at the door with my backpack held at arm's length, double-knotted in a garbage bag.

"I believe you brought some ants into the office today," he said.

I heard some laughter from the PhDs at the other desks.

At the bottom of the bag, an amorphous black mass moved in waves against the white plastic.

"I'm sorry," I said. "I was eating outside."

I took the bag from Jared and ran out of the building. I knew what they were saying about me inside. They already thought I was weird—too quiet, unwilling to ask questions, said yes to everything. Now I was the ant girl. I thought about triple-knotting the bag and stamping on the plastic until the mass of little ants gradually stopped moving. Serves them right, sneaking in somewhere they didn't belong.

Instead I found the tree on the quad where I'd eaten lunch and spilled the ants back out onto the dirt, the grass, the tree roots. I watched them rush out of the bag as quickly as they could, disappearing back into the dirt. It looked like a home-coming.

"I'm sorry," I said to the ants. I left my granola bar there as an offering.

Now I'm sitting under a different tree. I study the ground and see nothing moving beneath the blades of grass. For an hour I watch Bob play Frisbee as my stomach gurgles like a witch's cauldron. I never had that McChicken for lunch that I'd been dreaming of.

Finally I rise from my spot and walk over to where Bob's crouched, ready to lunge for the disc if it comes his way. I pull his hand and move him out of the circle of masculinity.

Just as in the pool, Bob comes with me easily. He's very sus-ceptible to being moved. I consider pulling him all the way to my car, but I imagine that would only strengthen his slavery accusation.

"Bob," I say. "Let's go home."

Curly-haired frat bro calls out to us, "Hey! There's a party at the house tonight. You guys should come."

The other boys in the circle shout out in agreement and whoops. The word *party* must be their rallying cry.

"Yes," Bob yells back to them, and they cheer.

"No," I say to Bob alone. "You need to come home with me."

"Not home."

I flinch a little at his words, though I should've been prepared for them.

"And you think these nineteen-year-old boys' shit-filled frat house is your home? You just met them."

I pull on his hand, and for the first time, he pulls away. Slowly, he looks me up and down. I feel suddenly exposed. I haven't looked in the mirror since this morning, but I can imagine what he sees: wet clothes, frizzy hair, dress shirt riding up over my love handles. It's not Bob that doesn't fit—it's me.

"I'm leaving," I say.

Bob says nothing.

I walk slowly off the quad, vowing not to look back until I cross the street. I imagine I'll see him running to catch up to me. Instead I just make out his silhouette in the dusk, jumping up to catch the Frisbee three feet above his head.

CHAPTER SEVENTEEN

I didn't get towed, but there's a sixty-five-dollar ticket stuck in the windshield wipers of my van when I return to it. I drive back to my apartment, avoiding the agricultural quad and those boys playing their stupid game. The vindictive part of me hopes it gets dark before they notice, and the dumb disc hits Bob in the face.

I shed my wet clothes as soon as I get in. Right on the threshold, I take off my socks and let the air circulate around my pruned feet. I peel out of my slacks and button-down shirt and leave them in a heap on the floor, as if I've rid myself of old skin. I glance at my phone and see a text from Elliott: See u soon!!!, with three emojis of a bearded woman.

And that's when I remember I'm supposed to be getting ready to be Elliott's beard.

I only have fifteen minutes. It's too late to cancel; he might already be on his way over. I pull on Spanx and the black velvet dress I tried on for Bob. I try not to wince when I see the glitter stains on the inside lining. In the bathroom I scrub my face and dot tinted sunscreen on my red spots. My mascara is old and clumpy, and the hairbrush just makes my hair frizzier.

"Shit," I whisper.

I use some old hair spray to weigh down the flyaways and cough uncontrollably on the chemicals.

As I ready myself to be Elliott's girlfriend, I try not to think about Bob. He made his choice. At some point soon, the frat boys will realize he's an impostor who doesn't watch football and kick him out. Where will he go then? I smear my mom's red Mary Kay lip gloss on my lips and remind myself that Bob somehow found his way to the hotel using my less-than-precise description of my commute. Surely, if he wanted to, he could return to the apartment where he spent his formative youth. In the meantime, Elliott's dinner will prevent me from pathetically staring out the window, waiting for my blob to return home from learning how to use a beer bong.

Elliott knocks on the door, and I run to the bedroom to grab my shoes and purse.

"Coming!" I yell.

I step outside, and there's Elliott in dark jeans, a black T-shirt, and sneakers. I rub the velvet fabric between my fingertips.

"Fuck, I'm overdressed," I say.

"You look beautiful," he says, and I almost believe him.

THE DINNER TAKES place at Elliott's parents' house, a mini mansion in a suburb inexplicably named Apple Wood. On the car ride over, Elliott tells me that his parents are itching to meet me.

"I told them we'd been dating a year," he says.

"A year?"

"Don't worry." Elliott smiles. "You don't have to know everything about me. Whatever you say, I'll play along. It's like improv."

"I've never done improv," I say.

He laughs as I fidget. "Are you nervous?"

"Of course." I tilt my head and try to see myself in the passenger side mirror. I wipe off the lip gloss on my arm. It makes me look like a clown.

"You know you're not really my girlfriend, right? This dinner has no consequence for your life whatsoever."

I glance at him and wonder if he's trying to make his lack of interest in me crystal clear. Maybe Rachel was the first of many straight girls he's had to fend off.

"I'm aware," I say.

We park in a circle drive crowded with new-looking cars and walk up stone steps to the house. I jump at the sound of the built-in sprinkler system coming on. On the threshold, Elliott squeezes my hand and says, "Here we go."

As soon as we walk in, I hear a loud din of laughter and Mandarin, and I regret saying yes. The ten-foot-high ceilings make the house feel cavernous, and in the foyer there's a dramatic wood staircase of the kind that I thought only existed in debutante films. A crystal chandelier hangs above us. I stare at it.

"It's fake," Elliott whispers to me.

His mom is the first to greet us, wearing a pink-and-white skirt suit with small flowers stitched onto the lapels. I'm relieved that I'm not overdressed; it's Elliott who's underdressed. She has kind eyes that crinkle when she smiles at us in greeting.

"Elliott," she says. She doesn't hug him but holds his hands in hers for a good five seconds. "We are so proud of you."

"And you're Vi." His mom turns to me and pulls me in for a tight hug. I smell a light, subtle floral scent on her hair and wonder if she can smell the lavender glitter lotion I doused myself in a few days ago.

"You have a wonderful home," I say, folding my hands and trying to make my body small, more demure—the perfect Chinese girlfriend.

In contrast, his mom laughs open and big. "It's nothing. I told his dad it's too tall."

"We'll talk later, Ma," Elliott says. "Let's get a drink." He leads me into the crowd.

From the built-in bar in the living room, I pour myself a glass of pinot grigio and Elliott grabs a stout beer. I decide that Elliott's girlfriend drinks wine, not gin, and doesn't chug but sips. For tonight I will forget about Bob and Luke and my shitty job and commit to the performance. I won't let Elliott down. If Bob can blend in with frat boys, I can blend in here.

I want to ask Elliott where his dad is, but as soon as the other partygoers notice that the guest of honor is in their midst, we're separated by a swarm of relatives—aunts and uncles, cousins and second cousins. Over and over again, I introduce myself as Elliott's girlfriend and watch the confusion move across their faces.

"Oh, his girlfriend," one teenage cousin says, and winks at me.

I'm pleasantly surprised that this is not a formal Chinese dinner—it's more like an open house with a long table pushed up against a wall and loaded with crispy duck, fried wontons, scallion pancakes, and pork belly. Normally I would've made a beeline for the food and stuffed my face to avoid talking to strangers. But as Elliott's girlfriend, I introduce myself and chitchat sweetly as I make my way slowly toward the food. I pick up a napkin instead of a plate, and delicately select a single fried wonton.

"Do you speak Mandarin?" asks Elliott's aunt.

"I'm trying to learn," I tell her as I eye the noodle dishes and steamed ginger fish. Everyone here speaks Mandarin, even Elliott.

When I was twelve, my dad took me to NYC to meet my Taiwanese extended family. I still remember my great-uncle Lee hugging me tightly, looking me over, and then asking, "Do you speak Taiwanese?" I shook my head, and he nodded sadly, like I had disappointed not only him but the Liu family ancestors. He was kind to me, taught me tai chi and let me rent *Lord of the Rings: Return of the King* on demand, but I couldn't fully connect to him. I blamed my dad. After all, wasn't it his job to teach me how to be Taiwanese? Instead all he did was listen to Josh Groban and yell at the TV during college football games. At home, I vowed to teach myself the language, even bought a Mandarin workbook that sat gathering dust on the top of my desk for months.

So it comes second nature to lie and say I'm taking Mandarin classes online. It's going slowly, but I'm learning. I tell Elliott's aunt that I can understand what everyone in the room is saying, I'm just having trouble speaking back.

"The tones are tricky," I say.

Once I start lying, I can't stop. Elliott's girlfriend wouldn't have dropped out of undergrad. No, she just finished her degree and is looking for jobs.

"I'm doing some freelancing, some consulting on the side. If you know of any companies looking for biochemical engineers, let me know." I fake laugh, and it sounds like a donkey braying. Elliott looks at me from across the room. I'm desperate for these strangers to like me.

And of course, everyone is smiley and eager to help. Elliott's cousin Julie works in pharmaceuticals and immediately pulls out her phone to email her boss about finding me a position, despite my insistence that it isn't necessary.

"It would be so fun to work together. Elliott's my favorite little cousin." Julie laughs and starts telling some joke about Elliott in Mandarin.

"Sorry," I say, and wince. "Just English."

IT ONLY TAKES me an hour to notice that everything around the house is Elliott-themed. A cake with Elliott's face sits on the kitchen with a star-spangled CONGRATS GRAD written in red, white, and blue icing. On the big-screen TV, a Power-Point slideshow exhibits photos of Elliott through the years: as a kid, playing tee-ball star, dressed up as the scarecrow in *The Wizard of Oz*. There are even pictures of him taped above the toilet in the bathroom—a tiny, serious-looking boy wearing a bow tie and cradling a violin.

"Only children, huh?" I joke, pointing to the banner that reads IN ELLIOTT WE TRUST. No one laughs except the guy next to me at the buffet. I gave up on the pretense of moderation after my second glass of wine, and my plate is full of food.

"I'm Ivan, Julie's brother," the guy says. "Another cousin."

He's twentysomething and cute, with that brush-away-from-your-forehead hair I've always been a sucker for. He's holding a wonton and rocking an *Ellen* look, blazer and white sneakers.

"Vi," I say. My chicken skewer is pointed at him menacingly. I slowly lower it.

"You and Elliott, huh?" he says.

"Yup," I say, trying to keep my voice casual. "Pretty hot and heavy."

"His parents have been praying for him to find a girlfriend for years."

"Here I am," I say. "The answer to their prayers."

Ivan follows me as I drift away from the buffet table, and I'm grateful for his monologue because it gives me time to think and eat. He's a graduate student at the university—a PhD in clinical psychology, an MA in English literature.

"So I can diagnose fictional characters with mental disorders," he quips.

He hosts a literary psychology podcast called *A Pod of One's Own* in which he reads aloud from a book and analyzes the author's word choices. A "Why does this sentence have a comma and not a period?" type of thing.

"Sometimes I discuss movie scenes. I've seen a lot of old films. Laura and I used to go to drive-in theaters all the time."

I pour myself another glass of wine as Ivan explains that Laura is his ex, a veterinarian with a heart of gold who lives in Minneapolis. He shows me a picture of her on his phone. She's naturally pretty, with curly brown hair and no makeup. Her Instagram profile bio reads, "There is no path to happiness. Happiness is the path." I stick another skewer in my mouth and try not to spear the back of my throat. Ivan explains that they broke up on mile five while running their first half-marathon together and couldn't cry because it would deplete their fluids.

"What happened?" I ask with my mouth full of chicken.

"It just didn't work out. We weren't in the same place."

"Mentally or physically?"

"Both."

There's an awkward pause that I know I'm meant to fill with something personal about my life. That's how connections form, supposedly.

"Sorry I've been talking your ear off." Ivan smiles and fidgets. He has a bouncy nervous energy that makes me think he'd be a phenomenal Ping-Pong player.

"I know what you mean," I say. "I had a breakup eight months ago. It's hard to let go."

I picture Luke running out of Denny's.

"Eight months? I thought you'd been dating Elliott for a year."

I choke on my wine. Before I can reply, Elliott appears from nowhere and grabs my elbow.

"Hey, can I steal you for a second?" he says, and pulls me away from Ivan and the party.

I follow him up the big staircase, grabbing the railing after I wobble in my wedges on the first landing. I have a premonition of myself tumbling down and breaking my neck.

"Steady," he says.

"What's up? Did I do something wrong?"

I hate the way my voice sounds all reedy and pathetic. Still a child looking for approval.

"No. I just thought you could use a break from Ivan. He talks too much."

I feel bad laughing, but I do.

"I think he knows I'm a fraud," I say.

Elliott shrugs. "He doesn't matter."

When we reach the top of the stairs, he leads me to what I gather is his old bedroom. It's as big as my living room, militantly neat, and monochromatic—blue paint, blue comforter, blue lamp, blue rug. I sit on the edge of his bed and immediately sink in.

"Did your mom redecorate after you moved out?"

"No, she's too sentimental for that," he says as he opens and closes the empty drawers in his desk like he's looking for something. In front of his family, he's been the life of the party—charming and natural. Now he looks restless.

"What's it like to be surrounded by family that loves you? I'm jealous."

I immediately feel guilty as I think of my mom packing my lunches, my dad taking me on walks so we could collect leaves from different species of trees.

"It gets old." Elliott gets up from his desk chair, sits beside me on the bed. He looks older in the lamplight; I can see the lines on his face, the bags under his eyes.

"But I know how to put on a show. I was an actor, remember?" Elliott lies back on the bed. "Now a lawyer, which is pretty much the same thing."

"I wish I could act."

I tried, once, to act like I was as smart as I looked. I can still smell the sterile 24/7 engineering library where I crammed for exams. Hidden behind the stacks, I slapped myself as hard as I could when I felt myself falling asleep.

I wince and change the subject. "It's going well, I think."

"Sure," he says. "But you know you don't have to lie for me. They wouldn't have cared that you worked at a hotel."

I snort-laugh.

"Or they would've cared, but it would've been fine. As long as you have a vagina, you can do no wrong. And go easy on the wine. My mom thinks anyone who has more than two glasses is an alcoholic."

I reach for my wineglass on the carpet, but it's empty. I'm drunk.

"I love your family," I say.

Elliott scoffs. "You just met them."

"I know, but I feel good here."

I've started to sweat into the heavy velvet fabric of my dress. Elliott's still cool and unrumpled. I lie back beside him on the bed.

"I don't think they'd care that you're gay," I say.

"They think *Modern Family* is the devil's television. They wouldn't get it."

"Maybe you're not giving them a chance. They might surprise you."

Elliott shakes his head and then shrugs. "Maybe."

"Julie said something about us getting drinks with her and Ivan sometime. You know, Ivan's really not that bad."

"What are you talking about?" Elliott says.

"I mean, he's definitely an oversharer, but—"

He shakes his head. "You never have to see these people again after tonight, okay?"

I don't want to argue, so I say nothing. It feels nice to lie here with him. Maybe we'll become friends after this. Go on double dates to the movies, me and Bob, him with some faceless, nameless boy. Afterward, over cocktails, Elliott and I will reminisce about this moment, us in his childhood bedroom.

WE RETURN DOWNSTAIRS just as Elliott's face cake, stuck through with lit candles, is wheeled out to the living room. A chorus of his relatives are singing "For He's a Jolly Good Fellow."

"It's not my birthday, you guys," Elliott says. He contorts his mouth into a big smile by force; I watch the muscles in his jaw pop.

The buffet table has been stripped of noodle dishes, replaced by coffee and tea samovars, plates of sliced mango and pear. Elliott's dad holds a plate and teacup in the back; I haven't been introduced to him yet, but Elliott's mother pointed him out to me. He's a tall, intimidating man in a sweater and collared shirt, with glasses perched on the edge of his nose—the opposite of my dad, who looks like a relaxed, round Buddha. He's not singing, but I detect a small smile. Julie waves to me, and Ivan stands beside her, pushing back his hair. I realize I'm surrounded by people who look like me. I'm part of the family.

"Make a wish anyway," one of his aunts calls out.

I stand in the frame with Elliott as relatives take photos. He closes his eyes and dutifully blows out the candles. Everyone cheers.

"What did you wish for?" I whisper.

"For this to be over," he says.

As Elliott cuts the cake, Julie comes up beside me and touches my elbow.

"My boss couldn't find you on LinkedIn. Do you have a website or anything?"

"Um." I look into her kind brown eyes and feel like she can see straight through me. "Hold on a sec."

I walk to the refreshment table and refill my wineglass. I down it in three gulps and refill it again.

Elliott clinks his glass and clears his throat.

"I want to thank everyone for coming. I feel so loved and supported, especially by my mom and dad. Without you two I wouldn't be here. Literally."

It's a rote speech, nothing original, yet somehow the crowd is affected. A few *awww*s break out, and Elliott's mom wipes away a tear, careful not to smear her makeup. Then Elliott gestures to me, and I return to his side. He takes my hands. He's a phenomenal actor; if there were any leads for Asian men, he could've been a big movie star.

"And thank you to my girlfriend, Vi, for helping me through this transition. I don't know what I'd do without your poise."

This incites many whoops, and one dog whistle from his uncle in the back.

"I'm so proud of Elliott." I raise my refilled glass. "I feel at home with you all."

The crowd claps, and tears prickle in my eyes.

"You are so kind. So accepting," I continue. I start to sway, and my wine sloshes back and forth. Elliott clears his throat and puts his arm around my waist to steady me.

"Keep it together," he whispers in my ear. "You're being paid to be here."

He looks down at me with a mixture of pity and frustration, and my happiness curdles into embarrassment. None of this is real, but for a second, I let myself believe it. Just like I had with Luke, with Bob.

"Don't you think I know that?" I say, too loud. I pull away from him, and my wine splashes onto the wood floor. They cut off the music for the cake cutting, so silence fills the room.

"I'm sorry for that, folks," Elliott calls out, as I stumble toward the door with my head down. "Vi's had too much wine."

Outside in the cool air, I collapse onto the front porch swing. After a minute the porch light comes on, the door opens, and Ivan steps out.

"Are you okay?" he asks.

"No," I say. "I'm an idiot."

"No use crying over spilled wine."

I grimace at his corny joke, and he laughs. He walks to the swing and sits beside me. I can't go back in now that they know what a mess I really am. Elliott never would've blundered the way I did. I imagine him inside doing damage control. "She normally doesn't drink," he'll be saying with a pasted-on smile. "She's just really nervous."

"I should probably go home soon," I say.

"Elliott's going to be swamped for at least an hour." Ivan gestures toward the house. "I can drive you. Where do you live?"

Ivan isn't judging me. His eyes are kind, and there's familiarity between us, like we've known each other for longer than just a few hours.

"Old brick building in Northside. Down the street from a cemetery. Where do you live?"

He gives a downtown address ten blocks away from me, the same street where all the undergrad clubs are.

"Been to any good parties?" I ask.

"No," he says.

We swing in silence for a few seconds.

"I always fuck things up," I say finally.

Our legs are dangling off the ground, and I feel like a child again.

"You haven't done anything wrong."

I turn to face him, and he's looking at me with such earnestness, it makes me want to cry. His glasses are slightly crooked, and his brow's scrunched. Before I can think of what to say in response, he's hopped off the bench and is walking toward the door.

"I'll just say my goodbyes," he says.

"It's crowded," I say. "No one will notice if you leave without saying goodbye."

Ivan smiles and raises an eyebrow. "They will."

I follow him to the door. Just like Elliott, Ivan belongs in there, with them. I don't want him to go back inside. What if he never comes back and I lose this moment forever? I grab Ivan's arm, turn him around, and kiss him.

"What," he says into my mouth, and his lips part, and we're kissing, or I'm kissing him, or he's kissing me—it's hard to tell.

"Sorry," I say when he pulls back.

I look up to gauge his reaction, and that's when I realize that we're in full view of the floor-to-ceiling window in the living room. Framed behind glass like a photograph is Elliott's family. They are staring at us. We're right below the porch light, spotlighted, as if we are putting on a play just for them.

In the movies, after something shocking happens, there's always a clamor. Gasps, fainting, maybe a scream. In reality, no one moves except Elliott, who immediately runs out of frame. Elliott's dad's face is frozen. I watch his teacup drop from his fingertips.

"Fuck," Ivan whispers.

The door opens, and we scramble backward. Elliott's on the threshold, and he's pissed.

"What the hell?" he yells.

"Cheating on my son, have you no shame?" Elliott's mom yells from behind him.

"It's not like that," Ivan interjects.

"We welcomed you into our family," she continues. "You ate our food and drank our wine."

I look to Elliott, expecting him to defend me and tell them the truth. His family keeps his childhood bedroom preserved as a shrine and has cakes made with photos of his face on them. Surely they won't care that he's gay.

But his expression is hard and his jaw set. The lamplight makes sharp edges of his cheekbones. He's going to let me take the fall and be labeled a cheating slut so he can remain the golden boy, the perfect son. I'm so mad, I can hear my heartbeat in my ears.

"Wait," I say. "It's not what you think. I'm not Elliott's girlfriend."

"What are you talking about?" his mom asks.

"Leave," Elliott says, and slams the door in my face.

CHAPTER EIGHTEEN

I run down the stone steps of Elliott's parents' house two at a time. I need to get as far away from this place as possible.

"Wait," I hear Ivan call out.

I don't look back. I don't stop running when I reach the curb. I'm not crying yet, just panting with my mouth open like a dog. With drunk speed I fly down the small streets, past the fancy houses that all look the same. I stop and open the Uber app, and my phone blinks: No Drivers Available. The fucking suburbs.

I can't stop thinking about what happened: Elliott's stone face, his mother's questions, the fallen teacup. There are so many things I shouldn't have done. I call Elliott once, twice, three times. I leave a voicemail.

"Elliott, I'm sorry. I'm an idiot. Please talk to me."

After I hang up, a wave of nausea comes over me, and I throw up at the base of an oak tree. The puke burns the inside of my nose, and I squat there for a few minutes, trying to get the taste of regurgitated beef out of my mouth. Daffodils bloom out of the mulch. My heels are digging craters into my Achilles, and when I wipe at my eyes, my hand comes away striped with mascara.

I walk in the dark cul-de-sac for twenty minutes refreshing my phone. Finally a brightly lit BP station reveals itself like a mirage. Outside, two men sit on the curb smoking. They barely look up when I limp into the parking lot in a velvet evening dress and smeared makeup. I reopen the Uber app, and a ride appears.

WHEN I GET home, I'm surprised by the dustless baseboards and scrubbed floors. My pretend put-together life smells like dampness and lemon Lysol. It almost tricks me into believing tonight never happened. Almost. I turn my phone volume all the way up, take off my dress, and burrow into my unmade bed.

I wake to the sound of my own front door opening and closing. It's around two in the morning, based on the amount of drool that's accumulated on my pillow, the pain in my eyes from sleeping in my contact lenses. My phone is still in my palm, heavy as a talisman. I poke my head out from underneath my blanket and breathe in the cool air.

I forgot to lock the door after I stripped, so the intruder could be anyone. Bob, or my neighbor who sometimes gets drunk, loses his keys, and sleeps on the patch of grass between apartment buildings, or a stranger here to steal my TV and *Veronica Mars* Blu-rays. I could get out of bed and confront whoever it is with the mace my dad gave me, which is stuffed under my bed, still packaged in plastic that I probably need scissors to open. Except the scissors aren't in my bedroom, they're in a drawer in the kitchen. Fuck it, I think, and close my eyes again. Maybe I deserve to get murdered. With my eyes closed, I can pretend the intruder is whoever I want.

The intruder's quiet footsteps make their way from the front door to the kitchen. The faucet runs and then stops. I hear the gulping of water as the footsteps make their way to the bedroom.

The floorboards creak as the intruder crosses the threshold and stops at the unoccupied side of the bed. My skin prickles and goose bumps as the mattress shifts under the new weight. I smell cheap beer. It's not until I feel the muscles in the intruder's arm that I know for sure it's Bob. Fully clothed, he wraps himself around my naked body and rests his chin gently on top of my head. I tuck myself into him and listen as he snores. Maybe everything will be okay, I think.

BOB FALLS ASLEEP like a rock thrown in the middle of a lake, hard and fast. Luke could never stay still in bed. Even in the beginning, when we were still in love and passing notes on coffee-shop napkins, Luke turned in circles when we slept together and wriggled out of my arms in the middle of the night.

"I feel like I'm pig wrestling," I said once when he squirmed away to his side of the bed, taking most of the blankets with him.

"What does that make me?" he mumbled. "The prize pig?"

"Maybe," I said, searching under the covers for an arm, a leg, some piece of him to hold on to.

I never understood what he found so objectionable about being wanted. He always made it seem like my adoration was annoying, a little gnat that wouldn't leave him alone.

Now I'm the one who slips from beneath Bob's arms. I can't sleep. It's 4:00 a.m., two hours before I have to relieve Paul from night shift, and I need to come up with a plan. I pace back and forth on the beige bedroom carpeting, avoiding the squeaky floorboards in the living room. I stare every now and then at Bob's unmoving form. He came back to me. The only question is, How do I stop him from leaving?

On my phone, I google "how to lock your house from the inside," and as Bob sleeps, I rig *Home Alone*–esque obstacles to keep him inside. I lock the window latches and duct-tape the cracks from the outside.

I google "hardware store near me" and find they're all closed, so I search under my kitchen sink for ideas. The cavernous mess escaped my deep cleaning last week; I find carpet deodorizer, a rusted cast iron skillet, and a Styrofoam cooler. I open the lid, and a stale lake-water smell hits me. Inside are bungee cords my dad used to secure the cooler when I brought beer on last year's ill-fated family canoe trip. Finally, something useful.

The trip was my mom's idea. It was right after Luke dumped me, and I temporarily moved into my parents' house to piece together my life. My mom was worried enough about me to get rid of the knives and the full-fat ice cream before I arrived.

"We never take trips as a family anymore," she said when Alex came over for Saturday-night dinner. Her smile was brittle, and no one wanted it to break, so we all nodded.

Swayed by the power of my mom's guilt and the promise that it would only be a day trip, we piled into the Subaru on a cloudless Sunday. My dad drove us to Kickapoo State Park with my cooler full of beer squeaking in the trunk.

We split into two canoes: Alex and my mom in one, my dad and I in another. My dad took the back seat without asking so he could steer, and I settled into the front, where I could pretend to paddle but really just pet the water like a kitten. I drank four beers in the first hour. I don't understand why people find nature relaxing—as I stared tipsily at the vista of endless green, the twisting shadows and sunlight on leaves, I felt nothing but dread.

The day was longer than promised because Alex insisted we paddle farther from our starting point than planned. "There's a clearing up ahead. Crystal clear. I saw it on the map," he repeated for twenty minutes.

We kept paddling, but there was no clearing, no transparent water where we could watch the fish swim and the turtles dive. Just cloudy river water, blue-green algae, and layers of overgrowth that, at that point, had lost all of its novelty. When we finally turned back, we were disillusioned, sunburned, silent.

Now, I leave the mess I've made of the kitchen and go back to the bedroom with the bungee cords. First I try to secure the door. I tie one end to the knob and the other to the kitchen cabinet, but it gives way easily, the elasticity working against my efforts.

I open the door to my bedroom and peek in at Bob. He hasn't moved. I tiptoe to the edge of the bed, the bungee cords still in my hand, and watch him. His hair has fallen into his eyes, and I push the locks back behind his ear so I can see his face. He doesn't flinch at my touch.

It's the perfect solution, I realize, as I finger the bungee cord in my hand. The stretch will still allow him to move around the apartment, just slowly, without the ability to bust down doors.

I start with his legs. His eyelids don't twitch as I remove the blanket from his lower half and loop the bungee cord around one ankle and then the other. I hook the cords together and tie a double fisherman's knot my dad taught Alex and me when we were little, an overhand knot commonly used by climbers—it's almost impossible to untie. I wonder if my dad would be proud that I still remember it.

I re-cover Bob's tied ankles with the blanket because seeing the ropes makes me feel like a villain tying a damsel in distress to the railroad tracks. Bob's hands are curled at his sides. I lift them gingerly, and hold my breath as I slip the bungee cords under his wrists. Bob's eyes open as I tug on the knot. I cover his hands with the blanket and pretend I'm tucking him in.

"Hi," I say. I feel desperate and sweaty.

He doesn't respond, just closes his eyes and doesn't reopen them.

When I leave for work, I drag my kitchen chair outside and tip it under the doorknob like I've seen in the movies.

RACHEL WALKS INTO the hotel thirty-five minutes into her shift, looking worse than I've ever seen her—watery red eyes, a makeup-free face revealing an outcropping of pimples on the corner of her chin, frizzy hair secured in a messy top bun with one of those thick grocery-store rubber bands that hold bunches of broccoli together. She's not even wearing her uniform, just plaid pajama bottoms and a white T-shirt.

"Is Walter in yet?"

I shake my head. "He has a meeting at the other Hillside until two p.m."

Rachel throws her bag across the desk and heads to the employee bathroom. Fifteen minutes later she emerges in a wrinkled dress shirt, with so much foundation and concealer caked on her face that she looks like an oil painting.

I pretend not to notice, just stare at my online Scrabble tiles, all low-scoring vowels.

"You're enjoying this," Rachel says.

I shake my head. Nothing about her dishevelment gives me pleasure; she looks as messy as I feel. I always imagined that underneath Rachel's girl-next-door act she was some evil archetype, Cruella de Vil disguised with a high pony. It turns out that what's underneath is just the same pathetic shit I wear on the surface. It's a depressing realization.

"What's wrong?" I ask.

"Derek broke up with me."

"The guy with the poodle? I thought you didn't like him."

Rachel says nothing, just types loudly on the computer, pretending she didn't hear me.

"I'm sorry. It sucks to get dumped," I say, and I think of Bob, hog-tied in my bed with bungee cords.

"Vi, can you please shut up?" Rachel says, and I do.

For the next few hours, we check guests in and check guests out. I take two bent keycards from a toddler with sticky hands. Rachel refills the cucumber water samovar. By the time Walter gets in, Rachel almost looks like her normal self.

"My girls," Walter says with a big grin as he walks up to the desk. He's carrying an old-school leather briefcase that makes him look like he's auditioning to be an extra on *Mad Men*.

"You're in a good mood," I say.

"It's a good day," he says, and pirouettes into the back office.

"Weird," Rachel says. I nod.

The rest of the shift goes by slowly. I'm terrified Bob will come rushing through the sliding doors like he did yesterday, but this time angry and bungee-corded. He'll point at me and start yelling, "Slaver, slaver, slaver!" as loud as he can. But he doesn't. I'm about to clock out when Walter pokes his head out of his office.

"Can I see you two for a second?" he asks.

We look at each other and shrug. Rachel grabs the cordless phone, and we walk into the back office to find our boss pouring a fifth of whiskey into three glass tumblers. We sit down, and he places a drink in front of each of us. He props his feet up on the desk, and I'm more convinced than ever that he's getting these tropes from TV.

"Well, I've been at this job for eight years, working tirelessly all day, every day, and finally my time has come. You're looking at the new Hillside regional manager."

Even in her weakened state, Rachel musters up some enthusiasm. She smiles, bounces in her seat, gives a few claps.

"That's wonderful, Walter," she says.

They both look at me, and I know I'm supposed to say something, but I've forgotten my lines. I gulp the whiskey. I never learned how to take a shot, so it sits stagnant on my tongue.

"The only bad news is, I won't be able to see your pretty faces every day," he says.

"We'll miss you," Rachel says. "Cheers."

They clink their glasses together and down their drinks in one swallow. I lift my empty glass ceremoniously. The charade makes me mad—Walter in his too-tight khaki pants toasting a promotion like he's cured cancer or something. I remember sitting across from him a week ago, him saying, *You and me. We're the same.* Now he makes big arm gestures as he explains to Rachel his new responsibilities, which amount to cross-hotel promotions and brand consistency checks. Is this how I looked at Elliott's party last night, so pitifully happy to be included that I lost all perspective?

"This is your dream?" I interrupt Walter midsentence. "To oversee more of these generic hotels?"

"Yes." Walter turns to me. "Unlike you, I care about this place."

"I just want to know why," I lean forward in my seat. In my periphery, Rachel's shaking her head at me, trying her very best to get me to stop talking. "You said it yourself. It's a thankless, meaningless job."

"I never said that."

"You clean up after other people who don't even see you," I say. "It's pathetic."

Walter's face goes tomato red, and he grabs my hand from across the table. "Pathetic?"

Rachel's hand goes to her mouth, and it's so cliché I almost laugh. Walter sees my almost-smile, and his grip gets tighter.

"You've never once taken me seriously, Vi. What am I, a joke to you?"

His hand moves up my arm and squeezes. It feels like when Slithers, my childhood snake, would coil herself around my forearm. The difference is, she was only playing.

"Stop," Rachel says. She moves to pry Walter's fingers off me.

He raises his left hand like he's going to slap her, but instead he releases me and takes a step backward, upturning a potted plant on the windowsill behind him.

His face forces itself into a Halloween-mask grin. "I'm just joking. Can't you take a joke?"

Outlines of his fingers are printed in red on my arm.

I once watched him water that plant he broke. He didn't know anyone was watching, and he talked to it as he pruned off dead leaves, whispering, "You are strong. You are strong."

"I quit," I say.

I DON'T REMEMBER driving home. I must've stopped at red lights, merged onto and exited off the highway, but I have no memory of it. I just arrive, suddenly, at home. Although the red marks on my arm have started to fade, my body still feels alien as I put my van in park and walk toward the peeling brown door into the basement. The chair is where I left it, propped against the doorknob, a good sign. I lift it aside, open the door, and water cascades out, soaking my shoes. My apartment is flooded in three feet of brown liquid. Popcorn kernels and Froot Loops float on top of it; tangled mats of my hair drift like lily pads.

"Bob," I yell.

I wade into the draining living room and survey the damage. My laptop is safe on top of the TV, but my modem router is submerged. On the bottom shelf of my bookcase the too-expensive biochemistry and physics mechanics textbooks I kept meaning to sell back are ruined. My recycling can has tipped over and spilled its contents into the water.

"Bob!" I splash my way to the bedroom, past floating chocolate wrappers and La Croix cans.

Just a few days ago I was vacuuming the carpet and scrubbing the kitchen floor on my hands and knees. I choke back a laugh. What an idiot I was.

He's not in the bedroom, not anywhere. In the bathroom the window is broken, half off its hinges, duct tape hanging limply to its edges. I stumble through water to the kitchen, the deepest point in my apartment, where most of the debris has accumulated. On the counter is a pool of blood, a butcher's knife, and the frayed remnants of bungee cords. A simple solution to untying an impossible knot: Bob must've sawed his way out of the cords, catching the knife blade on his lineless palm, before shimmying his way out the window. He didn't cause the flood; all the faucet taps are off. He was probably trying to escape it. I could've killed him.

I want to sink into the murk and drown, but instead I put my thumb in the blood and smear it across the white linoleum counter. As if it's a microscope slide I'm trying to examine, I lift my bloody thumb to my eye. One drop of blob blood—it looks normal, red, human. I put the finger in my mouth and suck it like a baby.

Fifteen minutes later I call my landlord Jerry, a creepy older man who blasts Rush Limbaugh and QAnon conspiracy theory podcasts.

"Shit," he yells into the phone after I describe the damage. "I'm on my way. Don't move a muscle."

I find a bag at the top of my closet and stuff dry clothes in it. My underwear and socks are safe. My bottom dresser drawer with jeans and sweatpants is full of water, so I pull out whatever's dry: old gym shorts, pajama pants, too-small skirts. I wait outside for Jerry on the narrow patch of grass, feeling a weird sense of déjà vu. Wasn't it just yesterday that my feet were wet, and I was watching Bob play Frisbee? The difference is now there's no hope of a dry and warm apartment to return to, no chance of Bob's arms curling around me in the middle of the night. You don't bind someone and nearly drown them and expect them to come back.

"Would you look at this?" Jerry says when he arrives and runs to the open apartment door.

Jerry hauls big buckets and a shop vac from his trunk. He's not a young man; he has a curve in his back, and he grunts and groans as he bails water out of my apartment by hand. I don't get up or offer to help. I lie back on the grass and close my eyes. For hours, I listen to the sound of water hitting concrete. When the water spray hits my face and legs, I pretend it's the ocean—I'm on a beach somewhere far from here. Luke never left me. The past year has been a vivid nightmare from which I'm just now awakening. I almost believe it. Blobs don't turn into men; everyone knows that.

Jerry leaves around eight after ridding my apartment of standing water. The carpeting is still soaked through, and the whole place smells like wet dog and mildew.

"You'll need to find another place to sleep tonight," Jerry says. "I'll call a carpet-cleaning service tomorrow."

He's sweating so hard, it looks like I'm seeing his face through a rain wall. If he saw the bloodstain in the kitchen, he says nothing.

I don't know what to do, so I take out my phone. I call Elliott, and I'm disconnected after one ring. I dial Luke's number next, and I'm surprised to hear it ring. Part of me wondered if I was blocked as well as unfriended. It's been months since we've spoken, and giving in to the impulse to call him feels like taking a long drag of a cigarette after trying to quit.

"Hi," I say.

"Hey."

His voice makes me cry, but I try to keep it out of my voice. He's heard me cry enough.

"My apartment flooded." I clutch my phone so tightly it hurts. "So I just called to see how you are. Have you seen any bison recently?"

Luke sighs, and I hear everything in that exhale.

"I'm not sorry," I say. "I'm not calling to say I'm sorry. I'm not sorry for anything."

"Okay."

The line goes silent. After a minute, I check it to see if he's hung up. He hasn't.

"Don't hang up," I say.

"Okay." I hear something in the background. The sizzle of something hitting the pan.

"What are you cooking?"

"Chicken breasts."

Probably bland and underseasoned, I think, meanly. He always had white-boy taste buds. I tear grass out of the ground by the handful. Did I call to hurt him or to hurt me? The next question I ask answers it for me, the words spilling out of my mouth before I can think of the door they're closing.

"Did you ever love me?"

For thirty seconds, the only sound is a spatula scraping the bottom of a pan.

"I don't know, Vi," he says.

Instead of pressing and probing, contradicting and questioning, I say thanks and hang up the phone.

CHAPTER NINETEEN

My parents' house looks smaller in the daylight. My mom's in the front yard, kneeling on a pink foam pad, picking weeds out of her flower bed. She's humming something sweetly under her breath, a nineties country tune that I recognize but can't name. When she sees me, she rubs her gardening gloves on her jeans and stands. I didn't call before I came, just got in my van and started driving. Her smile wavers as she takes in my puffy post-sobbing eyes and floodwater-brown shoes. She hugs me, and I feel her delicate collarbone press against my heart.

"What happened?" she whispers in my ear before letting go. "Something with Bob?"

I nod and walk past her into the house. My bag falls from my shoulder to the ground. I curl up on their new leather couch, let my face burrow into the white faux fur throw, close my eyes, and fall asleep.

I wake to the quiet murmur of my parents' voices in the kitchen. Even though I'm not sure where I am, the sound of their voices is comforting. It reminds me of being a child again. They're not talking about me—they're asking each other hushed questions about the minutiae of their own lives.

"Did you see the Bensons' new gazebo?"

"It's supposed to rain tomorrow, did you close your car window?"

"We should use up that asparagus before it goes bad."

I get up slowly. The blanket fell away sometime while I was sleeping, and there are indentations on my cheek from the couch seams. I yawn and stretch and realize my body feels more rested than it has in days.

"You're up," my dad says from the kitchen.

He's frying up scallion pancakes, a Taiwanese recipe he learned from Ama, my favorite. My mom's at the dining room table filling in a crossword puzzle in ink. I join her.

"Why are you here, Vi?" my dad asks, not unkindly, as he sets down a plate of flaky, sizzling layers of dough and scallion. He's curious, my appearance a confusing lab result.

"My apartment flooded," I say. "All my things are ruined."

"Oh no," my mom says.

"Everything?" my dad says.

I can see that they want to ask more questions, get to the heart of the problem. My parents are fixers by nature. When I stayed with them after Luke dumped me, they printed out WikiHow articles on how to get over a breakup and slipped the pages under my door. They learned quickly that the website was wrong. There was nothing to be done but watch as I slept, cried, and ate whole boxes of vanilla wafers. I dropped out of college three months later.

"I just need to stay here for a couple days," I say now.

My parents look at one another with expressions I can't read. I grab one of the scallion cakes from the plate and crunch down, listen to the hot oil bubbling between my teeth.

TIME PASSES QUICKLY at my parents' house—a day turns into three. I spend most daylight hours holed up in their guest room with the down comforter and dried flowers pressed into the bed frame. It has a wood desk with a quill pen and specialized stationery.

"In case anyone wants to write letters," my mom says.

"Who stays here? Emily Dickinson?" I ask.

A little rounded window looks out onto the backyard, and most days I can see my mom bent over newly sprouted flower seedlings or pulling up creeping Charlie.

"Do you want to help?" she asks me a few days into my stay. Usually I slink away with a breakfast doughnut and orange juice before she can ask me questions or force me to do chores like clean up dishes that I myself have dirtied. I'd planned on spending the day playing Candy Crush on my phone and scrolling through Instagram. To be honest, living at home hasn't been that much different than working at the hotel.

I want to say no, but something about the premature look of resignation on her face makes me want to prove her wrong.

"Okay," I say. "I'll help."

We start by moving a cluster of hostas that got scorched by too much sun last year. I'm tired within the first ten minutes as I kneel and push my shovel into the soil; meanwhile, my mom works beside me in double time.

"We'll transplant them here," my mom says and points to a shady spot under a redbud tree. It's in bloom, and the small clustered flowers shake as I cup them in my hand.

"It's beautiful," I say.

"Isn't it? It only blooms for a few weeks a year, but I think it's worth it."

It's silly, my mom's patient tenderness, but it makes me cry.

"Allergies," I explain as I wipe at my eyes.

On Saturday we have family dinner with Alex. Displaying his usual bluntness, he asks me straight out why I'm freeloading off our aging parents.

"Her apartment flooded," my mom says. "That's it."

My dad's bad at lying, so he stays quiet, moves food around on his plate. The truth is, my apartment is ready—the carpet cleaners have come and gone; Jerry called on the phone, saying "This is the best I can do" and "You have renter's insurance, don't you?" I just can't bring myself to go back to that place, to piece together a life I know will fall apart again. What's the point?

"Well, what happened with Bob?" Alex asks.

"I have no idea," I say—the truth, for once.

It's not that I don't care. Bob's presence in my thoughts is constant, a high-pitched hum I can't shake. Where is he? Does he have a place to sleep? I call the homeless shelters and ask if they've seen a man who looks like a movie star, and they laugh. At night, after my parents are asleep, I slip out of the house and take long walks through town. I tell myself I'm not looking for him, but I am. One night I walk all the way to the Back Door, and the dance music bass vibrates my feet as I study the empty corner where I found him.

I left a note at my apartment telling him where I am, though I doubt he's returned. *I'm sorry*, I wrote at the end. Pointless words. I told Jerry to leave the door unlocked, thinking that if Bob got hungry, at least he could take some food from the pantry. Maybe I could give him ramen noodles and Chef Boyardee—the only things I have left to offer.

"IT'S TIME TO go," my mom says, exactly five days after I showed up unannounced on my parents' doorstep.

"What?" I say, although I know exactly what she means.

"You're still paying rent on a place where you're not living." My dad hands me a big bowl of fried noodles and eggs, as if to lessen the sting. "It doesn't make sense."

They both tense as they watch my face, ready for an over-reaction, an explosion of tears or anger.

"Okay," I say. It's difficult to argue with them when they're so clearly right. They smile at me, relieved, as I eat my breakfast and go upstairs to pack up my dirty laundry.

"Things will get better," my mom says. She rubs her hand in circles on my back as I shove my bag into the back seat of the van. "When do you hear back from the Peace Corps?"

Part of me wants to tell them that I never applied, never even started the paperwork, but I can't, not when they look so happy that at least I have some sort of plan, a purpose in life.

"Soon," I say. "Any day now."

"I hope you get stationed in Madagascar. We'll visit. I've always wanted to see the lemurs," my dad says.

"I hope so too," I say, and turn the ignition.

They stand on the curb and wave goodbye as I pull away, like I'm a soldier setting off for war.

MY APARTMENT IS just as I left it—a swamp of garbage and mildew, a high-water mark on the bookcase, TV stand, and couch. Despite the carpet cleaner's best efforts, it still smells like a damp grandma's house. I check the cupboards, hoping some food is missing, a box of mac and cheese or a can of garbanzo beans, but everything is just as it was. Bob never came back.

I find some expired carpet-cleaning powder under the sink and pour it on the carpet until it's coated so thickly, I'm tempted to lie down and make a snow angel. I open all the windows and the door to try to circulate the stagnant air. Jerry hasn't fixed the window Bob broke. I catch an earthworm trying to crawl in through it and throw it back out onto the driveway. I'm at my empty fridge, looking into the void, when my phone dings.

We need to talk.

I rub my eyes, hoping Rachel's text is a hallucination brought on by sleep deprivation and will disappear in a moment. It doesn't.

huh? are u breaking up with me? I text back.

Let's go for a walk. Meet you at your place in 10 min?

fine

I assume she wants to convince me not to quit. She probably feels bad that she never texted me after what happened, but I don't blame her.

I've almost managed to disremember the hotel altogether. Sometimes my subconscious betrays me, and I dream about the mundane details, the diamond carpet pattern and Walter's scuffed brown shoes coming back to me unbidden. During the day, though, I bury the specifics, along with everything else I'm trying to forget.

It's advice my mom gave me after a traumatic lesson during which my piano teacher called me an "ungrateful brat" for not memorizing my scales. Right there on the piano bench after the lesson ended, as I sat there sobbing, my mom took my hands in hers and said, "Vi. You need to stop thinking about this. Do you hear me? Stop thinking about it." Lottie, Cole, and the dead bird on the porch: *Don't think about it.* "Shut up, chink" and regurgitated pool water: *Don't think about it.* Elliott framed in the doorway. *Don't think.* It gets easier with practice.

I throw on sweatpants and a workout shirt that I haven't worn in three years. Rachel shows up at my door just as I'm lacing up my tennis shoes, and I have déjà vu, almost expecting Bob to appear behind me half naked like a ghost. But no, it's just me and the mildew smell.

"It's so good to see you," Rachel says, and pulls me in for a hug. She looks tan and happy; she must be over the poodle guy. It's not as awkward as I expected to chitchat, although it's been a few days since we last saw each other. Part of me wondered if I was finally done with Rachel, my co-front-desk-attendant nemesis. Maybe we could go our separate ways, untethered by the hotel. I'm strangely relieved to find that we haven't. We walk toward downtown, through old cobblestoned residential streets.

"I'm not coming back," I say. "If that's what you're trying to do."

"It's not about that," Rachel says. She starts to walk faster, her arms pumping like she's on an elliptical. "I'm sorry about what happened, though."

"Me too."

We walk in silence. It's another perfect day, 70 degrees, the sky so blue it looks fake, like maybe we've stumbled onto a movie set by accident. We pass by Westside High, and construction wafts dust in our faces. They're redoing the building to add more windows and open spaces, fewer claustrophobic classrooms.

"I wish they'd tear it down," I say.

"I loved high school," Rachel says. I roll my eyes at her, and she laughs.

We cross the street and walk into Westside Park. In high school during gym class, we were supposed to run laps around the park. I walked with an AP Biology textbook in front of my face, reading and getting motion sick, until the gym teacher made me stop because I was a safety hazard.

"So, what did you want to talk to me about?"

Rachel points to a bench in the middle of the park, in front of the fountain of a mermaid with her tits out.

"Can we sit?"

We sit. The breeze offers us little droplets of water from the fountain every now and then. It feels good.

"You know your friend Bob?" Rachel asks.

I turn to look at Rachel. I blink once, twice.

"Of course," I say. "Do you know where he is?"

"Yes," she says.

She doesn't offer up any more information right away, just sits there silent with her hands in her lap. It's infuriating. It takes everything in me not to grip her like Walter gripped me, shake her, make her tell me everything.

"Well?"

"He came to the hotel again after you quit. He was hurt, his hand was bleeding, so I took him home."

Rachel fidgets with her hair and hands. She crosses and un-crosses her ankles.

"You took him home?"

"It just happened. Bob and me," Rachel says. "I'm sorry, Vi."

"What happened?"

I feel like Rachel's talking to me from the other side of a tun-nel. Something is getting lost in translation. I know she's trying to tell me something, but my brain can't understand what it is.

"We're together now. We live together."

Bob can't be with her. Bob is a blob I found next to a garbage can that I took home in the pocket of my sweatshirt.

"I want you to take me to him," I say, standing up. "Right fucking now."

Rachel says nothing. I think she's going to refuse me, tell me to fuck off, but after a minute she stands up too.

"Okay," she says.

IT ONLY TAKES five minutes for Rachel to lead me to her place. She lives in one of the new luxury apartment complexes gentrifying downtown, two blocks from the best brewery in the city. The water samovar in the lobby is glass, not plastic, and the whole place smells like fresh-baked cookies. It's way nicer than Hillside.

"Good afternoon, Rachel," says a man at the front desk wearing a satin vest.

She nods and smiles at him sweetly. It's surreal to me that a front desk attendant could have her own front desk attendant.

"How do you afford this place?" I ask as we wait for the elevator.

"My parents help out."

We get out of the elevator on the fifth floor and walk down a long slate-gray-carpeted hallway with citrus circles patterned on the walls. Rachel pauses at her door, the only one with a welcome mat.

"Are you sure you want to do this?" she asks.

I wipe my dirty white sneakers roughly on the mat.

"Do what?"

Rachel sighs and opens the door. Her apartment is clean, but not as glittery or pink as I imagined. She's opted for minimalist neutrals instead, warm brown throws and wood bookcases. The kitchen has an open floor plan, with stainless steel appliances, granite countertops, and mixed-material barstools. The rent must be at least fifteen hundred a month.

"Your parents must really love you," I say.

My sleep shirt, the one Bob was wearing when I left him bungee-corded in my bed, is folded on one of Rachel's brown leather chairs.

I run my fingertips over the fabric. It must mean something that Bob kept it—he didn't forget about me completely. Maybe he'll come back.

Rachel sees me looking at it.

"You can have that back," she says.

"Where's Bob?"

We call out his name with no response. It only takes a few minutes to figure out that Bob's not here. I walk through each room of Rachel's apartment anyway. I'm jealous of everything—the big windows with enough sunlight to keep plants alive, the glass-walled shower with a detachable shower head that probably doesn't take an hour for the water to warm up, the big white bed where Bob and Rachel must sleep together with their complementary bodies.

"He must be on the roof," Rachel says. "He loves it up there."

I want to laugh. They've been living together for a few days, and she's acting like they're married. We walk up the roof access staircase in silence.

The rooftop patio has a view of the whole town, twinkle lights, wicker furniture, and tiki torches, but I don't notice any of that when I step outside. What I notice is Bob with his back to us, standing on the edge.

"Don't," I say.

I move as quickly as I can, reducing the space between me and Bob. It's only when I'm closer that I realize he's not jumping, just looking out at the view.

"Hi," Bob says and turns to me. He looks comfortingly, reassuringly, the same. The man I created.

"Hi," I say.

He smiles, and I feel myself melting a little, tears springing to my eyes without my permission. He doesn't look surprised to see me.

"What're you doing here?" I ask.

"It's nice up here. You can see everything."

He's right. From here, I can see the houses on the far side of town in miniature, small enough to fit in my palm. In my basement, the only view is pavement.

"No," I say slowly. "What are you doing with Rachel?"

Rachel reaches us, and I realize that once again I've been cast as Bob's overly controlling girlfriend, the one he's with at the beginning of the rom-com before he meets the cool girl who helps him understand what true love really is. I could recite my lines: *You have to choose—her or me.* Everyone knows the movie doesn't end well for the ultimatum giver.

"She's my lover," he says.

Rachel moves to Bob, and he wraps an arm around her waist like he's made the gesture a hundred times.

"I keep trying to tell him that 'girlfriend' is more appropriate than 'lover,' but he won't listen to me," Rachel says.

"Lover. Love *her,*" he says.

I let the pain wash over me as I study them. They look good together—their toned bodies and white skin glittering in the sunlight à la *Twilight* vampires. Rachel has bought Bob new clothes to match her clean-cut aesthetic, dark wash jeans and a gray V-neck; he looks like a Gap model. Looking at this new version of Bob, I see what Rachel's doing. She's molding Bob into her own perfect partner, just like I tried to do.

But she doesn't know the truth.

"What do you know about Bob?" I ask Rachel.

She blinks, confused, then looks up at his square jaw and smiles.

"He's honest. I love the way he sees the world. Like everything's new."

I snort. "You have no idea who you're dating."

"What're you talking about?"

"He's not real. Nothing about him is real." My voice is rising, on the edge of hysteria. "He's a blob I found next to a trash can."

Bob stands frozen, looking back and forth from Rachel to me, like a puppet with its head on a swivel.

"He was just a creature when I met him. All he ate was cereal. He's not a real person."

Rachel shakes her head.

"Do you understand what I'm saying? He's not human. He's an alien."

"You're being really fucking mean, Vi," Rachel says, stepping away from Bob and toward me. I don't know if she's going to slap me or hug me. I don't know which would feel worse.

Bob steps between us, his brow furrowed in confusion. I look at them together, and I know it doesn't matter. Nothing I say will change anything.

"Forget it. You two are made for each other," I say.

I back away from them and walk to the door. I take the stairs two at a time, all the way down.

CHAPTER TWENTY

For four days I ignore my phone. I put it on the kitchen window-sill and try to forget. With my head under the comforter, the sounds, the dings and whooshes and rings, are muffled and weak. I pretend I'm listening to the faraway call of a rare, endangered species of bird.

Jerry my landlord texts: Everything okay with the apartment? other than the smell

Taco Bell emails about the new $5 Chalupa Cravings Box: You and the Bell. Has a nice ring to it.

Apple Alert: You have a new iOS update available. Introducing separate skin tone variations for couple emojis, more diverse voice options for Siri, and App Tracking Transparency.

Luke texts: I'm sorry about our phone call.

Instagram Alert: Bob, who you might know, is on Instagram.

Walter emails: Termination Paperwork.

H&M.com emails: You left this item in your cart!

iPhoto App: You have a new memory.

Hillside Inn and Suites emails: June Paycheck.

Walter emails: An Apology.

Rachel emails: Some News

Fitbit Alert: Your period is scheduled to start today.

Instagram Alert: Rachel Murphy has posted on Instagram for the first time in a while.

Apple Alert: Your screentime is down 100% from last week.

My dad texts: Are you coming by soon? You forgot your eye contact solution here.

My mom calls once, twice, three times.

My mom texts: Vi? Are you okay?

My brother texts: are you alive? mom's worried

My mom leaves a voicemail: "Vi, what's going on? You're not picking up your phone. Are you mad at us for asking you to move out? I thought we agreed you need to be on your own, learn how to be independent. Please talk to me. Love you."

My brother calls once.

My brother texts: You're being so selfish right now, making everyone worry about you for no reason. Pick up your fucking phone.

Duke Energy emails: Your statement is ready

Google Flights emails: Your tracked flight to Bozeman, Montana is now $199.

Luke leaves a voicemail: "Hey Vi. Been a while since I left you a voicemail. You never texted me back, so I assume you don't want to talk. That's okay. I just . . . When you called before, I was cooking chicken and you were talking about bison and floods. I was surprised to hear from you, you know? I didn't mean to hurt you. I just wanted you to move on. Hope you're doing well."

Hulu emails: Now Streaming: New Shows and Movies

Fitbit emails: Your watch battery level is low

CVS Alert: We miss you! New coupons available

My dad leaves a voicemail: "Vi, are you all right? Did you break your phone? We can buy you a new one, that's fine. Call us back. You don't know what you're doing to your mom."

My mom leaves a voicemail: "This isn't funny, Vi. I don't know what's going on or why you're not answering. I keep having nightmares where I find you dead in a ditch with worms all over your body. Call me."

Doordash Alert: Order it again? Free delivery for Maize Mexican.

Spotify emails, Jump back in to your music!

Apple Alert: Low battery. Your phone is at 20%.

My brother texts: sorry if my texts were harsh. U ok?

Harvey Jones *Spam Alert* emails: Urgent inquiry!!!

Jerry my landlord texts: are you in your apartment? I want to put a new drain in, should take a few hours to complete

Yoga with Adriene emails: Go all in for love. Start with yourself.

University Admissions Office emails: Fall Registration—Sign up for classes today!

IT WAS ALWAYS my mom who woke me up as a kid. Her footsteps on the stairs as she made her way to my attic bedroom, smelling of wintergreen gum and deodorant.

"It's time," she would say, and flip the light switch like I was a rodent who could be spooked out of my burrow by the dim overhead. It just made me close my eyes tighter, the sound of her voice washing over me like a white noise machine. I could tell what time it was by the length of her sighs, how much trouble I'd be in by the quickness of her steps.

"Now," she said when I pushed up against the limit of her patience. When time had truly run out.

It's not my mom who wakes me up after my four days in bed—it's Jerry the landlord. I'm drifting in and out of consciousness under my blankets, marinating in sweat and the natural smells of my unwashed body. I can feel my muscles atrophying. I'm not so far gone that I can't appreciate the poetic symmetry of the situation—now that Bob is human, I have to become a blob to maintain the natural order.

"Hello?" a male voice calls out into my apartment. I recognize it's Jerry by the coughing and shuffling of work boots. Under my blanket fort, I slip my hand out of my underwear. I don't respond to his yell, and I try to breathe quietly—I figure he'll do his land-lord business and leave me undiscovered.

I don't even realize Jerry's in my room until a hand rips my covers off. There I am, exposed, curled in the fetal position, my eyes blinking as they adjust to the natural light. Jerry screams. I don't know what he was expecting, but it wasn't me.

"Hi," I say. My lips are chapped, and my teeth catch on the skin flaps. I check to make sure I'm not naked, even though I know I'm not. I'm still wearing the sweatpants I put on to walk with Rachel.

"Sorry," he says, and puts the cover back down over me. "I thought you were a cat. No pets allowed. I'm here to fix the drain."

I tug the blanket down. "Okay," I say.

Jerry leaves the room. My teeth feel chalky, and my tongue fiddles with a strand of chicken that's trapped between them. It's official: I've hit rock bottom.

I could pretend he's not here. Keep lying in bed and refuse to be seen again for at least a year. Or I could get up. I sigh. There's really only one option, I know.

When I stand, I wobble on my legs like a newborn. I grab my phone from the windowsill. I see Luke's name and press play on his voicemail—his voice, all the way from Montana, speaks directly in my ear. *I just wanted you to move on.* There's distance in his tone—he sounds like a well-meaning stranger who's trying to tell me something I should already know. Surprisingly, it doesn't hurt.

I open the blinds. It's bright outside, midafternoon. Thursday. The only way out is through, I read once on a fortune cookie.

I walk into the living room, where Jerry is on the floor, studying the door hinge. It's humid, and a moldy smell fills my lungs. I cough to expel the tainted air.

"It still smells."

Jerry turns and examines me briefly, takes in my tangled hair and lack of bra. "I don't smell anything."

"You should get your sinuses cleared."

Jerry doesn't hide his frown. "Fine. I'll spray more."

He goes out to his truck and comes back with an unlabeled bottle that smells like vinegar. He showers the carpet until it's damp and glistening, like salad dressing.

"Happy?" he says.

"Very."

I go to the bathroom and shut the door. I wash my face. I brush my teeth, floss all of the leftovers out, run my fingers through my hair until flakes of dandruff and fuzzballs fall out. I practice smiling in the mirror, and my mouth obeys the order, rounds itself into the right shape.

Jerry's outside, hammering or nailing something, as I sit on the toilet scrolling through the rest of my notifications. I don't stop to let any of them sink in.

"Fuck," I say.

I ignore the messages and open Instagram. My favorite food blogger, the Korean Vegan, is making Kimchi Soondooboo Chigae, a spicy bubbling tofu soup in a stone bowl. As she cooks, she tells the story of going to college and losing the sounds of her mother's kitchen.

"I never realized how much I would miss them," she says as she chops scallions, separating the white parts from the green.

It reminds me of Elliott's family: the buffet table full of dumplings, his face printed in frosting on the graduation cake. I fucked things up, and I want to make it right. Before I can overthink it, I exit out of the video and pull up Elliott's number.

Hi. I'm sorry.

I hit send. The punctuation's stilted, and the text sounds inane, like a politician apologizing for getting caught with his pants down.

Why did you do it? he texts.

I read the question twice. I don't know what to say.

I was drunk, I type and delete.

You made me feel like an idiot, I type and delete.

I wonder if he's sitting somewhere watching the three dots appear and disappear on his phone. Everything I write feels like an excuse.

I was afraid. I type and hit send.

I see Elliott, Luke, Bob, all laid out before me. All the mistakes I made because I wanted to prove to myself what I never fully believed: that I belonged, that I was worthy. I struck out before I could get rejected or forced someone to reject me so I could leave on my terms. My isolation turned into a self-fulfilling prophecy. I've been a coward.

I stare at my phone, waiting for three dots to appear on my screen, but they never do.

I RETURN TO my notifications and click on the newest email. Fall Registration—Sign up for classes today! The banner shows racially diverse models posing as undergrads studying at the Starbucks in the Union, laughing with their mouths open so wide I can see their tongues. I only studied at the Union with Luke, on the brown leather couches in front of the fish tanks. Luke would type on his laptop with his noise-canceling headphones on while I tried to follow the movements of each individual fish with my eyes. I gave them names like Eileen and Harold and Levi.

I click on a link, and it takes me to a log-in page. I still remember my password (LukEy!14), and suddenly I'm back in the system, my old courses and grades staring back up at me: D in biochemistry, C-minus in organic chemistry lab, F in physics mechanics, probably the easiest class on the list. At the time the grade felt like a death sentence; now it stares up at me, innocuous, almost playful. I dropped out not because of the breakup or the Peace Corps but because I was running away from that F.

My only A during my last semester was in black-and-white photography, an elective I'd taken with Professor Baumgartner. He wore tan Tevas and drank lemongrass tea, gave off Yoda vibes as he taught us about focus, contrast, and perspective.

"No graveyards, no selfies, no flower close-ups," he said on the first day of class.

He was difficult to impress, only spending a few minutes critiquing photos he found boring.

"Familiar," he would say if he found the piece unoriginal. The word made the whole class wince.

There was one photograph of mine that Professor Baumgartner asked if he could keep. It was a portrait of a fortysomething woman who I found on her smoke break at the bottom of a concrete set of stairs by the cafeteria. When I asked if I could take her photo, she just shrugged.

"You have the eye," Professor Baumgartner said then.

Now I pull a scanned copy of the photo up on my laptop. It's in black and white, the woman shrouded in the darkness of the shadows of the stairs, but somehow her figure is illuminated. I can make out the embers of the lit cigarette she holds between her fingertips. She stares up at the viewer with her head tilted, not smiling. A challenge.

"Huh," I say.

It takes three hours in the bathroom, sometimes sitting on the toilet, sometimes lying in the dry bathtub, soap scum sticking to my back, to reapply for college. I transfer my major from biochemical engineering to general liberal arts. I apply for student loans and pick out my classes. Two photography workshops; an English seminar on Edith Wharton; a class on weather systems, Atmospheric Science; and a Philosophy of Mental Illness course. I scroll through my imaginary schedule, the times and room numbers of my classes, textbooks I need to purchase, and I realize, distantly, that I'm smiling.

"SOMEONE'S HERE TO see you," Jerry calls out when I'm still in the bathroom, no longer thinking about my future, just scrolling through Twitter cat memes and trying to avoid looking at texts from my mom. I'm surprised Jerry's still here—he must think I'm taking the biggest shit of my life. I flush the toilet and turn the faucet on and off, in case someone's listening.

"Knock, knock," says Ivan. He must've been out for a run—he looks sweaty in his workout clothes and tennis shoes, white socks pulled up too high. He bends his neck to fit his tall frame through my doorway. I never thought I'd see him again, and I feel suddenly shy. His presence brings back the longing I felt at Elliott's party, when I thought we might all become friends.

"Ivan. Funny meeting you here."

"I was in the neighborhood."

"Oh?"

"Well, your building's on my running route, and I saw your name on the mailbox, and I wanted to . . . I thought I'd check to see if you're okay."

He looks abashed for some reason. I can't tell if his ears are red from the run or embarrassment.

"I should get going," Jerry says. He walks between us to pick up his black tool bag. Clumps of dirt fall from his work boots to the carpeting, still sprinkled with carpet cleaner. "I couldn't get the drain in, but the mats should help with the flooding."

"Thanks, Jerry." I turn to Ivan. "I'm sorry for what I did at Elliott's party. That wasn't cool."

Ivan nods. "It wasn't."

"What happened after I left?" I ask, though I'm afraid to hear the answer. I've run through the scenarios in my head, and some of them are catastrophic.

"Elliott told everyone that you were telling the truth. You weren't his girlfriend, just someone he hired to pretend to be." Ivan pauses. "He didn't say why."

I nod and take a deep breath. Could've been worse.

"I would invite you in, but as you can see, I'm dealing with the aftermath of a flood." I gesture to the brown stains and waterlogged books.

Ivan studies the powder on the carpet as if the wave patterns are ancient runes.

"No worries," he says.

I expect him to leave, for this to be the end of the interaction; he'll go back to his run, and I'll try to piece my life together. But he stays, crouched in my doorway. I unfurl a roll of paper towels and grab some disinfectant from under the sink.

"Are you seeing anyone?" Ivan asks finally.

"Nope," I say as I wipe down dirt from the cabinets.

"Vi," Ivan says loudly, and I finally focus on him. "Would you like to get dinner with me tonight?"

I blink for a second and then look down at myself. I'm a mess. I've been wearing the same clothes for days and smell like BO. He's tall, sweet, could get any girl he wanted. Sure, he's a little neurotic, but in an endearing way, like Monk or Niles from *Frasier*. I picture his perfect match as a short Christian who volunteers at homeless shelters. Meanwhile I just recently made the decision to start living again.

"Are you kidding?" I ask.

"I'm sorry, it doesn't have to be a date, not if you don't want it to be."

"You know, I was lying back at the party," I say.

He nods.

"That's not who I am. I was just trying to get your family to like me."

"I know."

"Then why are you doing this?"

Ivan laughs, but sobers up when he sees I'm not smiling.

"I think you're interesting. I liked talking to you," he says.

It's not a poetic compliment, but I like it. It feels honest.

"Part of the reason why I've been running by your building is because I wanted to see you. Sorry if that's creepy."

Ivan looks down at his shoes, shoves his hands in his pockets, like he's just confessed to tapping my phone line or making voodoo dolls of me. He probably leaves a note when he bumps a parked car while parallel parking. We couldn't be more different.

"Yeah, okay," I say. "Dinner sounds nice."

AFTER IVAN LEAVES, I keep cleaning my apartment, though there's not much I can do after I wipe up the visible dirt. I could scrub forever, and it wouldn't be the same. I vacuum up the powder, but the smell lingers, sneaks up on me when I'm not expecting it. I give up after two hours and nap instead, curling my spine against my comforter.

For the date, I go for comfort over style—a black V-neck with the only pair of jeans that doesn't pinch my stomach fat. Ivan picks me up promptly at six, wearing black dress pants and a burgundy blazer. I resist the urge to ask him if he's interviewing to be the host of *The Price Is Right.*

His car is a puke-colored Honda Fit covered with bumper stickers like "To Pod or Not to Pod? That Is the Question." In the front seat, scholarly books and journals are piled haphazardly. "Sorry for the mess," Ivan says as he throws books into the back.

I can tell he's not a townie by the way he crisscrosses into town instead of going straight down the main road. I ask him where he's from, and he repeats what he must've already told me at the party; he just moved from the suburbs for grad school.

"Do you like it here?" I ask.

"I do. The little storefronts, slow drivers, big oak trees. It feels like the kitschy America my parents were promised."

"Don't forget the casual racism," I say.

Ivan glances at me, maybe trying to figure out if I'm joking or not.

He drives us to El Pollo Loco, a chain Mexican restaurant on campus, three blocks from his apartment.

"I love this place." Ivan smiles. "I come here all the time."

He opens the door for me, and I walk into the overly air-conditioned pseudo Pueblo style interior. I don't tell him it's a chain, or explain that there are at least three better Mexican places within a ten-block radius. Something about his childlike enthusiasm is hard to argue with.

Ivan leads me to a four-person table with a view of the street. A group of undergrads are already going out to the bars. We order margaritas, mine on the rocks, Ivan's frozen. He smiles at me and lifts what Luke, the alcohol snob, might call an adult slushy.

"Cheers," he says, and we clink glasses. I smile despite myself.

Ivan just orders rice and beans, guacamole, and chips to share. "I'm a vegetarian," he says in explanation.

"You do know *pollo* means chicken, right?" I say.

I order the double chicken platter, just to be contrary. We both gulp our drinks, and by the time our food gets there, we're already on our second margaritas and Ivan's lips have loosened. He talks and talks, monologuing whatever he's thinking.

"I like our waiter's beard. I can't really grow facial hair. Back when I was in college, I had a soul patch, but my girlfriend's mom made me shave it off. Right there at dinner, she got out the razor. Some of my hair got in the lasagna," he says.

"My dad got me that car when my mom died. I feel guilty whenever I drive it, like the two events are connected and I've somehow caused my mom's death because I wanted a new car. It's stupid," he says between bites of beans.

I already knew he was painfully honest, but I wasn't expecting this. Is he nervous, or does he always confess things to strangers? I'm afraid to ask if I'm a special case.

"What about you?" he asks finally. His straw scrapes the bottom of his second margarita. Mine has been empty for the past ten minutes.

"What about me?"

"You haven't told me anything."

I breathe into my empty glass and watch condensation form. He's right, his plate is licked clean, and somehow he's also been talking the whole dinner. I ordered too much chicken, and now the sight of it growing cold in front of me is making me feel nauseous. I've revealed nothing about myself.

"Well, unlike you, I can grow facial hair," I say. "I just bleach it."

"Good start." Ivan leans back in his chair. His eyes are heavy, and he has a bit of an Asian glow around his cheeks—he's definitely a lightweight. "What happened with that guy? The one you couldn't let go of?"

I'm not sure if he's talking about Luke or Bob. I tug at the napkin I've twisted into a pretzel. I could make up a million stories, but I'm inspired by Ivan's honesty.

"I tried to tie him down, and he escaped."

"His loss," Ivan says.

I resist the urge to contradict him, to enumerate my flaws and rehash every mistake. It's time to let go. Ivan smiles, and we sit in silence as he sips on his water.

"Fuck it," Ivan says, and grabs a piece of untouched chicken from my plate. He bites into it and moans.

AFTER HE PAYS the bill, Ivan asks if I want to go back to his apartment.

"I'm not expecting anything," he says as we head out of the restaurant and cross the street. "I just want to keep hanging out."

"Okay," I say, not believing it for a second.

On the stairs to his apartment, Ivan kisses me, and it tastes sweet and salty. I tug at his shirt and pull him in. I want him closer, I want to ingest him. He strokes my hair and then breaks away to unlock the door. I'm tipsy enough to know that I want to fuck him. I want animal, instinctual sex that makes my brain shut off, that takes me out of my body for a few minutes.

Ivan's apartment is as neat as I expected, his bed made with military precision. His apartment decor is all primary colors: reds, blues, and yellows. Over his bed is an abstract painting, big splashes of paint on a canvas with two distinct eyes sticking out of the shapes.

"Is it a snail?" I ask.

"Either that or an alien."

We don't talk after that. He's a good kisser, gentle and slow. I take off my shirt, trying to get to the main event, squeeze my small boobs together to make them more appetizing. He ignores them and kisses my fingertips, my wrist, my socked foot, instead. He takes the disparate parts of me in his hands like he's never touched a human before. I don't realize I'm crying until Ivan stops.

"Oh shit. I'm sorry," he says. "I'm so sorry."

"It's not you," I say as I pull on my T-shirt. "I fucked this up."

"No, no," he says and pulls my back against his chest. He holds me tightly. "You didn't."

We stay curled together like that, with all the lights on.

CHAPTER TWENTY-ONE

It's noon when I walk back to my apartment from Ivan's place. We didn't end up having sex. He loaned me a T-shirt and some extra-large basketball shorts, and we lay side by side in his bed, not sleeping. I finally started talking—about the flood, my sexual hang-ups, the layout of my mom's garden—and he recited step-by-step the recipe for his late grandmother's tomato and egg soup. It wasn't because we're both Asian, it went deeper than that—we whispered in each other's ears all night like teenagers, like virgins.

"Are you kidding me?" my mom says as I enter my living room. "You look fine. I thought you were dead."

My mom's standing with her arms crossed, tucked firmly against her chest like she's trying to stop herself from hitting or hugging me, I can't tell which.

"Sorry to disappoint."

"Stop it," my mom says.

"Just stop it," she says again, loudly, even though I haven't said anything.

My mom never yells or screams, and her voice sounds unnatural at that register. She usually runs cold, not hot. I sit on my couch and gesture for my mom to sit. She doesn't, just stands above me looking clean and sharp in her L.L.Bean floral button-up.

"Is this an intervention?" I ask, though considering the handle of gin in my fridge, maybe I shouldn't joke.

"It's family dinner," she says. "Go get changed."

WE DRIVE TO the house in silence. I don't follow her inside when we get there, I sit outside on the new porch steps, next to the gnome I bought her for Mother's Day when I was twelve. He's cracked on one side and the paint on his shoes and elbows has peeled off, but he still looks relatively jolly. Still has his red cheeks and big belly; a pipe in one hand, a frog in the other.

I gave the statue to her unwrapped, in the kitchen of the old house, the room I used to call hers because it was always full of her cooking and sad country songs. She'd just taken the dishes out of the dishwasher and her glasses were fogged. She cleaned them on a dish towel before taking up the gnome, examining him like a precious stone, a smile spreading over her face.

"A good choice," she said then.

"What's wrong with you?" she asks me now, from the doorway. In her hand is a mug of green tea, the type with brown rice, I can tell by the hanging string label. My favorite. She doesn't hand it to me.

"Nothing," I say. It's still too early in the season for mosquitoes and fireflies, the lawn looks lonely without creatures flying in it. "I'm just tired, Mom. I got tired."

My mom looks at me, frowning, like she's stumped on a difficult crossword answer. She doesn't understand why the world is so hard for me. Why being alive feels like wading deeper and deeper into quicksand. *Just don't think about it*, I imagine her saying as the shifting ground engulfs my torso, leaving just my head straining for air.

"Is this about Bob?"

"Not really," I say without knowing if that's true or not.

Bob was right—I had wanted to control him, to force him to adore me unconditionally and never leave. And maybe I thought he could save me too, baptize me in his own innocence, my personal blob savior. That wasn't love.

"I've always told you, you don't need a man to be complete," my mom says.

She sits down next to me and blows on the tea she's holding without sipping on it.

"Yeah, that's not something you made up, Mom, a lot of people say that."

My voice sounds small and mean.

"What do I need then?" I ask.

"No one can tell you, Vi."

I turn and stare at my mom's profile, the strong jaw I've always admired.

"This isn't a joke, Mom. I'm really asking. Tell me."

"I can't."

She rubs my back as I cry angry tears. I swipe the liquid away before it hits my chin. She hums a tune I don't recognize, passes me the mug of tea, and goes back inside.

"We were worried about you," my dad says when I finally stop crying and go in the house. My mom's retreated to the kitchen while my dad tinkers with some electronic circuit board at his desk in the corner of the living room. I know it pains him to look up, to lose his place and train of thought, but he does. He looks silly with his glasses dangling off the tip of his nose and I smile, just a little.

"I'm sorry," I say.

My dad looks me up and down, presumably searching for any physical wounds or signs of illness.

"Are you okay?" he asks.

"I'm good," I say.

He takes off his glasses, unconvinced. When I was little, before I realized that my facial expressions always give me away, I thought my dad could read minds.

"I'm the same," I revise. "And different."

My dad nods, satisfied with his examination, and goes back to his work.

I sink down into the couch, which is just as comfortable as when I fell asleep on it a few days ago. I know if my parents would let me, I would stay here, swaddled in brown suede and the concern of two good people who will never understand me, who I will never deserve.

WHEN HE GETS in, Alex walks through the living room without acknowledging my presence. Mom must've told him that I was alive and coming to dinner, because he doesn't immediately start laying into me, yelling that I'm a selfish brat, though I'm sure he's tempted. I consider getting up and trying to smooth things over with him before dinner but I don't. I stare at the ceiling and blow air on my greasy bangs.

"Time to get the food," my mom says, touching my dad's shoulder.

He tucks his circuit boards into one of the many containers full of his half-finished projects: a motion sensor for the shower, half-painted Star Wars figurines, Christmas lights synchronized to "Jingle Bells."

"You didn't cook?" I ask.

My mom shakes her head. "No. 1 Wok."

I cringe. It's a dumpy joint in a strip mall next to a liquor store and an abandoned Blockbuster that only serves American-ized Chinese food lo mein, orange chicken, and limp shrimp fried rice. I swallow the urge to ask if they picked that place just to punish me.

In the kitchen, I find an open bottle of white wine and pour it into a Garfield mug.

"That's a month old," Alex says without turning to look at me. He's already sitting at the table, a beer open. In front of him are some official-looking charts.

"Wine gets better with age."

I sip gingerly and the sour flavor floods my nose.

"How's feeling sorry for yourself going, sis?" he asks.

"I can't complain."

"Funny."

I look over his shoulder and read some words and num-bers from his papers without understanding what they mean: "acute myelogenous leukemia" "vasculitis," "30% blasts in bone marrow."

"Still working?" I ask.

Alex shakes his head, closes the chart that I'm trying to read.

"Just testing out a hypothesis that if I stare at a chart long enough I can change test results."

My brother takes a pull of his beer. He rubs his eyes and looks tired, older than his twenty-eight years. I sit down next to him at the table.

Ten minutes later, my dad comes in with three bags of luke-warm food and my mom sets the table with paper plates and plastic cups.

"Dig in," she says, sticking serving spoons in each plastic container.

I swirl General Tso's chicken in overdone fried rice, slurp bland wonton soup straight from the plastic container. My mom scoops plain white rice on her plate and picks shrimps individually out of the fried rice.

"I can't believe you like this place."

"It's fusion," my dad says as he bites into a half-cooked broccoli, chews it with his mouth slightly open. "Just like you."

"Ha, ha," I say.

It's a quiet meal. Toward the end, around when my brother's calculating his getaway excuse, my mom's yawning, and my dad's leaning back in his chair and sighing contentedly, I decide to tell them the truth.

"I never applied to the Peace Corps."

I look straight ahead when I speak, at some new abstract painting of flowers my mom has hung behind the table. I don't want to witness the disbelief, the anger, crossing their faces.

"What?" my mom says.

"I flunked out of engineering last semester. But I reapplied to college yesterday."

I hear my mom gasp like an actress in a 1920s film.

"You flunked?" my dad says.

"What are you going to study?" Alex says.

"I want to take some photography classes," I say.

I push the congealed orange sauce to the edge of my plate.

"I'm not Alex. I'm not a scientist, I don't have the brain for it."

Silence. I put the empty mug to my mouth and pretend to sip.

"You've always had a good eye," my mom says. "I remember your lightning photos. I mean, they were blurry, but you stood out in the rain for hours."

"How are you going to pay for it?" my dad asks.

"Loans," I say. My dad takes his glasses off and presses his fingers against the bridge of his nose.

"Is this all because of Bob? Or Luke?" Alex asks.

I shake my head. For the first time in years, I feel sure about something.

When I was nine years old, I fell in the playhouse my dad made and got a scar and a concussion. I'd been playing alone on the monkey bars, putting hand over hand when my fingers slipped. I hit my head on the wood platform and everything went black, like candles blown out on a birthday cake. When I woke, there were three faces above me: my mom, my dad, Alex. They were looking down, mouthing words I couldn't hear. Alex was crying, the snot in his nose bubbling and receding as he breathed. The lines on my mom's and dad's faces were deep and scary, drawn with ultra-contrast. I didn't know what they were saying but I felt their hands on my body, their hands holding my hands. In the emergency room, in the enclosed MRI, in the hospital bed, I still felt them.

Looking around the table at their faces now, I feel them again.

CHAPTER TWENTY-TWO

I'm in the car on the way back to my apartment when my phone rings.

"Are you not checking your email?"

No hello, no introduction, no chitchat. I almost smile because it's such a classic Rachel move.

"Good to hear from you too."

"Yes, hello," she says. I picture her pulling her hair behind her ear in irritation. Maybe she's pacing back and forth in her fancy apartment. I never thought I'd hear her voice again. "Have you read my email?"

"No, I just woke up."

"I sent it Tuesday."

"Right."

Rachel sighs. I wonder if Bob's there watching her, rubbing her back in commiseration, playing the part of a supportive boyfriend.

"I talked to Walter. He wants to apologize and offer you your job back."

"What?"

"I know I should've called you first. I tried and you didn't pick up."

"Well," I say.

I drive up to my apartment. It's drizzling again and I close my eyes, breathe the rain in and out.

"You'll come back?" Rachel asks.

"No. I can't. Thank you though," I say. "I mean that."

"I won't be there, if that's what you're worried about," Rachel says. "I quit. I'm moving to LA to give acting a real try."

There's a low murmuring in the background as Rachel talks. It takes me a second to realize it must be Bob talking to someone in another room. I unlock my door, walk in, and sink into the couch. Not so long ago, the only person Bob knew was me.

"And Bob's going with you?"

"Yes."

"I could see Bob being a good actor," I say.

"Me too. He already kind of looks like . . ."

She trails off, maybe thinks it's awkward to say he looks like a movie star.

"Anyway," she continues. "We have to get married."

I blink once, twice. I can see it now: Bouquets of expensive flowers. Monogrammed napkins. A big white cake with a topper that looks just like them. Bob and Rachel. Rachel and Bob.

"Have to?" I ask.

"It's Bob's whole immigration thing. He doesn't have citizenship. He's an orphan—doesn't even have a birth certificate.

"I need to ask you a favor. We're having an engagement party and we think it would look convincing if you were there. You're the only person who knew Bob and me separately. You know, he didn't get out much."

I get up and start pacing as the line goes silent again.

"Okay," I say finally.

"It's this Sunday."

She sounds happy.

"That's quick."

"I feel like I've already wasted too much time. You only live once."

"Yeah, I think I've heard that before."

"Okay," Rachel says brightly, probably freaked out by the heavy breathing on my end. "Well, I'll see you then. Six p.m. Invite's in your email."

The line goes dead, and I sit down hard on the carpet.

SATURDAY, TO GET out of my apartment and the mold smell I've come to find familiar, I rotate through coffee shops: first Kopi, then Espresso Royale, then Paradiso. The Paradiso baristas hate me because when I used to go there with Luke, we never tipped.

"They just pour coffee into a cup," he said and I never had a good enough come-back to convince him.

Now I buy a black coffee, tip two dollars, and sit in a wooden booth with my laptop and camera. I scroll through profiles of photographers on Instagram. An anonymous account with 15K followers takes night photos, long-exposures of a ghost figure in a sheet with two eyehole cutouts, standing in front of old churches. They look like postcards from the afterlife. *Wish you were here*, the caption says.

I don't realize it's open-mic-slash-karaoke night until the host comes to my table with a sign-in sheet.

"It's low-pressure," he says and pushes the clipboard toward me. I stare at his long hair, the small gap between his two front teeth—he looks exactly like what a coffee shop emcee should look like.

"No, no," I try to smile, push the clipboard back at him.

I've always hated live shows, even got detention once for leaving in the middle of a talent show. By the second minute of "American Pie," I just couldn't take it anymore. The earnest out-of-tune singing, the fumbling chords, the stupid bravery.

"Next time," he says.

A sandy-haired boy in a puka shell necklace walks to the makeshift stage, a wood platform with a microphone, holding an electric guitar.

"This one's for Sarah," he says.

I look around the café for Sarah but it's impossible to tell who she is or if she's here at all. I take my camera out. In the viewfinder, I look at the faces in the crowd. Flushed college kids, older men, a fiftysomething in a hemp skirt. I take a picture of her as she recites a poem about having sex on an anthill.

Next up are two women in matching jean vests who belt out a Robyn song. Then a skinny kid gives a passionate rendition of Radiohead's "Creep," gyrating his hips to the left and right during the instrumental breaks. Then a big tattooed dude with the voice of an angel croons a Frank Ocean song. "Thinkin bout You." The performances go on and on. What surprises me is not how good they are but at how willing they are to go up, to volunteer for the privilege of becoming an object of ridicule.

"Anyone else?" asks the emcee.

It's almost over. The crowd has thinned out, everyone's already performed twice. The barista is sitting on a stool and scrolling on her phone, probably waiting to close. Suddenly, I realize that I don't want it to end.

"I'll go," I say. I stand up and my knees shake as I make my way to the microphone.

"What's your poison?"

I name my song and the emcee raises his eyebrows.

"Rad," he says with a smile as he queues it up.

"A long, long time ago. I can still remember . . ." I sing.

The small crowd cheers at the familiar melody. I shift my feet from side to side with the beat, almost dancing, and I know I look stupid but I don't care.

The whole coffee shop joins in on the chorus, the jean vest girls raise imaginary lighters and sway them back and forth. I know the words by heart, so I close my eyes.

I KNOCK ON Rachel's door thirty minutes late to the engagement party wearing a floral dress I found in the back of my closet. It has a rip in the armpit that I'm hoping no one will notice and during the walk over, I keep reminding myself of all the movements I shouldn't make. No large hand gestures, no high fives, no throwing my hands above my head like I'm on a roller coaster.

"You made it," Rachel says when she opens the door.

Her face is powdered, eyebrows plucked, cheeks contoured. She pulls me into a hug and I try to keep the cold bottle of Prosecco I've brought away from her vintage-looking white lace dress.

"I made it," I repeat back.

Her apartment's already packed with shiny-haired people in dress slacks and skinny ties, jewel tones and delicate gold jewelry. It's decorated festively with silver and gold balloons, streamers, the word "LOVE" written on the chalkboard in the entranceway.

I make a beeline for the kitchen, carrying the wine bottle like a police baton. I don't see anyone I recognize, I don't know why I thought I would.

"You must be Vi," says a woman next to the kitchen island who's straightening the glasses and cocktail napkins. "I'm Rachel's mom, Nancy."

"Good to meet you," I say, grabbing a wineglass without thinking. Nancy immediately starts reconfiguring the setup.

"Sorry," I say and she gives me a close-lipped smile.

I don't ask how she knows who I am. In a sea of skinny white people, I tend to stick out.

Standing next to Nancy is John, Rachel's dad. Her parents aren't exactly the WASPs I was expecting. They're young, late forties, John's wearing a black T-shirt with an album cover of a band I've never heard of. Nancy exudes the type of effortlessness that can only be achieved by people with money. Her lilac perfume is subtle, her hair curled into perfect beach waves.

"We can't thank you enough for introducing Rachel and Bob," Nancy says. "We're so happy she found somebody."

As if on cue, Bob enters wearing a baby blue suit with silver cuff links. He shakes my hand like we're rival businessmen and it makes me smile. I glance at his palms, the lines that have formed in my absence.

"Good to see you again, Vi," Bob says.

"And you."

My heart is so full of tenderness it's almost bursting.

John pats Bob on the back. "We were just telling Vi how glad we are she found you."

Do you want to know where? I almost say. I don't look at Bob, afraid I'll start laughing and give myself away. I stare straight ahead as I pour my drink.

"Vi took me in," Bob says to Rachel's parents. "I had nowhere to go. No one to turn to."

I look up then, touched. I didn't know if he remembered how I cared for him. Kept him fed and watered.

"What exactly do you plan to do when you get to LA?" Nancy asks Bob.

"My mom encouraged me to get into acting. Before she died. Of cancer."

There's awkward hitches in Bob's speech, but no one notices. Nancy puts her hand on his sleeve in sympathy, John nods like a bobblehead. You wouldn't suspect someone like Bob of lying. He looks so earnest and at ease with his deceit, I almost wonder if he's come to believe it. That he's an orphan, that he's human.

"Rachel's given me the confidence to think I could make it," Bob shrugs. "I've always loved television."

"You'll be marvelous," Nancy says, stroking her fingers down his sleeve.

"Yes," I say, lifting my glass to toast although no one else has a drink. "Bob's the best of us.

"Excuse me," I say and leave the kitchen before I can embarrass myself further.

I WALK THROUGH the living room, past unfamiliar faces. On tall tables scattered around the room are trays of small bites—bruschetta, mini cups of gazpachos, shrimp cocktail shooters. Across the room I see the boy who threw the Frisbee at my face. I guess Bob really did make friends with some of the frat bros. He gives me a little wave that I pretend not to see as I shove a whole bruschetta in my mouth.

"Thought you might be here," says a voice from behind me.

It's Elliott with his button-up unbuttoned, shirt sleeves rolled to the elbows. He looks like a very hip mobster.

"At the party or at the food?"

"Both."

I finish chewing and wipe my mouth with a napkin, taking most of my lipstick with it.

"I'm glad to see you," I say.

I wait, expecting him to say something, anything, but he seems content just to stand near me in awkward silence. Maybe this is my punishment.

"I'm sorry," I say.

Rachel has hooked her phone up to a portable speaker and put on a "Party Chill" Spotify playlist that so far has just been a lot of Train and Vanessa Carlton.

"I was an ass," I say.

"Yes," he says.

It sits between us for a second. Elliott puts his hand on my arm and I feel a knot in my chest, one I'd become accustomed to, thought I might live with forever, loosen.

"What do you think of this Bob guy?" Elliott asks. With a whiskey in his hand, he sounds like a grizzled detective in a film noir.

"He's nice," I say.

"You know him, right?"

I nod, gulp down some wine. It's hard not to say anything more.

"You and Rachel made up?" I ask, changing the subject.

"Yeah. Figured it was time to stop holding grudges over kisses."

Elliott grabs a mini egg roll from the tray.

"It's time," Nancy announces, her crystal voice ringing through the small room. "For a game."

Everyone claps as Rachel and Bob move to the center of the room. I catch Rachel touching his hand—they look cute together, it's impossible to deny. Nancy hands Rachel and Bob whiteboards and markers, and has them sit in chairs facing each other.

"The Newlywed Game is simple," she says. "I ask a question, you write down an answer. The other guesses what you said."

Nancy whispers the question to Bob first and he nods seriously before scribbling on his board like this is a timed test. I wonder how long it took him to learn to write, if it's natural now or if he still has to think about the curve of the letters.

"What would your fiancé want as his last meal?" Nancy asks Rachel.

Rachel beams, her high ponytail bobs.

"Easy," Rachel says. "My homemade sweet potato pie."

Bob lifts his board. It reads, "Fruity Pebbles."

The room erupts into laughter, even Elliott smiles. My hands start sweating. I study their faces—Bob looks abashed, Rachel's blushing.

"I didn't even know you liked cereal," she said, not quite keeping the annoyance out of her voice.

The rest of the questions are boring: what dream vacation your fiancé wants to go on, what profession would they choose if they had to switch, where did your first kiss happen. The only exciting part of the game is that they get all of the answers wrong.

"Awkward," Elliott whispers in my ear.

Finally, Nancy whispers the last question to Rachel.

She gives Bob a wink as she writes on her whiteboard. "We got this."

To Bob and the rest of the party, Nancy announces the question, "When did your fiancé know you were the one?"

Everyone's silent. Bob furrows his brow like he does when he's confused. He looks around the room composed of mostly Rachel's friends and family like maybe they can answer for him.

"The one?" he asks.

"Like your soulmate. The person you'll be with until you die. The one," Nancy tries to help.

Rachel fidgets in her chair and pulls at the hem of her dress as Bob thinks.

"She doesn't?" Bob says finally.

Nancy's eyes widen. Clearly embarrassed, Rachel laughs too loud.

"He's kidding," she says as she gets up from her chair, turning to address the partygoers instead of Bob. "It was when he came into the hotel. He'd hurt his hand, lost some blood, and I bandaged him up and took him home. That's when I knew he was the one."

A few girls in skintight cocktail dresses clap. Rachel pulls Bob into a kiss.

"To the beautiful new couple," Nancy toasts and the whole room clinks their glasses together and drinks, turning back to their conversations.

"Elliott?" I say.

He turns. His whiskey glass is empty.

"Do you remember the night at the Back Door when we met?"

"Sure."

"That thing I showed you in the alley?"

Elliott's face is blank, a complete lack of recognition, and for a second, I wonder if he's forgotten. If it even happened at all. Then something sparks, he smiles and snaps his fingers.

"The blobfish."

I am ready to tell him everything. The whole absurd story. I brace myself for laughter, disbelief, an eye roll, a "You're fucking kidding me." But there's a hand on my arm. It's Bob.

"The man of the hour," Elliott says.

"Can I steal you for a second?" Bob says.

I nod. Just as a few weeks ago I was the one leading Bob, now it's Bob leading me, his hand on my shoulder, out of the apartment and up the stairs to the roof.

THE ROOF LOOKS pretty with twinkle lights strung across the railing and balloons tied to the posts. The day has cooled, leaving warm remnants, gentle as a baby bath. Bob turns to me and his face looks weird, the handsome features crunched up like he's constipated.

"Are you okay?" I ask.

He starts to pace. I wonder if he still climbs on the walls and does cartwheels. How many of Rachel's vases have been broken by Bob's high kicks?

"Vi, I don't know what to do."

"What do you mean?" I say.

Bob shrugs. He kicks a pebble off the roof and we both listen for the sound of it hitting the ground.

"You have it all figured out," I say. "Look at this apartment, this view, this life you've created. Most people would kill to have what you have."

Bob just shakes his head. I lean on the railing. I'm tired of standing, I shouldn't have worn these platform wedges, I can feel the straps digging into the back of my ankles.

"I don't know who I am," he says finally.

Instead of hugging him, I wrap my arms around myself and squeeze.

"I'm sorry," I say.

I can't pinpoint exactly what I'm sorry for. Creating him, using him, trapping him? Maybe I didn't take into account the world I placed him in, the way that even the best-looking life can test you, beat you to dust. Bob looks at me with his big blue eyes, so sad I want to cry.

"You should go back down," I say. "I'm sure Rachel's worried about you."

Bob moves closer to the roof's edge, his leather loafer hanging over the gutter. I know if I grabbed his hand and pulled him back, he would come with me.

"You made me," Bob says, turning toward me, away from the edge. "You can help me. Tell me who I am."

He runs his hand through his hair. He's attractive and wounded and for a second, I'm paralyzed. I love him like a teenage girl loves a boy band member. I want to hang a poster of him above my bed, kiss it every night before I fall asleep, keep him forever as a symbol. But he's not.

"You're human," I say.

"I don't know how to be though."

"No one does. I can't tell you how," I say. "And neither can Rachel. You have to figure it out for yourself."

I'm tempted to leave Bob there on the roof after I deliver my wisdom, to disappear into the night like a caped crusader, but I stay. Together we watch the lights on the hill. All the strangers eating dinner and watching TV and jacking off. Living lives.

I touch him then, just a hand on his shoulder. I have no idea what he's thinking or who he'll become.

"Okay. I'm ready," he says.

Together we go back downstairs.

ACKNOWLEDGMENTS

Thank you to everyone who saw promise in this book.

To my mentor, Leah Stewart, who guided me through each chapter. Thank you for suggesting I go gentler on Vi (and on myself). To Chris Bachelder, Michael Griffith, Elizabeth Eslami, and all of the amazing creative writing professors at University of Cincinnati, Indiana University, and University of Illinois.

To my incredible agent, Samantha Shea, who wrote me words of encouragement back in 2015. Your edits shaped this novel. To Sarah Stein, Charlotte Humphery, and everyone at Harper and Sceptre Books. Thank you for taking a gamble on me.

To every editor and journal who published my work along the way. Thank you.

To all of the generous writers who've offered feedback, advice, and love over the years. To Su Cho and Scott Fenton for helping me survive my early twenties. To Reneé Branum, my karaoke soulmate. To Lisa Low for all those freezing-cold walks. To Claire Kortyna and Maddy Wattenberg for your un-warranted, unwavering belief in me.

To my toughest animal critics, Daisy and Leo. To my weird, wonderful childhood friends. To my dad, brothers, and all of my family for your love and support. Thank you especially to my mom for giving me your love of reading.

To the first reader of everything I write. Andrew, this book wouldn't exist without you.